W9-AEW-863

The Guns of Evening

Books By The Same Author

* Written as Ronald Bassett

Historical novels

The Carthaginian
The Pompeians
Witchfinder General
Amorous Trooper
Rebecca's Brat
Kill the Stuart

World War II novels

The Tinfish Run
The Pierhead Jump
The Neptune Landing

* Written as William Clive

Dando on Delhi Ridge
Dando and the Summer Palace
Dando and the Mad Emperor
The Tune That They Play
Blood of an Englishman
Fighting Mac

Ronald Bassett

The Guns of Evening

ISBN 0 333 26281 6

First published 1980 by
MACMILLAN LONDON LIMITED
4 Little Essex Street London WC2R 3LF
and Basingstoke
Associated Companies in Delhi, Dublin,
Hong Kong, Johannesburg, Lagos, Melbourne,
New York, Singapore and Tokyo

Printed in Great Britain by
Redwood Burn Limited
Trowbridge and Esher

PART I

'We'll force the Kattegat narrows and land our own army on the Baltic coast of Germany'

Admiral Sir John Fisher, First Sea Lord, 1914.

One

The three warships, in line ahead, thrust their long hulls into a slate-coloured sea already hazed with evening mist thickened by the black smoke tumbling from the funnels, flattening over the wake that boiled astern and swirled around the battle ensigns fluttering from foremast and main like bloodied red petals. Bow waves creamed and lifted, knifed aside with ease by the bows ploughing through them at 24 knots, undeviating.

To the immediate eye they were identical, these three grey ships – powerfully sinister, each of 17,250 tons and mounting eight 12-inch guns that could hurl a broadside for almost ten miles, each crammed with a thousand men now tensed at battle stations, in magazines, engine rooms and control tops, bridges and flag decks. They carried the belligerent names that small English boys in sailor suits wore proudly on their caps – *Invincible, Inflexible, Indomitable* – and their massive, toad-shaped turrets were turning, lifting their long, hot gun-barrels to sniff at the sky southward, where the enemy was in sight.

Until now, visibility had never been better than 9000 yards, with the sea-clinging mist and thickening palls of gun-smoke allowing only occasional glimpses of the enemy ships which were turning away from the approaching British. From *Invincible's* bridge an enemy would be sighted, identified, and would be obscured again in moments, barely enabling the Spotting Officer to observe the fall of shot. But, they knew, *Invincible* was hitting. They had seen the dark red glow of high explosives bursting on *Lützow* and *Derfflinger*, and on a battleship that someone shouted was *König*. The time was 1830, and sunset was only ninety minutes away.

Rear-Admiral Hood cupped his hands around the mouth of the Director Control voice-pipe. 'Your shooting is very good, Dannreuther. Keep at it, man – and quickly. Every shot is telling.' They were the last words he spoke.

Invincible had been struck several times. A shell had burst in the Boys' messdeck, forward, and another had torn through the flimsy 2-inch plating below and abaft the after funnel to wreck the officers' bathroom flat and the chapel, which was being used as a casualty station. Several boats had been smashed by shrapnel, but a fire in the paint-store was under control and nowhere was fighting efficiency impaired. The ship still led the battle-cruiser line with flags flying and every gun that could bear on the enemy firing steadily.

Then, weirdly, the ubiquitous, fog-like smoke that had hitherto clung to the racing warships was wrenched aside like a theatre curtain and, at that moment, the sun on the westerly horizon thrust through the clouds. *Invincible* was exposed, silhouetted against a clear sky, only 8000 yards from the enemy battle-fleet. *Derfflinger*, already hit twenty times and with 180 casualties, had steered out of station to avoid further punishment, but she fired her last salvo at a target impossible to miss.

A 12-inch shell plunged through the armour of 'Q' turret, exploded in the gun-house, tore off the roof and flung it 400 feet skyward. There was a secondary explosion as ready-use cordite within the chamber erupted, and officers and gun-crew died instantly. The searing flash ignited the cordite in the gun-loading cages, roared down the turret trunk in which the protecting doors were open, and burst ferociously into the cordite handling room. 'Q' turret, trunk and magazine disintegrated. 'P' turret, adjacent, followed suit seconds later, and then all boilers ruptured in quick succession. A colossal mushroom of dense smoke rose, spreading over the sea, and, with the entire midships gouged out of her, *Invincible*'s back broke between her second and third funnels. She sank swiftly in a welter of flame, steam and spitting cordite, her masts folding inwards, together, as bows and stern rose simultaneously.

Two

In 1913 Steve Bundy was eighteen, a native of Stepney Green, and ordinary in everything. Being ordinary meant that he was undernourished but paradoxically as tough as rivetted leather, was usually hungry but would curse himself for a stupid bastard and give his last copper to the old woman with no feet who begged outside Lockhart's in the Mile End Road, because he adhered to a crude code of honour that was based on the laws of survival and not the laws of the land.

He was stocky, pale-faced, of barely average height, slightly bow-legged. His hair was closely cropped but conceded a single lock over the forehead, a cow-lick, which was customary for ordinary men, and he wore the uniform of the East End – a greasy cloth cap, a scarf knotted at the throat, trousers threadbare at the knees and broken boots. Steve Bundy could read and write laboriously, although he seldom did either, count his change and the spots on a playing card, and whistle through a gap in his front teeth. Any other attributes of higher academic quality would have been entirely superfluous in Stepney Green.

There were thousands like Steve Bundy, seldom venturing further west than Holborn or deeper east than Woolwich, and to whom places like Harrow, Watford or Hounslow were as remotely foreign as Bombay. They congregated nightly in gas-lit corners, blasphemed, boasted, punched each other, speculated on the virtue of every passing woman, and tried not to look in the direction of the workmen's cookshop on the corner with its steamed windows. There was always going to be work tomorrow, or perhaps the next day. There would be labourers wanted at St Katherine's, or the railway cuttings, or the omnibus company – but never today. Somehow the thought of working every day of every week was discomfiting. The ideal life-style, if it could be achieved, was one in which a bloke could work one day and earn sufficient to maintain himself in idleness for six. Frustratingly, nobody could calculate how.

It was hunger and Johnnie Spong that persuaded Steve Bundy to try his luck at Blackfriars. Johnnie Spong was several years older than most of Steve Bundy's immediate associates, and had the enviable if uncollaborated reputation of having once been a professional boxer. Certainly he possessed a flattened nose, a wealth of boxing terminology, and gave the impression that he had been personally acquainted with every champion since Gipsy Jem Mace.

When Johnnie Spong, chewing on a matchstick, mentioned casually that he was considering a stroll down to Blackfriars to pick up an easy thirty bob for six rounds, Steve Bundy was interested. Thirty bob, Johnnie Spong nodded, for anyone who was given a fight as a last-minute substitute, an extra quid if he won, and if the fight was bloody there would be nobbings – the coppers throw into the ring by the beer-fuddled crowd. It was money for old boot-laces.

Steve Bundy was intrigued. Thirty bob was a small fortune. 'If yer going, Johnnie,' he suggested, 'could I come with yer? They might want two.' And accompanying Johnnie Spong, who was known by all the promoters, would mean that he, Steve Bundy, could not fail to be chosen. 'If they don't, I can watch. I ain't never seen yer in the ring.'

Johnnie Spong shifted the matchstick from one corner of his mouth to the other. 'Well,' he considered, 'I might go this week an' I might not. It depends.' He studied his dirty fingernails. 'There's this bloke in Hoxton I got ter see about a fight in Manchester—' He saw the doubt in the other's eyes. 'All right, I'll tell yer what. I'll meet yer, but if I don't turn up, see, yer can go yerself. I 'spect I'll go, but in case I don't, I'll tell yer the dodge.'

'I'll jes' mention yer name,' Steve Bundy said, and Johnnie Spong nodded absently.

When the time came, Johnnie Spong did not appear, being apparently more urgently committed to a bloke in Hoxton. Alone, Steve Bundy walked from Stepney Green to Blackfriars, shrugged into his upturned collar, hands in pockets. It was a drizzling November night and the wetness seeped through the broken soles of his boots, but there were many like him, cold and wet. It was hunger that pulled a bloke down.

On his arrival the usual hangers-on were thronged under the lamp at the door. It was like a pen-sketch of Gustave Doré, of thin faces, defeated eyes and slumped shoulders, sodden caps and neck-cloths. He joined them, but nobody seemed to care. The gas lamp hissed softly and his belly yawned. Six rounds, Johnnie Spong had said, for thirty bob. He had never fought in a real ring. Christ, he had never fought anywhere except in the alleyways of Whitechapel against his juvenile fellows; at eighteen he had never fought a grown man. But thirty bob....

Don't let the bastards offer you anything less, Johnnie Spong had urged him. The blokes that got their names printed big on the bills got a quid for every round, and the promoter made hundreds. The bastard.

If the bloke asks, he had been advised, tell him you've been fighting up north – say Liverpool or Glasgow. Not that he'll believe it, but he's got to tell the crowd something. Of course, Johnnie Spong had sniffed, you'll get beat, but the cove you fight will keep you alive for four or five rounds, perhaps put you away in the last. He can't make it look too easy. Likely he'll cut you up; the crowd likes to see blood – but what's a smashed mouth or a filled eye against thirty bob?

If you win? Johnnie Spong had sniffed again, amused. Blokes like Steve Bundy didn't win. Mo Lyons' lot was made up of two kinds – tough, promising youngsters with their sights on the London Sporting Club and a championship purse, or scarred old warriors on the wrong side of the hill but knowing far too much for a boy from the street. Still, he could always try.

From beyond the closed door there penetrated, faintly, the murmur of the crowd, swelling occasionally and fading again, sometimes a muted roar. Outside, in the rain, someone hawked and spat, but nobody spoke.

When the door opened, quite suddenly, nobody was prepared. Steve Bundy smelled warm, stale air, and a man stood, silhouetted against the inner glare, unwilling to emerge too far into the drizzling gloom and waiting for the group to gather in the pool of yellow gaslight. 'Any middles?' he asked wheezily. 'I want a middle.'

Steve Bundy took his hands from his pockets, but another had shouldered ahead of him. The man in the doorway shook his head. 'No, not you, Wallace. I've told yer before. If you're making eleven-ten, man, you're starved. Yer ain't got the legs.' He peered further. 'Anyone else? Any middles? I ain't got all night.'

'Me, guv,' Steve Bundy offered, keeping his voice as deep as possible and, for good measure, wiping the back of his hand across his mouth – a gesture which, for some reason, was calculated to indicate belligerence.

'Let's have a look at yer in the light.' The promoter withdrew a pace. 'Gawd – how old are yer?'

'Nearly twenty,' Steve Bundy lied. 'I jes' look young, that's all.'

Mo Lyons took a stub of a cigar from his mouth and exploded into a paroxysm of coughing, his eyes watering and his face turning to turkey red. 'Gawd,' he gasped finally, and drew painful breath. 'Nearly twenty? 'Ow nearly? An' don't tell me yer've been fighting up north.' He reached forward a hand to knead the other's shoulder and upper arm doubtfully. 'We-ell—'

Steve Bundy wiped his mouth again and narrowed his eyes aggressively. 'I can take care of meself, Mister Lyons. Johnnie Spong sent me.'

'Johnnie Who?' Lyons enquired, then turned to the rain-slashed darkness beyond the open door. 'Ain't there any more middles out there? Eleven-ten or near it? No, *not* you, Wallace.' The fluctuating tide of human noise behind him had ebbed suddenly, and a single voice shouted an announcement, incomprehensible to Steve Bundy. Mo Lyons' sweating face was worried. 'All right,' he conceded. 'Come with me. What's yer name?'

'Bundy. Steve Bundy. I won't let yer down, Mister Lyons—'

'Bundy? That don't sound very spiteful.' The portly, wheezing promoter ushered his recruit into a long, narrow room of which most was left in shadow by a single, naked electric light bulb in mid-ceiling. There was a powerful reek of stale sweat, liniment and tobacco smoke. Six or seven men, in various stages of undress, sat on a bench against a wall that was scattered with old fight bills, disinterestedly eyeing another who bounced on his toes, punched at the air and snorted. Festoons of boxing gloves hung from nails, and everywhere – on the dirty floor, on lockers and shelves – were clutters of clothing, footwear, empty beer bottles and soiled towels.

'Palmer,' Lyons panted, 'get this'n some gear. He's going

in against Rowse, next on.' He turned to Steve Bundy. 'Six rounds, right? A quid, and a bit extra if yer win.'

Steve Bundy shook his head. 'Thirty bob, Mister Lyons. That's what Johnnie Spong said – and an extra quid fer winning. That's usual.' Only minutes ago he would have fought for a quid, but now, faced with the reality, his resolve had drained and, given any excuse, he would have cut and run. His belly twisted again, and not just with hunger. Christ.

'Usual?' Lyons heaved. 'What do you know about what's usual? An' who the bloody hell is Johnnie Spong? For all I know, yer might never 'ave been in a ring in yer life – and I ain't even put yer on the scales yet. I could walk out there' – he nodded at the door – 'and get ten like you ter fight fer a quid.'

Steve Bundy shrugged. 'Thirty bob,' he insisted. With luck, Lyons would tell him to go to hell.

'Is 'ee going ter want this clobber or ain't 'ee?' enquired the man Palmer. He was paunchy, like Lyons, but with a head as closely cropped as a Prussian's, eyes puckered by old scar tissue, and a grotesquely concave nose. 'There ain't much time.'

Lyons chewed on the cold stump of his cigar. 'All right. Thirty bob – and yer'd better bloody make a show. Get 'im fitted up, Palmer.' He paused. 'Bundy, did yer say? That ain't no good. Where d'yer come from?'

'Stepney. Mile End.'

'Stepney? Yer ain't a Yid, are yer?'

'No.'

Lyons frowned, breathing asthmatically. 'That's where Jack the Ripper came from, ain't it?' Steve Bundy, pulling off his shirt, did not care. He was experiencing an urgent desire to vomit, which was odd because he had eaten nothing since the previous day. He wished he'd never listened to Johnnie Spong. 'That's it, then,' Lyons nodded. 'Palmer – when yer take him in, tell the Major ter announce Jackie Ripper, the Mile End Killer.'

'Gawdalmighty,' Palmer grinned, and rolled his eyes.

The man who had been bouncing on his toes now bounced towards Steve Bundy and, still weaving and snorting, looked down at him speculatively.

'Fer Chris' sake keep bloody still, Rowse,' Lyons snapped. 'Now, listen. They ain't going ter like another substitute.' Presumably 'they' were the ringside crowd. 'So yer've got ter make it look good. Carry him fer two. Let 'im push yer about a bit, and act like it 'urts. Yer can start coming back in the third. In the fourth he can look after 'isself, and yer can do what yer like. After that—' He shrugged, glancing at Steve Bundy. 'D'yer get the idea, Bundy?'

'Yes, Mister Lyons.' He got the idea exactly, and it was depressing.

'Jes' don't get too cocky, that's all,' Rowse warned, 'or I'll bloody mince yer.' Steve Bundy nodded, pulling on leather ring shoes that were several sizes too large. Palmer loosened the lacings of a pair of gloves, and Lyons looked at his watch. 'All right,' he said again, doubtfully.

'Is that anyone's?' Steve Bundy asked Palmer. A broken sausage roll lay among pastry fragments on a greasy scrap of paper, surrounded by empty stout bottles. Palmer frowned at it, then at Steve Bundy. 'Yours, if yer want it. Jesus, are yer that 'ungry?' Rowse laughed, turned his back, and began upper-cutting viciously.

He disposed of the sausage roll in two hurried gulps, but it refused to be completely swallowed and lodged uncomfortably in his gullet. Palmer was pushing the gloves over his hands, and Lyons had opened the dressing-room door, his head cocked, listening.

'Where did yer say yer've been fightin'?' Palmer asked. 'Up north? Up north where?'

Steve Bundy swallowed on his clogged throat. 'I didn't say

I'd been fighting anywhere. I jes' said I could take care of meself.' There might still remain a chance of reprieve.

'Right,' Lyons shouted from the door. 'Next two. Don't fergit what I bloody said, Rowse. There some black ties out there, tossin' in a bit o' silver, so yer might do yerself a bit o' good if yer play it right.'

Steve Bundy felt Palmer's hand under his arm. 'What d'yer mean, yer can take care of yerself?' he hissed. 'Yer mean yer ain't fought *anywhere*?' He glared. 'Christ, this ain't a bloody tent on a fairground, son. It's the Blackfriars Ring.' He glanced over his shoulder. 'Mister Lyons – are yer sure—?'

Mo Lyons and Rowse, however, had gone, and several others had made a noisy entrance – two men in tights and shorts, waist-stripped and streaked with wetness, tugging off their gloves, one with a bleeding mouth. A third carried a small bucket, which he flung down and then groped under the bench for a bottle. 'Where's Mo?' he challenged. 'The Major's pissed again. I 'ad ter tell 'im twice what soddin' round it was.' Steve Bundy allowed himself to be propelled towards the door. The sausage roll was still anchored stodgily below his throat and he felt nearer to vomiting than ever.

'Look,' Palmer advised anxiously, 'yer'd better do like Mo Lyons sez, ter start with. Tuck yer chin in yer shoulder an' keep diggin' in yer left, straight. Keep movin'. Keep orf the ropes and *don't* get in a corner.' He could see the ring – a raised, roped island overhung by lights, a narrow aisle between terraces of seats, a sea of pink faces hazed by tobacco smoke. Rowse was already in his corner, jogging on his toes and scowling.

'Rowse ain't no bloody Tommy Burns, see,' Palmer went on, 'but he can fight nasty. Watch out fer buttin' and thumbin' – but he won't try none o' that unless he thinks he's being beat—'

They climbed under the ropes, and Palmer spoke briefly to a man wearing a shabby evening suit and sporting a huge cavalry moustache, who eyed Steve Bundy glassily and then belched. In the opposite corner Rowse pawed like a bull. 'That's the Major,' Palmer confided. 'Don't let 'im breathe on yer.'

The Major screamed for the attention of m'Lords, Ladies and Gentlemen, although the presence of any ladies in the smoke-choked auditorium was doubtful. The hubbub died momentarily, but then, at the mention of Jackie Ripper, the Mile End Killer, there was an eruption of angry laughter, cat-calls and shouts of 'Swindle!' The Major shrugged and spread his hands apologetically, then beckoned the two contestants to the centre of the ring.

'One day,' he promised, 'we're going to have shixteen bloddy names like they're printed on the bill. What's happened to Battersea Fowler? Doing drag for being drunk an' dishorderly?' He swayed towards Steve Bundy, who realised what Palmer had meant. 'I shuppose you've heard of the Quishberry Rules?'

'Fer Chrissake get on with it, Major,' Rowse gritted, 'before yer soddin' fall down.' From the obscurity of the surrounding seats came a tattoo of stamping feet. The Major steadied himself. 'All ri'. Go back to your cornersh. Three minish each round an' no bloody nonsense.' He waved them away.

'Remember what I told yer,' Palmer said with a lack of enthusiasm that Steve Bundy shared. At least, he told himself, it could only last for minutes, like having a tooth pulled. Later, it would be just an unpleasant memory. For now, he must just keep thinking about thirty bob.

Thirty bob. Thirty bob.

The bell clang-clanged, and Palmer gave him a push.

Rowse shuffled to meet him, snorting as if trying to dislodge some nasal obstruction. Tentatively, Steve Bundy stabbed out his left glove, which, to his surprise, jolted Rowse's head backward and made him stagger. The crowd hummed like bees and Steve Bundy was encouraged. Had he hit *that* hard? He tried again.

He never knew if his blow landed because, inexplicably, he was on his knees, clawing at the ropes, staring through a red mist at the Major's legs, his ears singing.

'Four. Five. Six—'

Jesus Christ. There was the salt taste of blood in his mouth, and he was angry. Rowse, the bastard, wasn't playing it right. For the moment he was unable to see Rowse, but he hauled himself upright, his legs like water. He could see the Major, but he still did not see Rowse when a second explosion full in the face hammered him to the canvas again, to all fours, with his senses in chaos and his vision blurred.

'Three. Four. Five—'

This time, before he rose, he looked for Rowse and, as the man advanced, flung himself away to put distance and the Major between them. He needed respite, time for the mist in his head to clear and his legs to steady. His apprehension had gone, and so had the fragment of sausage roll from his throat. If anger was not the same thing as courage it was a good substitute, and he wanted to hit Rowse with every savage ounce of his strength, just once, before he was cut down again. He gulped for breath, feeling stronger, angrier.

Rowse bobbed and swayed with the nonchalance of a man shadow-boxing in a gymnasium, and the crowd hummed venomously. Steve Bundy retreated, felt the ropes at his back and sidled along them, took a numbing blow to his ribs and lashed back. Rowse snorted, jabbed with both fists to the head, and Steve Bundy could feel the warm blood from his nose trickling over his chin. Again he flailed, and this time had the satisfaction of feeling the jolt of his knuckles against bone. Rowse paused momentarily, surprised and obviously shaken. There was a red smear on his cheek and now the crowd roared. Rowse shook his head, then came forward with his gloves moving like pistons.

Rowse, Steve Bundy realised, was vulnerable. He was more experienced, but he had been halted in his tracks by a solid blow, and he was overconfident. He was playing to the crowd, boxing flashily and with a disregard for the caution he might have shown against a more mature opponent. Twice, perhaps, he had been stung, but he was willing to be stung to demonstrate his stylish superiority. He bounced and shuffled professionally, head cocked, fists weaving and stabbing painfully into Steve Bundy's face, once, twice, three times. The one thing that Rowse did not anticipate was that the bloodied young man he was making a fool of should suddenly take the offensive.

Steve Bundy escaped from Rowse's reach, again felt the ropes at his back. He must do something now, he decided, or never; every punch he took was sapping his ability to counter. He drew another breath, then launched himself at Rowse with all the vehemence he could muster. A single, ungainly bound brought him toe to toe. He scythed wildly, knew that he missed with his left but felt his right fist sink home. Rowse grunted and drew away, hurt and insulted, stumbled backward over the Major's foot, and turned angrily. 'Yer drunken bastard—'

It was unfortunate that he should have taken his eyes away from his opponent just at that moment, because Steve Bundy had only one real punch left. It was an optimistic, crude swing that might have been easily avoided, to leave him unbalanced and reeling, but it smashed into the side of Rowse's half-turned head with a hammer-crack that drew a hungry 'Aaah!' from the crowd. Rowse's face was suddenly blank, and he went down as if his legs had been severed at the knees, outsprawled. The Major stared down at him stupidly.

Equally unbelieving, Steve Bundy stood trembling, listening to the delighted chant from the darkness beyond the ropes.

Thirty bob. Thirty bob. Christ, no. Two poun's ten.

In the dressing room Rowse, revived by cold water from a bucket and fortified by a bottle of stout, complained that he had been hit when he wasn't looking. 'Any referee that wasn't soddin' boozed would 'ave stopped the fight,' he claimed, and glared at Steve Bundy, who, with the same bucket, was gingerly washing the blood from his raw mouth. His nose throbbed painfully. 'It won't soddin' 'appen again,' Rowse promised. 'I weren't even trying. Next time, I'll bloody slaughter yer.' Steve Bundy believed him.

Mo Lyons entered angrily. 'One bloody round!' He scowled at both of them. 'Yer didn't do what yer was told. I said ter make it look good, didn't I? And yer didn't do one bloody round!'

'Yer only told Rowse, Mister Lyons,' Steve Bundy said. 'Yer didn't tell me. I warned yer I could take care of meself.' He announced it with more assurance than he had twenty minutes earlier. Rowse sat in disgusted silence.

'I told *both* of yer,' Lyons insisted. 'It takes two ter make a fight, don't it? I wouldn't bloody tell *one* of yer, now would I?' He peeled two notes from his wallet. 'Here's yer thirty bob, Bundy. Now sling yer 'ook.'

Steve Bundy paused in the act of pulling his shirt over his head. 'And a quid fer winning. That's what yer agreed, Mister Lyons.'

'Only if yer'd done what yer was told, Bundy.' Lyons shook his head. 'And yer didn't. Besides, that wasn't what I'd call a win. It was a bloody fluke. Yer could fight Rowse every night fer a year, and he'd beat yer every bloody time.'

'That's the soddin' truth,' Rowse agreed.

Palmer scratched his shorn scalp. 'I don't see it matters what might 'appen every night fer a year. It's what 'appened ternight. If Rowse weren't lookin', that was 'is soddin' fault.'

'Nobody asked yer, Palmer,' Lyons wheezed. 'You jes' do the job yer paid for.'

'There's bloody rules,' Rowse claimed, 'and they don't

include referees that's blind pissed and can't stand up.'

'So you're still rooking your fighters, are you, Mo?' The amused voice came from the open door, and they all looked up. A man had entered, elegant in evening clothes, a coat with an astrakhan collar, white gloves, carrying a silk hat and a silver-headed cane. He glanced briefly round the cluttered dressing-room, then back at Lyons. 'Give the boy his money, Mo. He won.'

Lyons was immediately respectful. He wrenched the cigar butt from his mouth and beamed. 'Why – Mister Seagram! It's a rare pleasure ter see yer at the Ring, sir. If I'd known, I'd 'ave offered 'ospitality.' He chuckled. 'The money? It was jest a joke. O' course I'm giving the boy his money.' He fumbled for his wallet. 'Mo Lyons 'as never bilked a fighter yet. That's what gives the game a bad name.' He patted Steve Bundy's shoulder. 'Palmer – get Mister Seagram a chair. Mister Seagram – now I know yer'd like a bottle o' champagne. Palmer – go across ter Bowler's and get two bottles, an' make sure they're cold. An' proper glasses. An' tell them ter send over three dozen Whitstables an' some pate.' He beamed again at the newcomer. 'It's a rare pleasure, Mister Seagram.' He paused. 'Now, 'ave yer seen anything ternight that's tickled yer fancy?'

Mr Seagram drew a handkerchief from his cuff to flick at the seat of the chair that Palmer had offered, sat carefully, then looked from Steve Bundy to Lyons and finally Rowse.

Lyons rubbed his hands together. 'I've got a good string jes' now – all honest fighters an' some that's very promising, Mister Seagram. They're all under contract, o'course, but yer've never found me difficult, and I've never wanted ter stand in anyone's way—'

'You're the biggest damn' Fagin in the business, Mo,' the other smiled, and brushed at an immaculate knee. 'But I doubt if you'd recognise real promise if you saw it, or know how to handle it if you did – which is why you're still managing thirty-bob-a-nighters in Blackfriars while I've got options on Wells, Carpentier and Gunboat Smith in Paris and New York.' He waved aside Mo Lyons' proffered cigar and reached for his own silver cigar case. 'However' – Seagram allowed Lyons to hurriedly strike a match – 'my boredom tonight was relieved by one of the youngsters out there. The Major introduced him as Jackie Ripper, the Mile End Killer. Only you could think of a name like that, Mo.' He eyed Steve Bundy, who was lacing his boots.

'Jackie Ripper?' Lyons frowned. 'Well, that was Bundy there, Mister Seagram, but I dare say the Major got the names mixed. He does, sometimes, when he's three sheets in the wind. I've been meaning ter do something about it.' He turned. 'It's Rowse yer really mean. Bundy ain't nothing special. As a matter of fact—'

'No, I don't mean Rowse. I mean Bundy, if that's his name. All Rowse has is a lot of bad habits. No, it's Bundy I'm interested in. Did you say you have him under contract?'

'Mister Seagram,' Lyons protested, 'I wouldn't want ter see yer waste yer money. What yer saw ternight was an accident, a blind fluke. Ask Rowse. Ask Palmer. Bundy shouldn't 'ave been in there ternight. It should 'ave been Battersea Fowler. Bundy can't bloody box, Mister Seagram.'

'Box?' Seagram shrugged. 'Of course he can't box, Mo, but he can hit – and that's what I want. I can teach anyone to box – or enough to get along with – but nobody can be taught how to *hit*.' He drew on his cigar and leaned back in the chair, gazing thoughtfully at Steve Bundy, who gazed back. 'The Americans are putting more and more niggers into their rings, Mo. They can't box, either. They fight by instinct, and they can take a lot of punishment to the head. I've seen some of them. They've got thicker skulls than whites, but they can be beaten if they're hit hard enough to the body. I've seen that, too.'

Mo Lyons said nothing. He had tried to catch Steve Bundy's eye, but had failed.

'Niggers aren't intelligent,' Seagram went on. 'They just keep coming forward, taking punches and throwing them, like Rowse there, until someone can't take any more and goes down.' He paused. 'It's not boxing, Mo – not even your kind. It's just attrition. But it's successful, and it's making a lot of money. Besides, sooner or later someone has to beat Jack Johnson.'

Lyons laughed and shook his head. 'Not a white fighter, Mister Seagram. There's no white 'eavy that can stand in the same ring as Johnson – not with a chance o' winning.'

'I think you're wrong, Mo, but I'm not too concerned about world championships yet, or even heavyweights, only in finding a few youngsters who might match up to the Americans in due course. Purses are getting bigger, and they're winning most of them. Tonight I saw Bundy put down twice, and get up twice. Then I saw him put Rowse down, and Rowse didn't get up. That adds up to something I can't teach anyone. I can teach him all the rest that matters – if he's willing to be taught.'

'Oh, he's willing ter be taught, Mister Seagram – ain't yer, Bundy?' Lyons winked in the direction of Steve Bundy, but the younger man had his eyes on Seagram. Was this really the legendary Maurice 'Gentleman' Seagram, who had a personal suite on a White Star liner, who staged world-news fights in London, Philadelphia and Sydney between men like Gans and Nelson, Burns and McCoy? Was this *the* Seagram? A worn bootlace snapped in his fingers and he wondered if it was worth knotting. Christ, he had two pounds ten, anyway. For two bob he could stuff himself sick with two helpings of pie, mash and gravy, or stewed eels, or faggots and peas. The excruciating problem was whether to stuff himself sick in Blackfriars or hug blissful anticipation all the way back to the Mile End Road.

Seagram drew out his watch. 'I haven't a lot of time, Mo. Now, about that contract. Do you want cash or a percentage?'

'Well, Mister Seagram,' Lyons suggested, 'if yer'd like ter step into my office—' Palmer had reappeared with two bottles in a bucket of ice. Seagram lifted one by its neck, looked at the label and winced. 'I'm not doing any horse-dealing, Mo. Do you want to sell or not? If you do, my legal man will make an offer.' He rose to his feet, then glanced at Steve Bundy. 'I suppose you *have* got a contract?'

'I don't know,' Steve Bundy said. 'I got two poun's ten.'

'As a matter of fact, Mister Seagram,' Lyons explained, 'I was jes' about ter sign him when yer came in. I'd decided that if he won he could 'ave regular billing and a retainer. O' course, there's nothing on paper at the moment, but yer can take it that I'm Bundy's manager—'

Seagram chuckled. 'And you can take it from me, Bundy, that you're a free agent.' He probed in a waistcoat pocket. 'Here's my card. My offices are in Albemarle Street, off Piccadilly. Call on me any day next week, but before Saturday, because I'm sailing for Quebec. And don't let Mo talk you into signing anything.'

'Won't yer 'ave a glass o' champagne, Mister Seagram?' Lyons pleaded. 'There might be other things o' mutual interest we could discuss.'

Amused, Seagram declined. 'Mo, after the last occasion I drank champagne made by Schuckert of Poznan I found I'd signed a bearded lady clog-dancer from Budapest.' He turned back to Steve Bundy. 'I'll expect you next week, Bundy – and before you come, spend some of your winnings on some soap.'

'Seagram?' Johnnie Spong gaped. 'Yer don't mean "Gentleman" Seagram, do yer? I mean, not "*Gentleman*" Seagram?' It was totally impossible, but Steve Bundy produced the business card. There was something irrefutable about an engraved business card, and Johnnie Spong held it to the gaslight in a dirty paw. 'Seagram Promotions,' he read slowly with eyes narrowed. 'London, Sydney and New York. Berwick Chambers, Albemarle Street, Piccadilly.' He paused. 'An' a bleedin' telephone number!' That proved it. 'Jesus Christ.' He returned the card reverently, momentarily speechless.

'I thought yer knew 'im,' Steve Bundy suggested. 'Yer *said* yer knew 'im.'

'Ah, well,' Johnnie Spong hastened to explain. 'I wouldn't say I *knew* 'im. Not exactly, that is. When I fought Tinker Taylor in Luton—'

'Luton?' Steve Bundy grimaced. 'What's bleedin' Luton? I mean – did he offer yer a contrack?' He was not quite sure what a contrack was, but two pounds ten shillings suggested that it was an enviable involvement. 'I got offered a contrack.' He still had a pound left and could afford to be condescending. Nonchalantly he jingled the coins in his pocket. 'I might 'ave ter go ter America and fight niggers.'

Johnnie Spong thrashed his thoughts into a degree of cohesion. 'What yer want, Stevie boy, is a professional adviser, see – a bloke what's done it all before—'

'I asked Mo Lyons,' Steve Bundy puzzled, 'and he'd never 'eard of yer. "Mo," I said, "yer must 'ave heard o' Johnnie Spong, who fought fifteen rounds wi' Fusilier Bailey?" and he said, "Who the bleedin' 'ell is Fusilier Bailey, never mind about Johnnie Spong?" '

'Ah,' Johnnie Spong nodded. 'It jes' goes ter show that Mo Lyons don't know much about the fight game, don't it? Never 'eard of Fusilier Bailey?' He snorted contemptuously, thumbed his nose fiercely, and flung a straight left and a right hook in the direction of the Prince Albert, opposite the workmen's cookshop.

Steve Bundy was unimpressed. 'Mister Seagram arst if I

might call at his office before he left fer Quebec. I knocked out Ernie Rowse, see, in the first round. Now I'm going ter fight niggers. Mister Seagram said something about Jack Johnson.'

Johnnie Spong's fists froze in mid-air. '*Jack Johnson*—?'

'Well, not next week,' Steve Bundy said hastily. 'I gotta be taught, Mister Seagram sez — but Johnson's going ter be beat sometime.' He had acquired a matchstick, which he shifted from one corner of his mouth to the other. 'Mister Seagram sez I got promise, and he can teach me what matters.'

Johnnie Spong searched for the fragment of cigarette harboured behind his ear. In the world of professional pugilism 'Gentleman' Seagram's position was arguably only slightly below that of God Almighty. Teddy Roosevelt had sparred in his New York gymnasium, and it was rumoured that King Edward had sought his advice about reducing weight because Mrs Alice Keppel had made certain oblique comments. Even *The Times* was respectful, if distant, towards Mr Maurice Seagram.

Johnnie Spong could see new, rainbow-hued horizons. 'I'd better come with yer,' he decided. 'Contracks can be tricky.' The fragment of cigarette was damp, and he sucked anxiously. 'Besides – yer never know – Mister Seagram might want two.'

'I might go, and I might not,' Steve Bundy shrugged. 'I ain't decided yet. Anyway, if I do, I ain't walking.'

'I'll pay me own fare,' Johnnie Spong volunteered.

Three

In later years it would only be when he had taken a whisky too many that Georgie Pope lost control of his accent and betrayed himself as Australian, and at these moments of carelessness his companions would be equally tipsy and unlikely to notice; if they did, they forgot with the morning's hangover. He avoided being identified as Australian by simply never volunteering the information. If asked, he did not deny it, but would change the subject of conversation immediately, and then, if his questioner persisted, remark that as he had an English mother he was really only half Australian.

Georgie Pope would have firmly denied, even to himself, that his reluctance to confess his country of birth was based on any sense of shame or inferiority. He might have said that he resented being an odd man out in English company, an object of polite curiosity or good-humoured badinage, but that would have been only a half truth. Other Australians more than held their own in such circumstances and did not seek to be excused. True, the other cadets in *Britannia* had laughed at his honest unsophistication, but not spitefully, and his cadet years were the happiest of his life. They had also laughed at the boy who arrived from Inverness in a kilt, at another whose mother had thoughtfully packed water-wings in his valise. They laughed at themselves, at authority, at life. That was the damnest things about these Limeys, Georgie Pope simmered – and they were born with Atlantic salt in their blood. He could outswim most of them even in the chilling Dart river, and he could walk on his hands, which was an enviable achievement. He cared less for mathematics or navigation, and detested Sunday stiff collars and white gloves – but that, they laughed again, was only to be expected of someone descended from a Botany Bay convict.

The jest hurt because it was not widely divorced from the truth. His father was Sir Arthur Pope, the rough-hewn owner of Sydney's largest department store and chairman of the Port Kembla Steel Company. Sir Arthur took pleasure in the boast that the first Pope had come to Australia in 1822 with a cargo of second-hand farm tools which he sold at an extortionate profit and then established a gin distillery that supplied every chandler, tavern and brothel in New South Wales. 'The Pope business, boy,' he told young Georgie, 'was launched on crank hardware and floated on rotgut booze – and don't you forget it.'

The family was now among the state's elite, wealthy and influential. Why young Georgie wanted to join the Navy – and the Limey Navy at that – was beyond his father's comprehension. But the boy had never been all Australian; there was a lot of his mother in him. She had forbidden swearing in the house and drinking before midday, disciplined him to tiny cucumber sandwiches, custard, and Sunday church, and he had submitted like a lamb. He smiled gently when he thought of it.

Georgie Pope's most treasured possessions had been several much-thumbed copies of Brassey's *Naval Annual* and an outdated issue of Jane's *Fighting Ships*. He entertained no desire to enter the Jervis Bay Naval College, which trained a mere forty-five cadets for an Australian Navy that mustered one old light cruiser, three destroyers and a handful of smaller, miscellaneous vessels of Victorian vintage. There had long been talk of additional cruisers being purchased from Britain – second-hand, of course – and even the building of a new battle-cruiser on Clydebank, but the expenditure of one and three-quarter millions pounds was something to which the Senate could not easily agree. After all, the Royal Navy,maintained by the British taxpayer, was already the world's biggest by far, and there was a treaty with Japan, the only country remotely threatening Australia, so why did Australia need a battle-cruiser? If Britain was involved in war, Australia could contribute a contingent of troops as she had to South Africa. Young Georgie Pope was disgusted. Was the Australian Navy never to be anything more than a comical little collection of old ships only capable of puffing around the Great Barrier Reef without venturing too far from land? He had seen a number of British warships, briefly visiting from the China station, admired their white decks, immaculate paintwork and burnished guns, the well-drilled pinnace crews. By comparison *Encounter*, the ageing flagship of the Australian service, was a shabby apology for a ship of war whose ensign would never be flaunted in the West Indies or Hong Kong, the Mediterranean or the Baltic.

'I think you're wrong,' his father argued. 'I'd not lift a finger to stop you, boy, if you've set your mind to it; you'd hate me for the rest of your life, but I still think you're wrong. Sure, there's a lot of things in Australia that don't measure up to the standards in England, but they've had a thousand years to get them right. By the same token, there are advantages we enjoy here that you've taken for granted; you'll miss them – like a quarter million acres without a fence, and beer in quart schooners.' He chuckled. 'Ah, you'll see eucalyptus trees in Kew Gardens, and 'roos shivering in Regents Park, and cockatoos in cages. You'll hear 'Strine in Earls Court and the British Museum, and you'll feel sick for the sight of Hervey Bay, or Elizabeth Street, or just a Sydney tramcar. There's no sundowners in London, boy, swearing about crutching and mustering, and dipping and yarding. Sure, you'll see a motor-car every five minutes, but never another cassowary dance, or hear a big green pigeon at five in the morning—'

Recalling his own experiences of English drawingrooms, Sir Arthur might have added more. He might have said that the upper-class sheilas were all pale-faced creatures who drank tea elegantly and talked in whispers about Mrs Langtry and Lady Brooke – and, of course, poor, dear Princess Alexandra – while their husbands swilled claret and winked at each other. But that would have been unfair, and he was a fair man. There had been at least one English sheila who had shown him, to his discomfiture, how to ride a big horse at a thundering gallop across heath and ploughed field, hedge and ditch, then asked him innocently if he would prefer something quieter tomorrow, just until he got used to it. He had married that English sheila and brought her to Sydney, watched an Australian sun bring peaches to her cheeks and gold to her hair, until she had died on the same day as the old Queen had died in distant, chilly England. 'Her Majesty the Queen,' chattered the telegraph, 'breathed her last at 6.30 pm, surrounded by her children and grandchildren.' But he had cared nothing, for his beloved sheila's cold hand was pressed to his lips, he willing it to stay warm, and crying like a man should never cry.

He had taken passage in the *Orontes*, mildly embarrassed when the steward had shown him to his first-class cabin on the starboard side and commented, 'Blimey – all this fer you, young 'un? There's room 'ere fer all my kids, an' I got seven.' Before he had embarked his father had given him a slim manila envelope.

'It contains two things,' Sir Arthur said. 'First, a letter of introduction to Rear-Admiral St John Primrose, RN.' He smiled. 'It's a damn rummy name, but there's nothing primrosy about Sinjin, boy. He is more like a cactus, I'd say. I haven't seen him for more than twenty years, and I don't know exactly where he is now, but you'll know, pretty damn quick, when he's around. He was my best man at my wedding and he courted your mother before I did. We fought each other to collapse outside Boodles, shook hands afterwards, and were both expelled for ungentlemanly conduct.' He frowned. 'I've never thought much of Limeys in general, but Sinjin's the whitest man I know.

'The other thing's different. It's a certified cheque for five thousand pounds.' He met his son's starried eyes. 'That's right, boy. Five thousand pounds.' It was more than the life's wages of a working man.

'I'll expect you to fight your own troubles, boy, as they come. Don't bleat or shout foul when you're whipped, and don't appeal to me – or you'll learn how deaf I can be. Sinjin Primrose won't show you any sympathy, either. If you go to him with your gambling debts or a pregnant actress he'll show you the damn door.'

He paused. 'But occasionally – *just* occasionally – something bloody disastrous can happen to a man that demands a lot of money, and fast. Do you understand?' He shook his head. 'No, you don't – and, b'God, I hope you never need to. Your mother might have lived if I'd sent a certified cheque to get that American surgeon off the *Ophir* instead of a polite note.

'I said something bloody disastrous. Remember that. If you ever cash that cheque I'll want to know exactly why – and, if I'm not satisfied, you'll repay every penny if it takes you fifty years.'

Devon was greener than he had ever imagined, a land of

sailors and cider, villages of lime-washed, thatched cottages, meadows and orchards, massive, gentle shire horses with beautiful names like Dancer, Rosie, Tip-Toe and Truelove. He had never seen tall hedgerows before, or wild blackberries, nor smelled honeysuckle at night, awakened to a chorus of thrush and blackbird, never listened to distant Sunday church bells that had sung the same loved carillons for three centuries. It was all that he had prayed it might be; it was England, his mother's country, and he had come home.

Dartmouth Naval College had recently been completed, replacing the old *Britannia*, anchored in the Dart river, and the smooth-cheeked cadets, schoolboys still, laboured over trigonometry and navigation, read Mahan and Colomb, rowed, swam, boxed, speculated on the Kaiser's brash ambitions and were arrogantly confident of the Royal Navy's superiority.

Georgie Pope made no attempt to establish a liaison with Rear-Admiral Primrose, but on several occasions he heard the name spoken – once by a gunnery instructor returned from Whale Island, who said that Primrose was a Henry Morgan with a dash of Bligh who ought to put on the retired list before he put Portsmouth to the sword. The letter of introduction and the certified cheque remained in their manila envelope in the Paymaster's safe.

He graduated from Dartmouth without particular distinction but with a reputation for being willing to try anything once, and he joined his first ship, *Albion*, at the beginning of 1907.

Albion was one of a class of battleships of modest size intended specifically for the China station. She displaced only 13,000 tons, mounted four 12-inch guns in two turrets, and in appearance was less formidable than the newly-joined midshipman would have wished. The gunroom, his new home, berthed eight sub-lieutenants and ten other midshipmen, a long table covered with green beize when it was not laid for a meal by a Maltese steward, a dozen battered leather arm-chairs, a dilapidated upright piano and a coal stove. He was the junior Snottie of the mess, he was told with satisfaction by the midshipman relieved of that predicament, and would remain so until the next new arrival. It meant that he would fetch and carry for his betters, brew the cocoa and toast the cheese, lash up watchkeepers' hammocks, and have his head punched whenever a senior felt so inclined.

He would have to submit to several years of general, usually menial, duties – running errands, handling a picket boat, taking libertymen ashore and bringing back fresh-killed meat, keeping a deck log – before he could specialise in gunnery, torpedoes, signals or navigation. During those several years, without an independent income, his financial situation would be tenuous. A midshipman's pay was 1s. 9d a day, to which was added a compulsory allowance of £50 a year from his parents, but he was required to donate 3d per day to the Chaplain for instruction in nautical astronomy. His advancement to a Lieutenancy in due course, with 5s. a day, would mean little improvement; most of his pay would be consumed by his mess bill and laundry bill, the Silver Fund and the Sports Fund, his tailor and outfitter. Georgie Pope occasionally thought wistfully of the manila envelope, but not for long. Walking miles to save the fare of a train or tram, or politely declining entertainment he could not afford to return, these did not constitute 'something bloody disastrous'. The cheque remained in the Paymaster's safe, and he envied the Able Seaman with his daily two shillings on which nobody had prior claims, his duty free shag and his tot of rum.

Albion's record, like her appearance, was less than distinguished. Built by the Thames Iron Works, at her launching in 1898 her wash had wrecked several temporary stands along the slipway and thirty-four spectators, mostly women and children, had been drowned. After four years in China she had joined the Channel Fleet and, off Lerwick, was rammed by the battleship *Duncan*. In February 1907, when Georgie Pope came aboard, she was attached to the Home Fleet at Portsmouth. With her sisters of the class, *Albion* was regarded by experts as being a second-class battleship even by pre-Dreadnought standards, and now, with Dreadnoughts in service, she was obsolescent. To Georgie Pope, however, she was the finest warship afloat.

'We did our speed trials yesterday,' he wrote enthusiastically to his father, 'and achieved 18¼ knots, burning 12½ tons of coal in one hour! Our forward main deck guns were swamped and the fo'c'sle was flooded!' To Pope Senior any battleship with guns that became flooded posed uncomfortable problems, but, he conceded, he was a layman in such matters, and presumably the Navy knew what it was doing. 'Tomorrow,' his son added, 'we are going to coal ship – 1200 tons!' That, decided Sir Arthur, was not at all surprising. At 12½ tons per hour the ship must be filled to the rails with damn coal.

'Ello, my 'andsome,' the pretty waitress in the Falmouth olde tea shoppe had greeted him, smiling. 'Are yew on that ol' boat with the guns, then?' It was not a boat, he corrected her. It was a ship, and he served *in* her. He would have a pot of tea, please, and strawberries and cream. Cornish cream teas, the notice in the window said, one shilling. He had twelve pence exactly and had counted them surreptitiously in his pocket to make sure.

She was a big country girl with fine breasts pushed high by her corset so that they threatened to explode over the top of her bodice, and she leaned over him to brush crumbs from the table, shrugging her shoulders slightly to afford an even franker perspective. 'They guns,' she asked. 'How do 'ee fire 'un, then?'

He was not prepared to explain to a waitress the intricacies of gunnery firing circuitry. 'With a trigger,' he simplified, 'and cordite.'

'Ah,' she nodded, as if she had always suspected as much. 'Cordite.'

She brought strawberries, cream, scones and tea, then leaned over him again. 'I bet 'ee's got a girl in every port. Yew sailors.' Georgie Pope was acquainted with very few ports, and not at all with girls.

She sighed deeply to protrude her breasts again for his benefit. 'I finishes at seven o'clock,' she confided. 'I was a-thinking o' going ter the Electric Palace fer three penn'orth o' dark, only I 'ates going alone, see.'

Ye olde tea shoppe, Georgie Pope decided, had suddenly become rather warm. He eased his starched shirt-collar with a finger. In *Britannia* and in the gunroom of *Albion* – except for occasional references to a mother or sister – the subject of women was taboo, but at eighteen he was aware that things like this happened. There were fewer inhibitions among the lower deck messes. The men talked easily about the 'parties' they had walked on Southsea Common or Portsdown Hill, and the fumbling exchanges that had followed. Listening to them – and they did not care that he did – it all seemed so easy. A man winked at a girl, she giggled, and then the resulting sequence of events was as sure as if both had rehearsed them.

Georgie Pope poured tea, then gave his attention to the strawberries and cream. The girl with the breasts served two elderly ladies at a far table and then returned. 'Do 'ee like moving pictures?'

He had watched moving pictures only two or three times and had not been impressed by either the flickering quality of the film or the slapstick nonsense it projected. The fairground was the proper place for moving pictures. Even so, the prospect of an hour in the darkness with the girl with the breasts stimulated a train of thought that caused him to cough on a strawberry. Silk stockings and garters. He felt himself redden. In the darkness nobody would see; he could remove his cap and turn up his collar.

'Well,' she whispered impatiently, 'do 'ee or don't 'ee?' She was three, perhaps four, years older than he was, a flirt, and his for the taking if he had the courage. He must be careful not to be seen in the street with her, but perhaps he could meet her outside the Electric Palace—

'Of course,' he said, and reached for another scone. The gunroom must never get to hear about this, or he might find himself sharing an embarrassing confrontation with his Divisional Officer, Lieutenant-Commander Wickwire, perhaps even the Captain. He glanced at the girl, feigning nonchalance. She probably wore only cotton stockings. 'Did you say seven o'clock?'

She nodded. 'There's five comicals and the Relief o' Peking, the Army manoeuvres on Salisbury Plain, the launching o' the *Mauretania*, and they conjurers, Maskelyne an' Devant.' Predictably, she giggled. 'O' course, I doant know 'ow much o' they pictures yew'll see – not in the dark.' Then she added, 'It's sixpence an' ninepence.'

Then he remembered.

'Er' – he apologised – 'I'd forgotten. I have to be aboard by seven-thirty – quarterdeck duty—' But he had excused himself too adroitly, and his stammer confirmed the lie. It was the girl's turn to flush. Then she tossed her head. 'It doant matter ter me, doant 'ee think that.' Her eyes were angry. 'An' if 'ee's finished, that'll be one-and-six.'

Georgie Pope struggled for comprehension. 'One and six?'

She pointed her breasts at him. 'One-an'-six, me 'andsome,' she confirmed, tightlipped. 'Or, if 'ee likes, eighteen pence.'

'I thought it was a shilling,' he protested. 'In the window it says a shilling, doesn't it?' He was absolutely sure that the notice had said a shilling. He had read it as he thumbed his pennies.

The white orbs of her breasts swelled again, just to show him what he might have enjoyed in the darkness of the Electric Palace; her bodice strained but held firm. 'Yew 'ad a cream tea, didn't 'ee – and that's a shilling – an' *tea*, and that's sixpence. A cream tea doant include *tea*.' It was all very simple. 'That's one-an'-six.' She shot a glance at the elderly ladies at the far table, seeking confirmation, but they were discreetly looking elsewhere. She returned her attention to Georgie Pope. 'One-an'-six.'

Georgie Pope suppressed an urge to run for the door. He counted his twelve coppers, yet again, into the palm of a hand. 'I'm sorry, I don't seem to have enough. I only have a shilling—'

She stared at him, amazed. 'Yew mean yew *can't pay*?'

The two elderly ladies had decided that they had an urgent appointment elsewhere, and departed with whispers and backward glances, leaving a gratuitous penny under a plate. Georgie Pope was alone with the waitress.

'I'm sorry,' he repeated, miserably. 'If you'll take an IOU—?'

'For sixpence?' she ridiculed. 'An' yew a Navy officer, smart as paint, an' talkin' about they cordite – an' yew doesn't 'ave *sixpence*?' She scooped the twelve coins into the pocket of her pinafore and took possession of the last uneaten scone.

'You have my absolute word,' he assured her, 'that I'll call when I'm next ashore – the day after tomorrow. My name's Pope – George Pope.' He hesitated, then added rashly, 'Look, if you like, I'll take you to the Electric Palace.'

'I'll believe that when I see 'un,' she shrugged, weighing the offer. 'I knows what yew sailors are.' When she considered, there seemed little choice. 'Us'll go in the nine-pennies, then?' she bargained.

Georgie Pope nodded.

He did not understand why it should be necessary to steam 375 miles to Bantry Bay to fire the ship's guns; the ocean seemed sufficiently wide and empty anywhere, but the six ships – *Exmouth, Albemarle, Cornwallis, Duncan, Russell* and *Albion* – pushed their ram-nosed bows westward until they met the long green rollers of the Atlantic and the black smoke from the tall funnels was whipped away by a salt, stinging wind. The ships rolled and the spray flew in sheets over the fo'c'sles, drenching. This, he told himself, was the real sea at last, something the blue-water cadets in Jervis Bay had never seen.

Until the turn of the century the gun-laying procedure in the Royal Navy – indeed, in all navies – had been a haphazard business and accuracy was abysmal. In 1897 the percentage of hits on a towed target, to rounds fired, was thirty-two percent. In ten years, however, three officers – Admiral Sir John Fisher and Captains Percy Scott and John Jellicoe – had revolutionised techniques, insisting on the introduction of Barr & Stroud rangefinders, and organising 'battle practice' test-firing under realistic conditions in which every ship's gunnery efficiency could be assessed and compared with her sisters' on a competitive basis. By 1905, for the first time, hits exceeded misses, and in 1907 had reached seventy-nine percent.

'To begin with, Pope,' Lieutenant-Commander Wickwire, the Gunnery Officer, had said, 'you'll be my "doggie", which means you'll follow me like a shadow, watch, listen and learn, and run like a hound when I send you off somewhere. Understand? I hear that your most notable achievement is walking on your hands. I thought all Australians walked that way, upside down.' It was not very funny, but Georgie Pope laughed politely because the Gunnery Officer was a fierce, unapproachable officer held in only slightly less regard than the Captain, who was God, and to be addressed with such familiarity was comforting. It was a good start. Wickwire went even further. 'Perhaps,' he pondered, 'you should be my dingo.' Georgie Pope laughed again.

'Take your binoculars, a stop watch and a signal pad,' Wickwire ordered, 'and position yourself in the forward starboard six-inch casemate. We'll be firing main armament to starboard, forward turret first. Time the shots and observe the fall. I'll be doing the same from the conning tower, but we may have trouble with smoke, so we'll hedge our bets.'

Forward on the main deck the 6-inch gun casemates were mounted in sponsons – bellied protruberances from the ship's side – which allowed them to be fired directly ahead as well as abeam. Through the open, nine-inch sighting port Georgie Pope could see the streaming bow-wave, only twelve feet immediately below him, the horizon rising and falling gently, and a narrow ribbon of sky. If he turned his head he could watch *Russell* and *Duncan*, wallowing in line, but he focused his glasses on the floating target, 7000 yards away to starboard. This was almost the real thing. This was where the casemate officer would be if the distant target was the *Braunschweig* or the *Hessen*. From the nearby voicepipe to the conning tower he could hear Wickwire talking to someone else. In a way, Georgie Pope told himself, he was the Assistant Gunnery Officer. He wished he had remembered to sharpen his pencil.

The 6-inch gun crew lounged idly on the main deck behind him; they were not involved in the long range shoot. He could smell forbidden tobacco smoke, and wondered if he should order pipes out. 'Begin first shoot,' he heard Wickwire say.

'Don't yer want the shutter closed, sir?' the petty officer

asked him at his shoulder. The muzzles of two 12-inch guns were only thirty feet away.

Georgie Pope was not aware that there was a shutter to close. He had brought a handful of cotton wool but had been reluctant to plug his ears because he could see nobody else doing so. For a fleeting moment he did not understand what the petty officer was saying. Then he did, but it was too late.

When he regained consciousness he was lying in a suspended cot in the sick bay, without his shoes and with his clothing loosened. A surgeon probationer leaned over him and, beyond, Wickwire and the Surgeon-Commander stood in conversation. His head ached and the light hurt his eyes.

'Concussion,' the Surgeon-Commander was saying. 'There's an Ordnance Committee report that measured thirty pounds of blast pressure per square foot as far as a hundred and fifty feet from the muzzle of a twelve-inch gun. I'm not surprised that anyone exposed at only thirty feet should be rendered senseless.' He shrugged.

'He's coming to, sir,' the probationer reported, and the Surgeon groped for his stethoscope. 'Good,' he grunted. 'How do you feel, lad?'

Georgie Pope was bewildered. 'A bit queer, sir. Dizzy.'

'Well, your ear-drums seem to be intact, and you're lucid. Can you manipulate your extremities?'

Georgie Pope experimented. 'Yes, sir.'

'Any pains other than your headache? Any nausea?'

'No, sir.'

The Surgeon held up a splayed hand. 'How many fingers?'

'Four, sir,' Georgie Pope frowned, 'and a thumb.'

'And do you know what six nines are?'

'Fifty-four, sir.'

'How many cats have nine tails?'

Georgie Pope considered. 'None, sir. Cats have one tail each, unless they're Manx—'

'All right, Pope.' The Surgeon nodded. 'Your brain seems to be in one piece, anyway, but you'll stay in that cot for today and tomorrow. Fluid diet, and perhaps a purgative later. We'll screen off the light. Just keep quiet and try to sleep.' In the passageway outside he turned to Wickwire. 'We don't know a lot about concussion. I remember an able seaman in the *Empress of India* who was comatose for six days, and afterwards couldn't spell his name or remember where his mess was, or tell red from green. And he urinated in the Captain's gig. Eventually he was discharged unfit, but I never did decide if he had genuinely lost his memory or if he was just a damn good actor. He remembered the price of a jug of ale as soon as he got out of the dockyard gate.' He chuckled. 'Anyway, I don't think young Pope has suffered much damage. You can have him back in a few days – and perhaps you'll keep an eye on him. I'll dare say he'll be nervous about sitting in a casemate again when the twelve-inch are firing broadside.'

'He's going to,' Wickwire said, 'as soon as he's back to normal duty. The best thing for anyone that comes off at a fence is to get right back in the saddle and do it again. The next time, I'll wager, he'll have the damn shutter closed – and he'll never forget it.'

'We-ell—' The Surgeon was uncertain. 'Sometimes I think you drive these youngsters too hard, Wickwire. They're not made of brass, y'know.' They had reached the upper deck, and both gazed at the Irish coastline, blurred and purple to northward. 'This beggar-my-neighbour obsession with bigger and bigger guns, flying machines and submarines – well, there's got to come a time when mere flesh and blood can't keep pace.' He frowned. 'Do you know that, scientifically, we've advanced further in the last fifty years than in the whole previous history of man? It's too fast, and we're still accelerating, scientifically, all the time. But human fibre stays the same, and the day must come when it's no longer adequate. *Homo sapiens* was never designed to be hurled through the air, or breathe under the sea, or be exposed to the concussion of high explosive. What are we going to do next? Fly men to the moon? Ah, it'll happen – perhaps not in our lifetime, Wickwire, but it'll happen.'

'I'll not deny it,' Wickwire nodded, 'but there's something else that's going to happen a lot sooner – a war between the major powers. It's going to be the most vicious war of all time, and young men like Pope, on both sides, are going to fight it. The country that survives is going to be the one with the biggest ships and the biggest guns, the most submarines and the fastest flying machines.'

'And flesh and blood,' the Surgeon added.

'And flesh and blood,' Wickwire nodded again. 'That's why I drive my young men hard. They've got to be better, tougher and more determined than the young men on the other side. The Germans are building some damn fine ships, perhaps – who knows? – better than ours.'

Two days later the Surgeon-Commander examined Georgie Pope again.

'You've got a slight temperature,' he observed, 'but nothing exciting.' He stabbed with his stethoscope. 'How do you feel now?'

'Just a little out of sorts, sir, with an occasional headache and not much of an appetite.'

The other grunted. 'Not for boiled fish and tapioca pudding, I dare say. And you've got a slight rash on your chest.' He frowned. 'Likely it's this confounded sick bay; it gets too damn humid at sea. The probationer will give you some coal tar soap. If the rash persists, come back to see me – or if you experience any urinary trouble, vertigo or memory lapses.' He hummed as he penned a note on the midshipman's history sheet. 'All right, lad. I'm recommending daymen's duties for a week, plenty of fresh air, no alcohol, plenty of exercise but nothing violent.' He paused, smiling. 'If you don't get blown up again, or otherwise brutally destroy yourself, Pope, I'd say you'll live to see old age – always allowing they don't hang you in the meantime.'

Georgie Pope returned to duty in due course, free of all concussion symptoms and, to all appearances, a normal healthy young male. True, from time to time during the years that followed, his rash reappeared briefly and faded again. It was a mild annoyance, but nothing more than that – prickly heat, perhaps, or a nettle-rash, eczema, or, as the senior Sub-Lieutenant sniffed, a sign of his long delayed puberty.

He had no way of knowing, nor had the Surgeon recognised – because he was deceived by circumstances – the hallmarks of a disease to which no teen-age midshipman was expected to expose himself. It would have meant far more than an embarrassing confrontation with his Divisional Officer.

Georgie Pope had tried hard to forget the girl with the breasts, the guilty lewdness in the darkness of the Electric Palace and, worst of all, the shameful conclusion in the library gardens from which he had finally run in disgust and disillusionment.

The disease within him was quiescent now, like a sleeping animal, but one day it would stir and stretch its claws. Then, slowly, tertiary syphilis would begin to manifest itself in all its ghastly forms, in bones, heart, throat, blood-vessels, in impotence, incontinence, epilepsy, gradual paralysis and madness.

Four

For as long as Albert Selley could remember he had shared the lumpy mattress of a narrow, truckle bed with his younger brother, Martin, and beyond a string-suspended blanket that bisected the room his two sisters, Harriet and Kate, occupied a similarly narrow bed under the window. The boys slept in their shirts and kept their socks on in the winter. It had always been that way. He knew every crack in the low ceiling, and if they had been a network of rivers could easily have navigated the shortest route from the door to the big brown stain in the far corner.

It was a small room, but no smaller than the one adjoining, in which his parents slept in a bed that had double doors which could be closed over it. The separating wall was thin, and when Albert grew to understand certain things he would sometimes lie with his ear to the plaster, listening to the murmur of voices, the creaking of old bed-springs and sometimes his mother's protesting plea, weaving intriguing visions behind his closed eyes of what was happening, until overcome by sleep.

If he lifted the curtain from the bedroom window, which he seldom did, he would see below a tiny yard enclosed by a decaying brick wall, the roof of the water-closet, a rusting, over-spilling dustbin and an old, galvanised iron bath hung on a nail. The dark, cobbled street stretched to right and left, terraced by narrow houses that backed on to others precisely similar and equally grimy. There was always a smell of dampness and stale urine. Had he lifted his eyes he would see a tangle of chimneys and slate rooftops hazed with smoke and, distant, the cranes and derricks of Leith Docks, where his father worked.

Below stairs was the living room, shabbily furnished, with a black, iron stove and a brass fender under a mantelpiece and a cheap German clock. There was always a filled kettle on the stove, and at night the room was lit by gas that hissed gently. A door opened into a diminutive, stone-floored scullery housing a sink with a single water-tap and a cupboard for foodstuffs. A small, tarnished mirror hung behind the sink, partnered by pulpy soap in a saucer and a communal towel. The scullery's outer door, under which a puddle always formed when it rained, led to the yard, the water-closet and the street.

Albert would not have considered his circumstances unfortunate. There were many poorer homes in Edinburgh; the Selley family had three of its members earning and a fourth was promised. His father, Donald Selley, had once been employed by Hawthorns' shipbuilding yard, but the bottle had always been his ruin, and he was now reduced to unloading the timber, veneers and grain from the ships of the Baltic trade that docked almost daily. He got drunk on Saturdays and usually on Sundays, continuing daily until he was spent out. Mrs Mary Selley climbed from beside her snoring husband at 4 each morning to walk through the dark in her cloth cap and shawl to Princes Street, where she scrubbed floors and stairways, and Albert delivered for Coleman's Bakery for four shillings and a weekly bag of stale and broken. Harriet, who was thirteen – two years younger than Albert – had her name taken by the Leith Fish Importing Company and would be given a knife and a place at the bench as soon as the next woman was laid off for fighting, soliciting or pregnancy.

Donald Selley was a large man, florid, with bad teeth and an uncertain temper when the whisky was in him. His homecoming behaviour was always unpredictable. He might sweep every cup and plate from the table or toss a ha'penny to the children, smash a fist into his wife's face or order her upstairs to wait for him with her breeks down. There were times when he reeled home with a bloodied mouth after a confrontation with some other docker as belligerent as himself, and on such occasions it was wise to be elsewhere.

They were forbidden to be elsewhere when the galvanised iron bath was taken from its nail in the yard and brought into the living room. The kettle and every available saucepan steamed on the stove, and while the children waited in kitchen or bedroom Donald Selley enjoyed the privilege of the first water, a new inch of yellow soap and a dry towel. The girls followed in turn, then Albert and Martin. The latter would reach adulthood before he experienced bath-water that was not grey, scummed and tepid, a towel that was not sodden.

Bath night, however, had its compensation when all had been cleared away. It was the night for fish and chips – 'a penny and a ha'porth six times' from the shop in the next street – newspaper wrapped, drenched in vinegar, hot and succulent. On balance, fish and chips were worth a bath.

Fortnightly, Donald Selley cut the boys' hair, cropping it brutally close to the scalp but leaving an inch of fringe over the forehead – to no apparent advantage, but it was the accepted mode. The girls' hair was combed with paraffin to discourage vermin. Clothing was infallibly second-hand and further handed down from older to younger. There were still children in Leith who went barefoot on weekdays, or wore elders' cast-offs, or women's shoes with the heels cut down, but every year the Selley boys had boots from the festoons in Macintyre's oilshop, armoured with hob-nails that could gouge sparks from the cobbles of Inkerman Street in defiance of their father's warning that if he saw them 'tearin' ye bluidy boots ta pieces I'll gie ye a bluidy thrashin' ye'll no bluidy fergit'. The girls wore pinafores, clean weekly, with a single pocket to carry a 'wee bitty rag' for nose-wiping, pen-wiping, or staunching the blood of a grazed knee – a frequent consequence of the street's juvenile warfare.

The family's bitterest experience had followed the day that Donald Selley hauled a well-dressed corpse from the dock with, more important, pockets that contained twenty-three sovereigns and a monogrammed gold watch. The corpse was unmarked and, with such possessions, death could hardly have been the result of foul play. At the time Selley was penniless, but he was also cunning. He deposited the corpse behind a pile of Swedish timber, raced home to hide the sovereigns and the watch, and relieved Mary Selley of all the money in her purse, a total of three shillings and two pence which included the week's rent. These coins he placed in the corpse's pocket and then reported his find to the dockyard authorities.

The police, wise in such matters, ordered Selley to turn out his own pockets, and he did so indignantly. Bluidy hell. His pockets were empty, but the corpse had three shillings and two pence. Bluidy hell. Did the police think that he'd stoop to robbing a dead body? The police did, but for the moment they were defeated.

Donald Selley returned to Inkerman Street once more, briefly, to collect the twenty-three sovereigns, and then embarked on an orgy of drinking that lasted for two weeks. During that time the Selley family saw nothing of him, but they heard of his unsteady progress from tavern to tavern, from Portobello in one direction to Corstorphine in the other. When he did reappear, he was unshaven and dirty, his eyes red-rimmed. He stank of beer.

He stared at the salt pork belly and bread which was to have been the Selleys' only meal of substance for the day. 'Ha' ye nothin' better than this?' he snarled, and flung it to the floor. His wife's purse, this time, was empty. He glared at her, unbelieving.

'There's nae mair till Saturday,' Mary Selley pleaded. Likely she could rescue the pork belly, and Albert could beg a stale loaf from the bakery. 'Och, it's been hard, Donal'—'

He snorted, still glaring at her. It was alcohol he needed, desperately, not a woman's whining. He could have smashed her mouth, but it would have gained him nothing, and it was certain that he had lost his work at the dock, where he might otherwise have wheedled an advance of a few shillings. There was only one thing remaining; the gold watch.

The police had not lost interest in Donald Selley. The drowned man's identity had been established and a missing gold watch, valued at forty guineas, had been exactly described to them. They had watched Selley's drunken itinerary of the past two weeks, and might have questioned him on the source of his wealth a dozen times, but they were not new to this game. Selley could have a little rope; sovereigns were not monogrammed, but the gold watch was. Sooner or later, they knew, the soverigns would be spent, and when they were – given twenty-four hours – Selley would try to sell or pawn the watch, his cunning dulled by two weeks of inebriation. Every pawnbroker and jeweller in the district had been warned and were waiting for a Leith docker to proffer a forty-guinea watch that his father had left him but which, tragically, must be sold to feed six hungry mouths. It was so easy, it was almost unfair.

Donald Selley, dock labourer of Inkerman Street, Leith, was sentenced to six months imprisonment with hard labour. He was fortunate. The coroner had already declared that the deceased had taken his own life while the balance of his mind was disturbed. Otherwise the Leith Police, after so much trouble, might have pressed more serious charges.

Life without Donald Selley was more peacefully predictable. The loss of his weekly wages – or that part of them that he surrendered – threatened difficulties, but in compensation he was being maintained by His Majesty, and then Harriet was summoned by the Leith Fish Importing Company to split and gut herrings while the drifters were landing. Mary Selley worked longer hours in Princes Street and took young Katie into her larger bed, leaving Harriet to sleep alone under the window. Albert considered that he, as the senior, might more deservedly enjoy exclusive sleeping accommodation, but could think of no permutation that would allow it. He was, however, now the man of the house and the younger Selleys accepted it with only a degree of resentment. He sat in his father's chair and put his feet on the brass fender, but was not yet ready to claim the first bath water; with Donald Selley's return only six months away it was probably wiser to forgo that privilege entirely. He had no taste for tobacco, but he occasionally eyed the Montrose Arms on the corner of Inkerman Street, wondering if he dare, at sixteen.

Harriet returned daily from Leith docks, locked herself in the scullery and washed the fish stink from herself with a kettleful of hot water in the sink. The language of the women at the gutting benches, and their lewd topics of conversation, had initially shocked her, but her more sensitive instincts had soon hardened and she was capable of making tentative contributions of her own, to her companions' amusement. Och, the wee lass could talk when she'd had her hokey-pokey, and not before. Sexual experience, it seemed, was an initiation to an inner circle.

For the two youngest, Martin and Katie, life had also begun a new chapter. There was no apprehension of their father's mood, no running from his oaths. This year there would likely be no boots from Macintyre's, either, but there were others without boots. They could brawl in the streets later at nights, swing on lampposts, pilfer from barrows or scramble for fragments of ice on the fish dock. There were no occasional ha'pennies, no fish and chips, but no thrashings either.

Albert had finished his deliveries, swept out the bakery and had been dismissed early. Except that he was free of work, however, there was little advantage in an early return to the empty house in Inkerman Street. He hesitated outside the Montrose Arms for a long moment, speculating as he had before. If a man worked, and had the money for it, there was no harm in a jug of ale, was there? He had heard his father say that, only his father, after a jug or two of ale, went on to whisky and then more whisky until his eyes reddened, his voice slurred, and his every penny was gone. Albert turned away, then halted again, jingling the few coins in his own pocket – too few for whisky, but a man had a right to a jug of ale after a day's work.

Inside, with an air of unconcern he did not feel, he called for a pint of ordinary, and the potman drew it up with a grin. 'Ye're no wasting any time, then, laddie? Wi' ye feyther awa', we were thinking o' gang bankrupt.' He glanced at the coppers on the bar. 'Och, nae sovereigns?' He chuckled.

Albert drank his ale in silence, then ordered a second, just to show. 'Ye're over thirteen, I suppose?' the potman enquired, and winked. 'I dinna want tae lose ma licence, ye ken.'

The second jug was as much as Albert could comfortably consume, but it had generated within him a warm glow of confidence. 'I'll tak' another o' the same,' he said, and sniffed. Ale was nothing; it was just the bulk that was discomforting. He was beginning to understand why a man drank whisky, but he had no more money with which to experiment. He disposed of the third jug determinedly, and when he regained the street he perceived that life had golden horizons of which he had never previously been aware. He almost fell at the kerb.

Harriet was at the scullery sink, washing herself, and she was completely unclothed. She had locked the inner door but had forgotten the door to the yard. She twisted desperately; her clothes were beyond reach. 'Och – Albert—!' He closed the door, grinning as the potman had grinned, and looked at her.

It was strange, when he thought about it, that he had never regarded Harriet as anything but a young sister, anything but a flat-chested juvenile who occupied a bed with another even younger sister beyond the hung blanket. Familiarity had long dulled any curiousity. Now, however, quite suddenly, she was different. She was still thin, almost waif-like, but her body was no longer that of a juvenile.

'Ye've sprooted a wee pair o' bubs,' he observed, and reached for her. She retreated, but the sink was behind her, and he took one of her small breasts in an appraising hand. Her flesh was damp. 'Albert!' she pleaded, shocked. 'Ye shouldna.' He toyed with the bronze coin of her nipple, and she allowed him, watching his face flush. Then he lowered his hand to the top of her legs.

She made a token effort to shrug free. 'Albert – I'm ye *seester*, d'ye no ken?' She was frightened, but his hands were exciting her. 'If ye feyther knew—'She drew a deep breath. This was what the women talked about, on the fish dock. It was shameful, but shamefully satisfying. And it was flattering that Albert, always her uncaring senior, should suddenly decide that she was interesting.

'If he knew,' Albert said, 'he'd likely be doing the bluidy same as I'm gang ta.' He had never remotely thought of his sister's puny body as sexually desirable, but he pulled her to him and kissed her on the mouth, clumsily, fumbling at his own buttons. 'Och, Albert,' she breathed, and then, comprehending, twisted away. 'Ye mustna! If Martin or Katie came in—' She stooped for her tangled clothes.

Albert swayed. 'I'll ha' ye,' he promised, 'when I feel like it – so dinna fergit it.'

He had her that same night, waiting until Martin, at his side, breathed evenly in sleep, and then inching himself from the bed. On the other side of the suspended blanket Harriet was still awake in anticipation, her emotions a confusion of fear and curiosity. She dreaded the fulfilment of Albert's earlier threat but could not erase the excrutiating hope that it would be. When he slid beside her, groping, her inhibitions lingered momentarily, then fled. She would have submitted if only for the reason that her brother had always been the dominant senior, albeit off-hand, justifying her acquiescence by reasoning that the responsibility was his, not hers.

In the intimately gregarious environment of the narrow houses of Leith there was no hiding of sexual anatomy until puberty imposed a reticence to expose oneself before the gaze of others. Children were aware that there were differences, but they were not relevant differences. Boys played aggressive football, fought in gangs and despised girls. Girls played with dolls and hoops, wore curl-rags and giggled in groups. The twain did not meet; there was no common ground until stirring adulthood began to generate interest in new, different values.

It was different now. His hunger was different and so was her response to it. Both were naive, and if anyone had suggested that what they were doing was sordid and incestuous they would not have understood either the words or their implications. A few moments of mutual incitement, clumsy but exhilarating, provoked the final experiment. His vehemence startled her, but he was quickly sated, and it was she who sought to prolong the exchange when he shrugged free and left the bed without a word. Harriet was shocked, ashamed, and yet curiously gratified. She recognised more clearly now what the other women meant; she had something for which Albert, her presumptuous brother, had an animal desire, and from tonight he would no longer be her lord but her vassal. Harriet smiled to herself in the darkness. And she would hold her own among the ribaldry at the gutting benches.

Albert avoided her eyes, said nothing of consequence, and left early for Coleman's Bakery. He walked with his hands deep into his pockets, his head bowed in thought. By even the warped values of Inkerman Street he was aware of having done wrong, but it could not be undone now. Even in Inkerman Street, where youths boasted and lied about their sexual adventures, nobody boasted of having enjoyed a sister. He fought to expunge the picture of the humiliating episode from his mind, but it reasserted itself repeatedly during the day. If his father, Donald Selley, ever heard of it, Albert could expect a merciless thrashing. Bluidy hell. He hoped that Harriet would have the sense to keep a shut mouth. She, too, would get the buckle-end of her father's belt. Aye, she'd keep a shut mouth.

By the end of his working day he felt more assured. Bluidy hell, but it must never happen again. He walked homeward with his bag of stale and broken, paused outside the Montrose Arms, fingering his four shillings. He owed three to his mother and retained one for himself. A man was entitled to a jug of ale, wasn't he?

He could not have sworn that he wanted a jug of ale, but he took one. It delayed his return to the house, and, when he re-emerged from the Inkerman Arms after consuming three jugs he no longer experienced any qualms. He almost fell at the kerb.

When the table had been cleared and the crocks washed,

the last hour of the evening in the Inkerman Street house was a sterile period during which Mary Selley darned or sewed a losing battle with the ravages in the childrens' clothes, or hung dank washing on a string over the stove, Harriet pinned her hair, and young Martin counted and re-counted grubby cigarette cards on the table. There were no books or newspapers; there had once been a phonograph, but Donald Selley had wrecked it during one of his drunken angers. Conversational exchanges were brief and confined to the superficial. The yellow gaslight hissed quietly and the cheap German clock ticked until Mary Selley, her chores finished and aware that she must rise at four, retired to her bed with Kate, ordered Martin to do the same, and warned Albert and Harriet that they were burning gas they could ill afford. Harriet, unwilling to remain alone with Albert, quickly followed upstairs, leaving her brother with his feet on the fender and staring at the dying glow of the fire.

He had no intention of repeating his adventure of the previous night. It would never happen again. He had persuaded himself that it was he, Albert, who had suffered an injury to his status; in a moment of weakness he had allowed himself to be exploited. Now it would not be easy to reassume his authoritive standing when Harriet's eyes mocked him with their knowledge. And what if she whispered of it to Kate, or, worse, let slip some careless comment at the gutting bench on the fish dock?

His resolve, and the resentment that bolstered it, lasted just until he reached the bedroom. Martin breathed steadily, his face in the crook of an elbow, but Albert could see the grey square of the window in the darkness because the hung blanket had been eased several inches aside. Then he heard Harriet stir, and knew that she waited. He groped his way towards her, felt her hand take his and draw him to the bed.

The date of Donald Selley's release from prison was only two weeks away when young Martin made his move, and he chose his opportunity very carefully. Albert and several of his fellows had gone to watch football at the Hibernians' ground, Mary Selley with her oilcloth bag and worn purse would be absent an hour or more at the Saturday market, and Kate could be in any of a dozen locations but would not return before dusk. Martin even waited until Harriet went to the bedroom to sort the least-darned pair from a half dozen stockings before he followed, to regard her from the open door.

'I ken what ye're doing wi' Albert when he goes to ye bed o' nights.'

Harriet froze momentarily, then whirled. 'He doesna!' But her face had reddened.

He nodded. 'Och, he does. I'm no asleep like ye think. Ye've been having ye breeks doon.'

There was silence, and then Harriet drew breath. 'I dinna ken what ye're talkin' aboot.'

'Aye, ye do. D'ye think I'm a bairn? I've listened to ye fer weeks.'

Harriet stared at him angrily. 'Ye've a dirty mind, Martin Selley. If ye feyther was here, and I told him, ye'd get a thrashing—'

'He'll be here in two weeks, aboot,' he agreed, 'and I've a mind to tell him mesel' – but I'm no sure who'll be gettin' the thrashing, ye ken.'

There was another silence. Harriet looked at the stocking twisted tightly around her knuckles, then swallowed. 'Ye wouldna!'

'Wouldn't I?' He laughed nervously, wetted his lips. 'Aye, I would – but I wouldna want, if I was doing the same, would I?'

She did not immediately comprehend. 'The same?'

'If I was doing the same as Albert,' he explained, watching her face. 'I wouldna want anyone to know, would I?'

Now Harriet understood, and her flush deepened. Her eyes met his, contemptuously. 'Ye filthy pig! Ye're only thirteen, an' ye think—?'

Martin was unsure of his ground, but he had gone too far to withdraw. 'Not o' nights,' he bargained. 'Only sometimes, when the others are awa' from the hoose.' He paused. 'Like today, ye ken.' Harriet was still staring at him with her lips tightly clenched. 'Weel,' he shrugged, 'I'll no ask ye again.' He half turned.

'No—' Harriet gasped. 'Martin – if I let ye – sometimes – ye'll swear ye'll not tell ye feyther, or anyone?'

He grinned, both relieved and elated; it had been easier than he could possibly have imagined. 'Och, I dinna have to swear. How could I tell anyone?'

Harriet, torn between abhorrence towards her brother's proposal and her terror of her father's savage temper, would have liked to play for time. She nodded. 'I'll tell ye when,' she choked, but he had closed the door behind him.

'I'll tell ye when,' he corrected, his eyes on her. 'Now.'

Five

The Mercantile Marine Training Ship *Worcester*, moored in the Thames off Greenhithe, was not the same as Dartmouth, where, it was said with a disdain not untinged with envy, the gentlemen cadets had bandsmen servants and cucumber sandwiches on white-covered tables. The *Worcester* provided cadetship training on the cheap, and, for Hedley Bellman's father, cheapness was important. It was difficult to understand how the Reverend Francis Bellman managed to provide any fees at all from his modest stipend; Hedley realised why his father was always such a threadbare figure, why he had relinquished his pipe of tobacco and even his once daily glass of sherry, why he separated the rare silver coins from the coppers in the church collection with such care, smiled sadly over the metal trousers button that appeared on three successive occasions. 'There's one more to come,' he predicted, 'and then one of my flock will face an embarrassing predicament. I'll pray for him.'

Most of *Worcester*'s cadets, destined to serve under the red ensign of the mercantile fleet, would have stoutly affirmed that this, and only this, was their chosen vocation; few would have confessed any regard for the Grey Funnel Line. Yet there was no doubt about the envious eyes that greeted the appearance of a cadet of the senior service with his smarter uniform and superior mien, nor any doubt about the number of *Worcester* cadets who competed for the two or three Naval Cadetships offered by *Britannia* to *Worcester* annually. The examination candidates feigned unconcern, agreeing that none of them was really trying. The successful few, hiding their elation, shrugged and conceded that, as they had won the scholarship, well, they may as well accept it.

Hedley Bellman had never allowed himself to even contemplate the possibility of a 'King's Cadetship'. Even had he the ability to achieve one, which he doubted, the expenses involved were still prohibitive. He counted his blessings and blessed his father. He was going to be a red duster man, and more likely aboard Masefield's dirty British coaster with a salt-caked smoke stack than in one of the ocean giants of Cunard or White Star.

These were hard days, particularly in winter, when no concessions were made to rain, snow, or the cutting wind that blew from the estuary. Decks were scrubbed and paintwork scoured, ropes spliced with numbed fingers and boats lowered and raised. It was warmer below in the classrooms, but only just, as they boxed the compass, wrestled with latitudes and nautical miles, maritime law and cargo manifests, the Beaumont scale, tides, berths and buoys, bunkering, lights, flags, ballast, pumps and bilges. In his second year Hedley Bellman was a Petty Officer Cadet and had achieved firsts in five subjects, a standard that recommended him to the Allan Steamship Company and an appointment as Fourth Mate in the old twelve-knotter *Corinthian*, of 6270 tons.

A few days before Christmas, 1913, Hedley Bellman returned to the Chelsea rectory on his last furlough before reporting for his sea-going appointment.

'This is my son, Sinjin,' the Reverend Bellman beamed, as he entered the drawing-room. The formidable figure in front of the fire turned and thrust out a ramrod hand.

'Good morning, young man. Rear-Admiral St John Primrose, Royal Navy. Your father and I were at Charterhouse together, many years ago – until we each took to a cloth of a different colour.' The Admiral wore civilian clothes, but there could be not the slightest doubt about his calling. He had a tanned face, a close-trimmed, pugnacious beard, jutting eyebrows and eyes like chips of blue ice. He stood with feet apart and well-braced, his head forward on square shoulders, conforming precisely to the popular prototype of an old sea dog. 'This' – Primrose nodded towards his less formidable companion – 'is my niece and ward, Imogen. We've come up for the Christmas shops, y'know – although we'd get the same things cheaper in Portsmouth, I shouldn't wonder, and with a lot less trouble.'

'The Admiral's come from HMS *Excellent*, Hedley,' the Reverend Bellman added, as Hedley muttered something. Imogen was a stunner, and he wished he had got his hair cut before leaving Greenhithe and worn his better suit. She was all peaches and cream, with hair of spun gold, hands of the most delicate porcelain and with lips that pouted deliciously. He felt positively uncouth. It was impossible that such a creature could be of the same genealogy as the craggy Rear-Admiral Primrose. Hedley struggled to gaze at the exquisite Imogen while simultaneously giving polite attention to her uncle.

'Your father was the best scrum half the school ever had,' the Admiral recalled. 'He ran like a whippet.' It was difficult to believe, and, anyway, Hedley hated muddy ball games, but he narrowed his eyes and nodded. 'You play, of course,' Primrose assumed.

'Of course, sir,' Hedley said, showing mild surprise. 'Scrum half.' He had not the remotest idea what a scrum half was, but he smiled resolutely in the direction of Imogen.

'Splendid,' Primrose boomed. 'You must bring a side down to Whale Island. I'll send your commanding officer an invitation.' Hedley nodded. 'We'll look forward to it, sir.' Thankfully, he mused, he would be aboard the *Corinthian*, somewhere off the west coast of Africa, when the cadets from *Worcester* were being pulverized by the seamen gunners and marines of HMS *Excellent*.

'I'll come and watch, Hedley,' Imogen promised. Hedley realised for the first time that his name sounded like music when spoken by an angel. Hedley. Hedley. If Imogen was watching, he'd pulverize *Excellent*'s fifteen single-handed, running like a whippet. For a wild moment he considered sending *Corinthian*'s master a telegram, requesting that the ship's departure be delayed because he was playing scrum half in the presence of Imogen Primrose, but it was doubtful if any unpolished, insensitive sea captain would understand.

The Reverend Bellman was pouring sherry at the sideboard on which, Hedley observed, stood bottles of brandy, whisky and port. They must have cost the old boy every silver coin for months, and only for the Admiral.

'I am told that this is very good,' said the Reverend Bellman, beaming, with a glass in each hand.

'Ah, I should have told you earlier,' the Admiral frowned, and raised a hand. 'I'm a total abstainer. In fact I'm the president of the Portsmouth Division's Temperance Union, and I've not touched alcohol – except for medicinal purposes – for twenty years. Miss Agnes Weston is absolutely right, y'know. Every time you open a liquor bottle you let Satan loose.'

The Reverend Bellman shot an apprehensive glance at the open sherry bottle. 'Yes – I suppose—'

'You have taken a brandy occasionally, Uncle,' Imogen reminded him, 'when the weather has been very cold.'

'True, true,' Primrose nodded thoughtfully. 'I think that

can be called a medicinal purpose. Nobody takes medicine because they like it.' He gazed in the direction of the sideboard. 'Since you press me, perhaps I will have a brandy. Just one. The weather is rather cold.' Imogen's eyes met Hedley's, and he thrilled. She was not only stunning, she was very intelligent.

The Admiral, reluctantly, took a brandy while Hedley, his father and Imogen sipped sherry. No, he would not have soda; it only made more of it. 'When I was in the old *Swiftsure*, in the Pacific,' he reminisced, 'we played the Samoans. They had bare feet, so we allowed 'em five extra players, but every time we got near to going over the line the spectators attacked us with sticks, and dozens came on the pitch to help their men in the scrum. Our ship's carpenter lost half an ear – bitten off, would you believe it?' Hedley and his father believed it, and made sympathetic noises. The Admiral, protesting, allowed himself to take a second brandy.

'Play to win, I always say,' he went on, 'but if you can't lose like a man, then don't play.' He glared at Hedley. 'You must come down to Whale Island for a weekend in the New Year, young man. Bring your boots.' Hedley, who had been trying unsuccessfully to exchange a few pleasantries with Imogen, agreed that he would. He could, he told himself, always sprain an ankle on the journey.

'That will be wonderful, Hedley,' Imogen sighed, and Hedley glowed. He might sprain both ankles. He refilled the Admiral's glass, which Primrose appeared not to notice until too late, when he remonstrated but finally conceded that, since it was poured, he may as well drink it.

'Foreigners have never understood the importance of the playing field,' Primrose resumed, a little thickly, 'which is why we always knock the spit out of them on the battlefield – and we always will, mark my words. Have you ever heard of a German hitting fifty before lunch?' They shook their heads. 'Or bagging two hundred brace in a day? Of course not.' Hedley was a hopelessly inept batsman and had never shot so much as a sparrow, but he snorted knowingly. 'That is why,' the Admiral rasped, 'we shall knock the spit out of the Kaiser's navy if he ever comes out to bat.' The terminology was a little confusing, Hedley decided, but it was comforting.

Corinthian was exactly as Masefield described. With her single, thin funnel emptying black smoke she butted through the Channel to Gibraltar, thence southward to Bathurst, Freetown, Accra and Lagos, loaded with printed cottons, shoddy blankets, telegraph wire and old red army tunics, returning with cocoa, copra, hides and gum arabic. Her hull was streaked with rust, her upperworks with soot, and every scuttle and hatch leaked brown water.

In a first-class merchant ship Hedley Bellman would have been rated midshipman or apprentice, but the title of fourth mate sounded more important ashore even if it meant the same and the crew knew it. *Corinthian* always seemed to be undermanned, and he had his hands to a rope or tarpaulin as often as any of the hands, and even worked in the galley when the cook had been carried aboard drunk in Las Palmas. 'Twin bloody screws, all of 'em,' the Bosun had nodded in the direction of a squadron of battle-ships off Portland. 'Some of 'em's got *four*, mate, an' burning coal like it was free. They can turn out two 'undred men ter 'oist one soddin' boat. *Six* 'undred, if they want. Whistles, bugles, soddin' marine bands – and *we've* got six ABs in each watch.'

It had been a matter of little consequence that the owners, on engagement, had insisted that his name be submitted to the Admiralty as a candidate for the Royal Naval Reserve. He had signed the necessary documents, and his feelings on learning that he had been accepted were mixed; he was mildly flattered, but annoyed that every alternate year henceforth he must give four weeks to the Royal Navy for the study of gunnery, torpedoes, strategy and courtmartial procedure. It was going to be a month wasted from his three-years qualification for his Master's Certificate of Competence, without which he would remain one of the hundreds of signed-off deckmen who thronged the shipping offices of London and Liverpool seeking berths, in any vessel, bound anywhere. His father, however, was more impressed. 'My son,' he would introduce Hedley. 'Fourth Officer of the steamship *Corinthian* and of the Royal Naval Reserve. If there is a war, you know, he will be summoned to the Fleet.' He said it as if summoning Acting-Sub-Lieutenant Hedley Bellman to the Fleet was England's indisputable answer to the growing threat of the Imperial German Navy.

The officers of the regular service would not have agreed. There was considerable resentment towards the Reserve – not so much towards junior reservists like Hedley Bellman but towards the captains and commodores of the mercantile marine who, in the event of war, would be given ranks and responsibilities which rightfully belonged to those whose career the Navy was. Hedley Bellman's reception aboard the cruiser *Aboukir*, when he reported for his first two weeks of training, was not unkind but it was offhand. 'Ah yes,' the Commander nodded, then glanced at the clock on the bulkhead. 'Bellman, Allan Line. That's the West African run, isn't it? Coconuts and all that?' He frowned. 'Well, find yourself a corner in the Gunroom, will you, Bellamy? Try to keep out of the way. Tomorrow I'll have one of the Snots show you around—'

'To be frank,' said the senior Sub-Lieutenant, Bradshaw, 'I don't really know why they send you chaps. I mean, what are you expected to *do* if there's a war? It can't last more than six weeks.' Bradshaw knew exactly what would happen. 'The French Army will sweep across the Rhine. We'll reduce Wilhelmshaven, Bremerhaven and Cuxhaven to smoking heaps of rubble, then force the Kattegat narrows and land our own army on the Baltic coast of Germany. By the time you fellows have packed your gunny-bags, got ashore from your banana boats and reported to your port divisions, it'll be all over.'

Hedley Bellman had the temerity to suggest that it might be the Germans who swept across the Rhine, and the German Navy might not be content to merely fight defensively in the Kattegat narrows. Besides, a war could begin somewhere else, quite beyond the reach of either the French Army or the Royal Navy.

Bradshaw laughed. 'You mean this sordid business between Austria and Serbia?' He shook his head. 'It'll come to nothing, mark my words. The Russians will growl, the Austrians will pipe down, and that'll be the end of it. No, if you ask me, the war will begin between France and Germany, probably over Alsace and Lorraine – and I'd say in 1916. By that time I'll have my second ring – I might even have a command.'

There was, however, the twice-weekly consolation of Imogen's letters. When they arrived he read them first quickly, for a second time slowly, and then thirdly and carefully dissected certain sentences in search of any suggestion that he and Imogen had reached a tacit 'understanding'. Sometimes he was *almost* sure, but never completely – not so that he could write back to pour out his well-rehearsed confession of love for her. He also nursed a carefully prepared verbal exhortation for that convenient opportunity which, however, never seemed to present itself, or, if it did, he lost his nerve.

He had visited Portsmouth several times since their first meeting, choosing occasions when there was no possibility of any rugby football being played, although Rear-Admiral Primrose had suggested that he might like to 'try a few runs' with the field guns crews. Primrose drank brandy for medicinal reasons, and Imogen played the piano. True, she addressed him as 'dear Hedley' or 'Hedley dear', but she was equally familiar with her uncle's secretary, Lieutenant George Pope, a serious, well-groomed young man with a very slight facial twitch that annoyed Hedley. Pope was disarmingly polite and not at all condescending, but Hedley wished that Imogen would not smile at him quite so often. Besides, Pope enjoyed an unfair advantage, so often in Imogen's company while Hedley Bellman was sweating off the coast of Senegal or, now, confined to the shabby gunroom of *Aboukir*. It was totally unjust.

At 5 pm on 3 August 1914, the German ambassador in Paris announced that his country 'considered itself at war with France', but during the early hours of that morning Contre-Amiral Rouyer, commanding the Second Cruiser Squadron of the French Navy, in Cherbourg, had received two signals. The first informed him that the German fleet had passed through the Kiel Canal from the Baltic, and the second told him what he should do about it.

'3 August. 0030 hours. Proceed to sea immediately and forcibly intercept the German Fleet anywhere except within British territorial waters.'

Almost all French naval forces had been sent to the Mediterranean on a gambling assumption that, in the event of a war with Germany, the British would assume responsibility for the Channel and the North Sea, but at dawn on 3 August neither the British nor yet the French were at war with Germany. Rouyer had three old cruisers, *Gueydon*, *Montcalm* and *Dupetit Thouars*, in Cherbourg's roadstead. There were a few destroyers at Dunkirk and several submarines based on Calais – the rag-tag of a navy that had for decades been deteriorating in efficiency and might be considered flattered to be listed the fifth in importance after the British, German, American and Japanese. For Rouyer the prospect of challenging Admiral Scheer's High Seas Fleet, with its thirteen Dreadnoughts, six battle-cruisers, thirty pre-Dreadnoughts, forty-five cruisers and a hundred and fifty destroyers, was shuddering.

But honour must be served. The French crews threw overboard their wooden furniture, the wardroom pianos and all other combustibles, including the flagship's account books. The captain and officers of *Dupetit Thouars* wrote their wills and mailed them to their families. Then Rouyer hoisted his rear-admiral's tricolour and ordered his squadron to sea.

For the last few hours of the day and throughout the night the three old cruisers steamed up-Channel, apprehensive but determined, but off Dover there came blessed relief. A British destroyer hailed them, conveyed the compliments of the Flag Officer Commanding, and suggested politely that the French should all return home. Britain had presented an ultimatum to Germany which expired at 11 pm British time. If there was going to be any shooting it would be done by the Royal Navy.

'My son,' the Reverend Bellman told everyone, 'has been summoned to the Fleet.' Hedley Bellman, in fact, had never got ashore from *Aboukir*; there had been no time. The Navy's reserve ships, manned for a rehearsal mobilisation on 15 July, had not been dispersed because of the darkening international situation, and now Britain was at war with Germany.

Hedley Bellman had hurriedly changed the badge on his cap and the buttons on his jacket; it might be months before he could get to a naval tailor despite what Sub-Lieutenant Bradshaw had said about the affair being all over by bonfire night. Bradshaw was annoyed. Everything had happened too soon. It was clear that, if the Navy was going to force the Kattegat narrows, the four-funnelled *Aboukir* and her class sisters *Cressy*, *Hogue* and *Bacchante* would not be involved.

The four gaunt old ladies had already been marked down to be scrapped, or sold to some South American banana republic. It destroyed a man's moral fibre, Bradshaw said, and had the midshipmen doing Swedish drill on the quarterdeck at 0600 in their pyjamas until Captain Drummond ordered him to keep these damn Snotties out of sight – or Bradshaw would find himself inspecting seamen's kits in the drill-shed of Chatham Barracks. Bradshaw sulked.

Sub-Lieutenant Bradshaw's campaign plan for the war against Germany, however, was ignored by the Admiralty. There was no battle for the Kattegat narrows, no landing of an army on the enemy's Baltic coast. All the Dreadnoughts, the battle-cruisers and almost all the sleek-hulled new cruisers with their reputed thirty knots and quick-firing guns withdrew northward to Rosyth, Cromarty and Scapa Flow. It was incredible to Bradshaw, as he repeatedly lectured Hedley Bellman and the gunroom in general, that the warships nearest to the enemy consisted of a few destroyers and light cruisers based on Harwich and Dover, and the Live Bait Squadron – the 7th Cruiser Squadron of *Aboukir* and her arthritic sisters. 'There are times,' he lamented, 'when you wonder.'

Hedley Bellman did not feel qualified to either agree or disagree. His immediate problems were enough – where to sling his hammock, how to occupy the hours of every day, or, more accurately, how to keep out of everyone's way, whether he was sitting in someone else's chair, and, in brief, how he could pretend to justify his existence aboard *Aboukir*. Nobody seemed to want an Acting Sub-Lieutenant of the Naval Reserve with a Temporary Certificate.

There were others besides young Bradshaw who were concerned, for different reasons, over the Live Bait Squadron's activities. The four ships, sharing sixty years of service between them, had been ordered to the Broad Fourteens – that nasty slice of North Sea between the coasts of Norfolk and neutral Holland – an area of choppy shallows, minefields, the U-boats' corridor to the Atlantic and a likely place for meeting the fast, hit-and-run cruisers of the Kaiser's fleet.

The majority of the Navy's ships were equipped and belligerently ready to fight. *Aboukir* and her matronly sisters, however, were not members of that majority. Most of their crews, totalling nearly 3000, were reservists of the Nore Command, drawn from the Medway towns of Chatham, Rochester, Gillingham, Maidstone and Sheerness. They possessed English middle-aged courage and the phlegmatic calm of old sailors who had done this all before. Few of them had any experience of submarines or aeroplanes, those new-fangled things that would never amount to anything. There would always be time to peel off a coat, spit on palms and take a fresh bite of chewing baccy before loading the gun and getting down to business.

By dawn on 22 September the squadron's number had been reduced; *Bacchante* was undergoing repair and her replacement, *Euryalus*, had also returned to harbour to coal. The remaining three steamed in line abreast at ten knots, only twenty miles from the Hook of Holland and on a north-easterly course. For days the sea had been whipped by gale-force winds, and the destroyers which would normally be within call had run to Harwich for shelter. *Aboukir*, *Cressy* and *Hogue* had remained determinedly on station, rolling ponderously through the spindrift and the high-flung spray. Now, this dawn, the weather was moderating, but they were alone and as perilously vulnerable as three old ladies in a street of brigands – and as unconcerned.

Hedley Bellman lay in the warm cocoon of his gently swinging hammock with eyes closed, listening to the noises of the ship as the comparative quiet of the night was terminated by first the Reveille bugle and then the call-boys' shrieking pipes moving through the lower deck messes.

'Wakey, wakey, lash up and stow! Men under punishment muster on the quarterdeck. Cooks to the galley.'

The old cruiser, Hedley sensed, was riding more comfortably than she had been, which probably meant a following sea and the barometer easing. He turned lazily onto his back and stretched his toes into the hammock nettles. Five more minutes. This morning, perhaps, there'd be coffee and bacon instead of the cocoa and biscuits of the last two days. It was damn odd, he mused, how the smell of coffee and bacon was the only smell that a man's morning stomach could tolerate with equanimity. Inches above his eyes the deckhead was streaked with condensation. Someone was opening a protesting scuttle – probably the gunroom steward – so it must be light. He groped under the head of his mattress for his watch; it was 0620 and he had the forenoon watch. If he got to the showers early he'd have the best of the hot water.

Today, with luck – or perhaps tomorrow – the light cruiser *Lowestoft* and the 3rd Destroyer Flotilla would take over the Broad Fourteens patrol, and *Aboukir* could return to Harwich for coaling and provisioning, more red lead to hide the creeping eczema of rust, dockyard artificers shaking their heads over the ageing engines, Sunday divisions and the church pennant hoisted, mail and shore leave. There would be letters from Imogen . . . .

To his amazement the hammock in which he lay suddenly lifted violently towards the deckhead, convulsed, and then turned completely over. Hedley Bellman heard the steward's shout and, a second later, found himself sprawling on the deck with mattress and blanket spilling over him. He struggled for comprehension. If this was somebody's joke then it wasn't bloody funny, but beneath him the coir-matted deck had positively tilted, and plates, cups and cutlery were cascading from the mess table. A heavy deadlight crashed shut, and there were other men on hands and knees among tangles of bedding, swearing. The steward swayed in mid-deck, whimpering at a hand of which four fingers were a bloody pulp. The deck lurched again, and the steward fell to his knees. 'Christ,' someone shouted. 'We've hit a mine.'

The presumption was irritatingly unreal to Hedley Bellman. He pulled himself upright. More likely the ship had touched bottom; these were shallow waters, and a north-easterly heading would put the squadron very close to Zandvoort or Ijmuiden. Given the bad weather of the last few days, it was not inconceivable that Captain Drummond had been steaming significantly further eastward than he had realised.

But why was *Aboukir* heeling to port? No, she wasn't. She was righting – but then, alarmingly, she continued rolling slowly to starboard. Somebody had wrenched open the water-tight door, beyond which was the ladder to the upper deck, and damp, chilling air flooded the gunroom. There were distant, incoherent shouts and the chutter of feet on steel rungs. A bugle was teetering 'General Quarters', and Hedley Bellman remembered, confusedly, that his action station was the Sick Bay, although for what purpose he had never understood. He scrabbled for his shoes among a tangle of mattresses and blankets, but could not find them, and, frustrated, tore an oilskin from a peg.

When he reached the upper deck he realised immediately that *Aboukir* had sustained serious damage; she was listing dangerously to starboard now and her bows were down. Men were pouring from every hatch in various states of undress, some still seeking their action stations, but the bosuns' pipes were shrilling from forward again. Everything had happened in such rapid sequence that there was no time to consider anything but that the ship, incredibly, was sinking. He clung to a hatch coaming, taking stock.

There was an eruption of steam from the starboard side, its source beyond sight. Underfoot, the damp deck lurched, tilting still further, and he could hear the new shouts. 'Hands to abandon ship. Hands to abandon ship.' Was this *really* happening – with such numbing swiftness?

He could see several ratings doggedly clearing away a 3-pounder gun, but they would never have time to fire it. Coal-blackened stokers – the black gang – were stumbling from below. Hedley Bellman hauled himself, hand by hand, to the port side. One boat had been released from its davits but had become fouled; the ship's red-leaded belly was exposed, and dozens of whitely naked or near naked men were lowering themselves around the 6-inch casemates towards the lapping sea that seemed to recede from them as *Aboukir* rolled. There were obscenities as barnacles, as spiteful as broken glass, tore skin from feet and buttocks. Hedley could see *Hogue*, a half mile distant. She was stopped and was lowering boats. One of her 12-pounders opened fire, then a second and a third, but it was impossible to see what they were firing at. Beyond *Hogue*, and only vaguely visible in the half light, *Cressy* had turned her bows and was closing with her four tall funnels vomiting smoke. Within *Aboukir* there was an ominous rumble, as if massive machinery shifted, the hiss of steam.

Hedley Bellman eased himself into the sea among scores of threshing swimmers, bobbing heads and unrecognisable flotsam. The water was icily cold, wrenching the breath from his lungs, but he struck out, anxious to put distance between himself and the stricken ship before she rolled for the last time. Christ, it was cold. A choking man clawed at him, but he tore free.

He could see no other he knew, but it would have been difficult to identify any of the chalky faces with their slate-coloured lips, wetly-plastered hair and blood-shot eyes. He turned onto his back just in time to observe *Aboukir*, with a noise like thunder, roll completely among debris and floating filth, presenting her keel to the sky with, ludicrously, one of her screws still slowly churning. 'She ain't gone yet,' someone sobbed, and there were exhausted swimmers struggling to climb up the slimed hull bottom. Hedley Bellman shouted a warning, but his voice was a croak, lost in the general clamour.

He never saw *Aboukir*'s final plunge because, from somewhere else – and momentarily he could not understand from which direction – came the unmistakeable drumfire of a massive explosion. He twisted again as, around him, desperate throats cried, '*Hogue*!'

Hedley retched, slavering caustic brine. The sister cruiser, stationery, and with almost every boat lowered and pulling for *Aboukir*'s survivors, was obscured by a vast pall of brown smoke through which the flashes of her smaller guns could just be seen. Already she was listing, and the boats were rising and falling in the grey swell, oars tangling, their crews uncertain whether to continue in the direction of the sinking *Aboukir* or return to their parent vessel, which was obviously in difficulty. God Almighty – was it another mine?

As they stared, all further groping speculation ended abruptly when a second explosion tore upward from *Hogue*'s starboard side, lifting a great mushroom of debris and dense smoke for two hundred feet. Involuntarily the boat-crews cringed over their oars, and there were moans and curses from *Aboukir*'s desperate swimmers, the weaker clinging to anything that floated – an upturned whaler, gratings, fenders, mess-stools and sodden hammocks. It was all impossible, but it was happening; all unbelievable, but the horror could not be denied – that both *Aboukir* and *Hogue* had been struck by torpedoes. It meant, Jesus Christ, that they were being attacked by submarines *that they could not see*.

Hedley Bellman turned his attention towards *Cressy*. The cold was agonising. He could just see the third ship of the squadron across a mile of choppy, white-flecked sea. *Cressy* had obviously paused briefly to lower her boats, for her davits were empty, but now she was working up to full speed and steering directly towards her stricken sisters. She made a brave show with her tall, streaming funnels, her bow wave lifting and her guns firing, but Hedley Bellman had the sickening feeling that he was watching the last act of a tragedy and that he knew exactly how it would end. After this, if he survived, nobody would tell him that submarines were gimcrack things that could only operate from sheltered waters. The projectiles from *Cressy*'s forward guns were falling uncomfortably close to the hundreds of begrimed and choking men in the sea, and there were fresh shouts of protest, but the shouts were weaker now. There was despair in many of the white, skull-drawn faces; lungs and muscles were surrendering to the paralysing cold. A corpse, with bared teeth snarling in a clay-coloured face, jostled against Hedley, and he elbowed it aside. Then he recognised, shocked, that it was Sub-Lieutenant Bradley.

Cressy, with pounding engines and her old boilers straining, suddenly shuddered like a charging buffalo met full between the eyes by a heavy bullet. Her bows plunged deeply into a lake of white froth, and for an awful moment it seemed that she might continue steaming downwards into the sea as hundreds of tons of water enveloped her fo'c'sle, but she shook herself and slowly, slowly came up, stopped in her tracks. To the desperate men in the sea it was if they were watching a moving picture for the third dismal time. Ink-black smoke poured from *Cressy*'s ventilators and hatches. Gun crews were still at their stations, uncomprehending, searching vainly for some sign of the enemy, but already the decks were tilting threateningly, and there was no doubt that the old warship had only minutes to live. Deep within her a boiler ruptured with a grinding crash, and there were screams as steam-scalded, blinded men with flesh like boiled pork fought hopelessly to climb the ladders from the inferno below. The whistles were shrieking the same, detested order that had been given on *Aboukir* and *Hogue* and, as in a nightmare repeated, hundreds of men were scrambling over the side, lowering themselves into the cold, leaden rollers.

Fewer than 800 survivors from the three ships were dragged from the sea by rescuing ships – first the small Dutch coasters *Titan* and *Flora*, then the English trawlers *Coriander* and *J.G.C.* The number might have been higher if a fifth vessel, unidentified but allegedly flying a Dutch tricolour, had not turned away and fled from the scene. When the light cruiser *Lowestoft* and her accompanying destroyers, summoned by *Cressy*'s last wireless transmission, reached the position three hours later, nothing remained but a few floating dead, splintered timber and refuse.

In Harwich the Great Eastern Hotel had been commandeered by the naval authority for the survivors' accommodation. Most were shoeless with lacerated feet, many in pyjamas, borrowed blankets and sacking. Hedley Bellman gulped at scalding soup, then sat under a hot shower, wincing but ecstatic as the steaming water drove the aching cramp from his muscles. The hotel lobby was filling with local next-of-kin, desperately searching for a familiar face, questioning, unconvinced that a loved one was not among the chilled and dirty rescued, but that day, in the Medway towns, fifteen hundred homes would have their curtains drawn and the gaslights lowered.

Six

They had only glimpsed Mr Seagram through the half open door of the inner office.

'Steve who?' he frowned. 'Bundy—?'

'That's 'im,' Steve Bundy whispered to Johnnie Spong, who nodded respectfully and straightened his cap.

'Ah, yes,' they heard Seagram say, with a disquieting lack of enthusiasm. 'I remember. Well, send him across to the gymnasium; I'll telephone Charlie. Has my baggage gone to the *Empress of Britain*? Good. And send a telegram to Roberto in Rio de Janeiro. Five hundred and his passage – that's our final offer. Who's this Jess Willard—?' The door closed.

The gymnasium occupied a basement, a short walk away, and smelled like the dressing room at Blackfriars. There was a roped ring in which two sweating young men punished each other, punch bags, Indian clubs and Charlie, middle-aged and predictably cropped, nose-flattened and tattooed. 'That,' hissed Johnnie Spong from the corner of his mouth, 'is Pom-Pom Charlie Sawyer.'

'Which of yer's Bundy?' enquired Charlie.

'Me,' Steve Bundy volunteered. 'Mister Seagram sez—'

'Never mind what Mister Seagram sez,' Charlie sniffed. 'Take yer clothes off.'

'Here?' Steve Bundy glanced around. 'All of 'em?'

Charlie shrugged. 'Why? 'Ave yer got something different to everyone else?'

Johnnie Spong chuckled knowingly. 'I do a bit meself,' he confided. 'Johnnie Spong. And I'm Steve's adviser.'

'Then advise 'im I can't wait all day while he takes 'ee's bloomers orf,' Charlie growled. Steve Bundy undressed hurriedly, to stand naked and self-conscious. 'There,' Charlie nodded. 'Your'n is just the same as orl the others, give or take.' He reached forward. 'Cough 'ard.' Steve Bundy coughed. 'If I was the Duchess o' Devonshire,' Charlie suggested, 'yer wouldn't be so fussy, would yer?'

Steve Bundy submitted to being thumbed and prodded, weighed and measured. He hung by his hands and pedalled with his legs, touched his toes and skipped with a rope as Charlie watched, expressionless, and Johnnie Spong yawned as if it were all a familiar business.

'All right, Bundy,' Charlie said at last. 'Now – can yer 'it?'

'He put away Ernie Rowse last week,' Johnnie Spong offered, 'in the first roun'.'

Charlie ignored Johnnie Spong. He indicated his own generous midriff. ''It me there,' he told Steve Bundy, 'as 'ard as yer can.'

Steve Bundy hesitated. 'Yer mean *really* 'it yer? Are yer sure—?'

'O' course I'm bloody sure – and I mean *'ard*. Don't worry, I won't 'it yer back. That comes later.'

Reluctantly, Steve Bundy supposed the other knew what he was doing. He bunched his fist, drew it back, then drove it with all his strength at Charlie's solar plexus. It was like hitting a bag of wet sand, and he felt his arm jar to the elbow. Charlie only rocked slightly on his heels and grunted. 'Well,' he conceded, 'I jes' felt it. Get yer clothes on.'

Steve Bundy dragged on his trousers. 'Don't yer want ter see me in the ring?'

'Gawd, no,' Charlie declined. 'Now, listen. I'll tell Mister Seagram I'll take yer on trial. Yer can start 'ere Monday at eight sharp. Ter begin with yer'll get yer meals an' yer fares paid, and ten shillings fer yer pocket. No smokin', no booze, no tarts, and no late nights. I'll be training yer, and if yer don't do 'zactly as yer bloody told, yer'll be out. If yer show promise, Mister Seagram 'll put yer under contract, put yer in lodgings; and arrange yer fights. That means yer'll get a percentage o' the purse, which won't be much fer a start, but they'll get bigger if yer do good. Don't think yer going ter be a champion next week. Yer ain't; yer'll probably never be. There's 'undreds that start, but only a few get anywhere – but most of 'em start too late, or they're taught wrong, or they're pushed too fast. That's why Mister Seagram likes ter catch 'em young, before they're spoilt, an' teach 'em from the beginning. Yer lucky, Bundy, but don't count yer chickens. It's likely I'll kick yer out after two weeks.'

Johnnie Spong made his bid, jauntily. 'I was jes' saying – I'm Johnnie Spong.' He paused. 'Johnnie Spong. I've done a bit meself—'

Charlie gazed at him. 'Why don't yer do yer bit somewhere else?'

Those first four weeks were cruel to Steve Bundy. He trotted, jumped, skipped, swung clubs and punched bags until, by each afternoon, every muscle in his body cried out for respite, and he had a shower every evening, which seemed a wholly needless extravagance. Charlie Sawyer's warning that he should refrain from drink, women and late nights was unnecessary; when he reached home he had thoughts only for sleep. The nightly horseplay at the street corner had lost its appeal, and he groaned as he rose stiffly from his bed at dawn to catch the workmen's early train to Oxford Circus.

He thought he knew how to stand on his feet, until Charlie Sawyer made it clear that he had been doing it wrongly for eighteen years. Charlie showed him how to breathe, how to hit with the knuckles, how to present a narrow profile to an opponent, how to retreat on the balls of his feet. Charlie, despite his years, was very difficult to hit; he was astonishingly nimble, and could duck and weave as Steve Bundy flailed harmlessly. When he hit back, it was with the power of a steam hammer and as unerring. 'If yer stick yer chin out,' he nodded, as Steve Bundy wiped the blood from his mouth with a water-soaked sponge, 'yer get it clouted. Next time, I'll clout yer proper.' Steve Bundy dreaded the prospect.

He was not sure how he survived those first four weeks. There had been moments when, dispirited, he had been tempted to chuck the whole thing and return to the less strenuous environment of the Mile End Road. Others of his age appeared at the gymnasium in their shabby caps and knotted scarves, all hungry, aspiring champions. Some did not progress beyond Charlie Sawyer's initial scrutiny, or remained for a week, perhaps two weeks, and then, for reasons beyond Steve Bundy's understanding – and Charlie Sawyer did not explain – no longer presented themselves.

Something, however, was happening to Steve Bundy, and he could feel it. True, solid food helped – bacon with bread and tea at eight, beef stew and dumplings at midday, and all the bread-and-dripping he could eat at six, after his shower, with a bottle of stout. This was what it meant to be fed like a fighting cock, and it made a difference. There was something else. He felt fitter and more confident, his daily, aching stiffness was disappearing and his muscles were hardening. His reflexes quickened and he could face Charlie Sawyer with less apprehension – and he knew he was beginning to get punches home, because Charlie grunted more often, and gave ground.

He was at liberty to spar with others in training, but

Charlie Sawyer did not care to see novices matched with novices. Nobody learned anything proper that way, he said. There was a continual stream of down-and-outs and broken-down fighters – not unlike the ragged men that Steve Bundy had seen gathered outside the Ring at Blackfriars – ready and willing to exchange blows with a youngster for the price of a meal and a doss-house bed. They were seldom good for more than a couple of rounds, but they were cunning, and aware that Charlie Sawyer wanted his youngsters introduced to such things as low punches, butting heads and gouging thumbs, and they could provide them. There was no profit in crying foul. 'It's yer own bloody fault,' Charlie would shrug. 'You're fighting 'im, I ain't. Yer've got ter learn.' And they learned.

On the next occasion that Steve Bundy saw Mr Maurice Seagram the promoter was accompanied by two swarthy gentlemen, one young and flashily dressed, the other older, who talked rapidly in Portuguese and gazed about the gymnasium with arrogant unconcern.

'This,' Mr Seagram told Charlie Sawyer, aside, 'is Petulio Roberto, the Brazilian Wildcat. He's going to demolish every middle-weight in Europe, according to his manager – starting in London – and he also expects to meet the King, the President of France and Mrs Patrick Campbell.' He tapped ash from his cigar. 'But I've seen some of these dago wildcats before, Charlie, and I'd like to know if he's as strong as his perfume. Have you got a youngster that might wipe the smirk off his face?'

Charlie Sawyer rubbed his stub of a nose with a finger. 'There's none of 'em that's 'zactly ready, Mister Seagram, but young Bundy there might give yer friend a bit o' trouble. He's got a good dig, and don't fold up easy. There's one or two others wi' more experience, but I'd say Bundy's the best fer your man.'

'Get him into the ring, then,' Seagram nodded, 'and we'll

see.' He turned to the two Brazilians, politely. Could the Wildcat be persuaded to spar a round with one of the novices? Of course the youngster would be hopelessly outclassed, but everyone wanted to see the great Petulio Roberto in action. It would be an education—

The Wildcat's white teeth flashed in a smile. He shrugged. Of course. He laid aside his hat and cane, removed his coat, waistcoat and cravat, then unbuttoned his silk shirt. He stripped magnificently, golden and muscular, with broad shoulders narrowing to a lithe waist. After carefully combing his hair he vaulted the top rope into the ring and offered his hands to be gloved.

'Don't let repertation frighten yer,' Charlie Sawyer told Bundy. 'Keep ter the middle o' the canvas and make 'im do the dancin'. Don't try ter outsmart 'im. Yer won't. Jes' wait fer yer chance. When yer see it – whammo!' There was no time for more.

The Wildcat glided towards Steve Bundy, deceptively nonchalant, smiling. His left hand was like the flick of a whip. It was like fighting Ernie Rowse all over again, Bundy thought – but this was no Ernie Rowse, no thirty-bob-a-nighter. This man was fast, faster than old Charlie Sawyer, moving with easy grace, jabbing, jabbing, and always smiling. One, two, three—the punches snapped into Steve Bundy's face, jolting back his head. He jabbed back, angrily, but Roberto had gone.

Don't lose yer temper, he told himself. Wait fer yer chance, like Charlie said. No, this wasn't the same as his first fight at Blackfriars; he had none of that sickening apprehension, no fragment of sausage roll clogging his throat, and his legs felt good. He took two more punches, this time high on the head, as Charlie had taught him. Yer skull's thicker than yer chin, he'd said. In bare-fist fights there were blokes that broke their knuckles.

Roberto swayed from the hips, hit, then swayed again,

condescending, almost taunting, with hardly a hair of his greased head out of place. Bundy tucked his chin into his left shoulder, adhering doggedly to the centre of the ring. His legs still felt good, but he was being punished, and he had hardly laid a glove on his opponent. Christ, this man was fast. He could feel warm wetness under his right eye, and knew he had been cut. It didn't hurt much; it just stung.

Don't lose yer temper, he told himself again. That's what the man wants. He took a left to the mouth, a right to his ribs, stabbed hard at Roberto's face and saw his smile vanish momentarily, only to reappear. That was better. If he had to take two punches to give one, well, it was something. This dancing Wildcat was fast, and no soddin' mistake – but he hadn't hurt much, only cut. There was the familiar taste of salt in Steve Bundy's mouth.

That was it. Roberto didn't hit to stun; he hit to cut. He cut a bloke's face to raw meat until he was blinded, until he was coughing on blood from nose and mouth, his face a red mask, and then he was finished. Well, that wouldn't happen in one round, but Charlie always said that a bloke that punched from his toes didn't punch his weight; he'd been taught wrong. And blokes that couldn't deliver a full-weight clout usually didn't like getting one.

It was one thing, however, being aware of an opponent's weakness and something soddin' else to take advantage of it. Wait yer chance, did Charlie say? Bleedin' famous last words. Roberto chopped at him twice more, and pirouetted, relaxed. Then, as he smiled, Steve Bundy hit him, just above the belt-line, and felt his knuckles sink into yielding flesh.

Roberto's jaw dropped, his eyes widened with shock, and he stopped dancing. Then he moaned, retreated several unsteady paces and stood with both gloves clasping his middle. Bundy rammed home one more blow, too hastily for accuracy, but the Wildcat's nose burst like an over-ripe plum, spilling crimson, and he turned desperately to the ropes, to his manager beyond.

'That'll do, Bundy,' Mr Seagram said quickly. 'Dammit, you're only sparring.' He shrugged at the Brazilian at his side. 'My apologies, Señor. Young Bundy hasn't learned discipline, I'm afraid.' He shot a worried glance at the Wildcat, who was climbing ill-temperedly from the ring, tugging off his gloves. 'I hope your man isn't hurt. Charlie, give the Wildcat a clean towel. Later, I want to see you and Bundy in my office.' He frowned. 'Señor, are you quite sure that your man is ready for Europe? Of course, it was probably just a lapse of concentration—'

Charlie Sawyer wiped blood from Roberto's biscuit-coloured trousers with a wet sponge. The Brazilian snarled and wrenched himself away. Charlie winked in the direction of Steve Bundy. 'Yer oughter be ashamed, Bundy,' he shouted. 'Yer ain't supposed ter lose yer temper wi' visiting guests.' He lowered his voice. 'Yer ought've hammered 'im clean through the soddin's ropes instead of jes' tapping 'is claret.'

'The nex' time, eef I come back,' the Wildcat promised, 'I will kill heem.' His manager nodded. 'Nex' time,' he threatened, 'he will kill heem.'

'Never mind the next time,' offered Steve Bundy, feeling the cut under his eye and suddenly feeling belligerent. 'What's wrong with bleedin' now?'

'That'll do, Bundy,' Mr Seagram snapped. 'I'll see to you later. Señor, if we could walk across to Albemarle Street, perhaps we should reconsider your plans. It might be a good idea if the Wildcat had a fight or two in the provinces before he goes in with our middleweight champion. I can put you in touch with promoters in Manchester, say, or Dublin.'

'If I was you, Bundy,' Charlie Sawyer advised, 'I'd pack me bags.'

'You reckon Mister Seagram's going ter sack me, jes' fer that?'

'I mean pack yer bags ready ter move ter digs,' Charlie said. 'Yer've prob'ly saved Mister Seagram a thousand quid wi' that dago. I told him yer 'ad a good dig, but yer've got ter learn ter cover up, or yer'll never go fifteen rounds, and that won't do fer Mister Seagram. Tomorrer we'll start teaching yer how ter stay out o' trouble.'

Steve Bundy never did learn how to stay out of trouble. He allowed himself to be hit too often, and he cut easily. If any of his fights went further than five or six rounds, Charlie Sawyer advised, he would lose it because he'd never see out of his eyes. Fortunately young Steve Bundy could hit unusually hard – as hard as someone two stones heavier – and that balanced the odds. He would never be a boxer in the classical mould; he would only hold the middle of the ring with head lowered, revolving slowly on braced feet, taking punch after punch from a more agile opponent but watching for the inevitable, careless moment. Then he would hammer home a fist that stiffened the other in his dancing, glazed his eyes and turned his legs to jelly. After that, all was predictable and the crowd loved it – clubbing blows that drove the dancer to his knees, bludgeoned him to the canvas or had him clawing helplessly at the ropes. Jack Cooke, the will-o-the-wisp from Cardiff, out-boxed and tormented Steve Bundy for three rounds and then, over-confident, jigged into a brick wall in the fourth. Battling Joe Marco, the Terrible Turk, born Patrick O'Flynn in Dublin, failed to survive one round. Only Sailor Hobbs stood on his feet for six, but Sailor Hobbs was made of solid teak with tarred seams, no teeth to be loosened and taking a swig of rum between every round. It was touch and go. Sailor Hobbs almost destroyed Steve Bundy, who subsequently needed eight stitches over his right eye and brow, four in his upper lip and another four to adhere his left ear to his head.

It wouldn't bloody do, Charlie Sawyer swore. So far, Bundy had fought only small-print boxers. Sure enough, he was winning, and that was difficult to quarrel with, but he was paying a price each time. Sooner or later he would find himself facing a man who made no mistakes, who refused to be hit or, when he was, merely shook his head. What followed after that would be nasty to watch from Steve Bundy's corner.

Steve Bundy shrugged, fingering the newly-healed scar over his eye. What were a few cuts? He had money to jingle in his pocket, a room of his own in King's Cross and good victuals. He bought himself a biscuit-coloured suit, a cravat, patent leather shoes with pointed toes, and a malacca cane. Then he sprinkled a little cologne on his shirt front and took a train to Mile End.

They were gathered, as always, in the pool of gaslight opposite the workmen's cookshop, from whence came the smell of frying liver and onions. Several tossed ha'pennies against a wall, but they were less noisy than usual, and others stood talking in low voices, sucking on stubs of cigarettes and gazing absently at their feet. Steve Bundy's reception was disappointingly less than effusive. They eyed his biscuit-coloured suit respectfully, gave him polite attention when he described how he had whipped Joe Marco. 'Twelve quid I got,' he told them, 'fer one round.' He chuckled. 'And ter think there's blokes that fight six fer thirty bob.' They nodded indifferently; even Johnnie Spong seemed unimpressed, which was annoying.

'Next week,' Steve Bundy said, 'I fight Max Kunze, a German.' He offered around a packet of Gold Flake.

Johnnie Spong shook his head. 'Not nex' week, you ain't,' he sniffed. 'Not nex' week, or the week after.'

It was even more annoying, particularly after he had distributed Gold Flake. He abandoned his earlier intention of treating a selected few to pie and mash in Lockhart's while he explained how he had hammered Sailor Hobbs to defeat; there was a limit to generosity.

'Next week,' he repeated. 'Next Saturday, in Birmingham. It's billed fer eight rounds, but' – he winked – 'not if I can 'elp it.'

Johnnie Spong hawked and spat. 'Ain't yer read ternight's papers, Stevie? There's going ter be a war.'

'A war? Yer mean this shindy over the Austrian bloke that was shot?' Steve Bundy laughed. 'There's always wars in that part, nearly every week. Austrians an' Serbs?' He snorted. 'If Mister Seagram feels like it, 'ee might bring 'em all over ter fight at the Albert 'All.'

Johnnie Spong took his time, puffing thoughtfully at his Gold Flake. 'The Germans 'ave marched into Belgium. *We* 'ave given the Germans an ultimatum.' He explained. 'An ultimatum's a sort o' warning, see, only it's different. If we don't get a satisfact'ry answer by ternight, we'll be at war wi' Germany termorrer – and I don't suppose they'll start by sending a bloke ter Birmingham fer eight rounds.'

'Oh, *that*,' Steve Bundy shrugged. 'I know about *that*.' He did not; he had heard scraps of conversation, references to Germany, Belgium, France and Russia, but they had meant little, and on the rare occasions that he scanned a newspaper he never ventured far from the sports columns. 'It won't come ter nothing. There's too much at stake.' Mr Seagram had used that expression only yesterday, and it had an authoritative ring. Anyway, it was difficult to imagine Mr Seagram, who had associates in New York and Sydney, allowing his plans to be upset by a war.

'We was thinking o' strolling down ter Whitehall,' someone else said, 'ter join up.'

'Blimey,' Steve Bundy marvelled. 'The Guards, o' course.' He laughed again. 'Yer'll catch me joinin' up fer two bob a bleedin' day, I *don't* think.' Not, he vowed, when he could earn twelve quid in one evening – but for these blokes, who didn't have his talents, he supposed that two bob a day, with all found, must seem attractive. And to think he was once one of them! Really, he should never have come back to the lamp-post; he had left all this behind him. He was lowering his standards.

'Well,' he decided, breezily, 'I gotta be going. Give my regards ter the Kaiser. If yer do 'appen ter be in Birmingham next week—' When he got his next money he must buy a watch and chain, like Mr Seagram's, and perhaps have some business cards printed.

A summons to Mr Seagram's office in Albemarle Street was always intimidating.

'This fellow Kunze,' the promoter told Steve Bundy, 'won't be coming up to scratch now, that's certain. The fight has been taken off the bill.' Seagram gazed at Bundy with lips pursed, calculating, then leaned back in his chair. 'As it happens, Paddy Donovan has had to withdraw from his fight with Craddock on the Sporting Club's programme – in London on the same night – and I've decided to put you in, Bundy, as a substitute.'

Steve Bundy stared. 'Me, Mister Seagram?' Donovan was the leading contender for the British championship title, unbeaten in fourteen consecutive fights. For several days the newspapers had been relishing, almost spitefully, his forthcoming match with Chris Craddock – an American who was perhaps a little past his best but with immense experience and who had fought the front-runners on both sides of the Atlantic. Chris Craddock – or, more usually, 'Grit' Craddock – could, in the opinion of many experts, know too much for the handsome young Dublin middleweight. Donovan, it was being whispered, spent too much time in the bed of Lady Llanstephan, who had an insatiable appetite for handsome boxers, guardsmen, chauffeurs, and even – in moments of deprivation – for her fourteen-year-old garden boy. Donovan was going the way of so many others of humble origin who could not resist the temptations of national acclaim. He was a promising, potentially brilliant, boxer, but the female head-hunters had got to him; he had become arrogant. Almost, the experts were hoping that Donovan would be thrashed.

'Gawd, Mister Seagram,' Steve Bundy frowned, 'Craddock's world class—'

'*Was* world class,' the other nodded, 'and he's still very good – far too good for you, Bundy; he could eat you alive. But at his age he has no future other than a slow run down hill, with every fight getting harder and the halls getting smaller. Craddock doesn't want that. He wants to breed horses in Kentucky, which means he needs dollars in the bank *now*.'

Steve Bundy tried to look as if he understood, which he did not.

'As for Donovan,' Seagram went on, 'well, I have an idea that young man is on the slippery slope back to obscurity, but he'll make a fine-looking footman for some dowager duchess. However, you needn't worry about that. You just give Craddock an honest fight, Bundy' – he looked hard at the younger man – 'and you could win.'

It was inconceivable and, later, Charlie Sawyer was almost noncommittal. 'Jes' fight yer usual fight,' he sniffed, and that was all. The newspapers, disappointingly, wasted few column inches on Paddy Donovan's indisposition and his replacement by Steve Bundy, 'the up-and-coming young middleweight from the Seagram stable'. Far more important things were happening – the savage German rape of brave little Belgium, the dashing French invasion of Alsace, the bloody nose being given to bullying Austria by heroic Serbia, the immutable Russian steamroller and, justifying the biggest headlines, the ramming of a German submarine by the cruiser *Birmingham*. All the usual topics of conversation, the score at the Oval, Aston Villa, Jack Johnson, Steve Donogue, and the ridiculous Women's Suffrage agitation, had been relegated to the inside pages.

The fight against Craddock was more bewildering than anything else. Within seconds of the opening bell Steve Bundy knew that his opponent, as Mr Seagram had suggested, was capable of eating him alive, but only Steve Bundy could see the disinterest in the other's eyes, and recognise that the craggy American's punches were feigned. Finally, in the fifth round, Craddock went down from a blow that Bundy would never have considered particularly damaging, winked at him from the canvas and then closed his eyes as the referee counted to ten.

Again, annoyingly, newspaper acclaim was brief and short-lived – the Germans had overrun the Liège forts, the road to Brussels was open, and scores of thousands of enthusiastic young Britons were flocking to recruiting offices to fight for honour and liberty – but one journalist did suggest, in print, that 'either Chris Craddock is a spent force or Gentleman Seagram has discovered in Steve Bundy a young gladiator who may soon challenge Al McCoy for the championship crown.' Charlie Sawyer snorted.

'What's wrong with that, Charlie?' Steve Bundy enquired angrily. 'I bleedin' won, didn't I?' Secretly, he was not entirely convinced that he had, but the record book would always say so, and only that mattered. 'What was I *'spected* ter do?'

Charlie Sawyer sighed. 'Yer did everything right, Steve. I ain't getting at yer – it's jes' that I don't like seeing yer being used, see.' He shook his cropped head. 'Gentleman Seagram ain't quite the gentleman yer might think. I shouldn't tell yer this, but yer must 'ave thought it was rum – the way yer beat Craddock. He was odds-on.' He paused. 'Well, Mister Seagram spread a lot o' bets, very careful, all over the country –

on you – and he won a bloody fortune; a lot more than he paid Craddock ter throw the fight, and that was a packet, I can tell yer.'

'I don't bloody believe it.' Steve Bundy stared. He did believe it.

'It wouldn't matter much,' the other resumed, 'if that was the last of it, but it won't be. Yer see, Stevie, yer a good young 'un, with spunk, but yer ain't ever going ter be a champion. Yer get caught too often and yer cut too easy. Al McCoy, did that bloke say?' He shook his head again. 'McCoy jes' murdered George Chip in forty-five seconds o' the first round. Ah – yer can earn good money, Stevie, so long as yer don't aim too 'igh. But that won't do fer Mister Seagram.'

Steve Bundy said nothing.

'Yer'll win yer next eight or ten fights,' Charlie explained. 'Some of 'em yer'll win proper – because, as I said, yer ain't bad – but some of 'em yer'll win because Mister Seagram fixed 'em. He's going ter build up yer repertation until yer the Great White 'Ope, only yer'll never be arf as good as the record book sez. Then, when yer big day comes, and it's you carrying all the odds, yer'll find yerself up against someone who ain't been paid off.'

Steve Bundy frowned. 'But suppose I still win?'

'If there's any doubt,' Charlie Sawyer shrugged, 'Mister Seagram 'll tell yer not ter try too 'ard, see, because he'll 'ave thousands o' pounds on the other bloke. O' course, he'll give yer a sweetener – a couple of 'undred.'

'I won't bloody do it!' Steve Bundy retorted. 'I ain't going ter throw a fight fer anyone!'

Charlie lifted his eyebrows. 'There mightn't be any need, Stevie. By then yer'll be fighting in a class yer should never be in; it's more likely yer'll be chopped ter mincemeat anyway. Remember yer contract. Mister Seagram decides who yer fight – or if yer fight at all.'

'And when I'm beat, what 'appens then?'

'Well—' Charlie Sawyer grimaced. 'It's back ter Mo Lyons fer thirty bob a fight, until yer've been punched out an' finished, then 'anging around gymnasiums ter spar a couple o' rounds with a young 'un, or fighting all-comers on a fairground, or chucking drunks out o' pubs. Then yer can carry gents' luggage outside railway stations, or clean shoes or sell newspapers. After that—' He sniffed.

It was too absurd to be believed, he decided after thinking about it. Gentleman Maurice Seagram was no Mo Lyons; he was too well established, too respected a figure to be involved in such chicanery. Charlie Sawyer was being spiteful, resentful of his own failed ambitions and jealous of those of a younger man. Steve Bundy felt comforted. Why should his defeat of Craddock be questioned? The journalist bloke could be right on both counts, couldn't he? Craddock was in decline while he, Bundy, was a new, rising star. Hadn't he also hammered Jack Cooke, Joe Marco and Sailor Hobbs? He fingered the scar tissue over his right eye. Nobody could tell him that Sailor Hobbs was paid to lose. He had bleedin' near won.

Still, an uneasiness lingered. His next fight, six weeks later, was against the Glaswegian middleweight Cockie Forsyth – the 'Cock o' the North' – who stood toe to toe as the crowd roared for five rounds and then went down, sprawling, in the sixth. Steve Bundy gave Forsyth the benefit of any doubt; it had been as good a right hand as he'd ever thrown, and it would have felled a bullock.

His disquiet returned, however, after the match with Matt Roper, the Nottingham Blacksmith, who had already beaten the Swedish champion, fought a gruelling draw with the British title-holder and, before each fight, amused the crowd by twisting straight several iron horse-shoes with his bare hands. Despite Bundy's string of successes, not even the kindest sports writer gave him more than a one-in-five chance of embarrassing Matt Roper – but it was Roper, after four rounds during which Bundy hit him at leisure, who threw in the towel from his corner as his own seconds stared in disbelief.

In the dressing room Steve Bundy confronted a wooden-faced Charlie.

''Ow much did Roper get paid fer *that*?' he snarled. 'A bloody packet, I shouldn't wonder. And 'ow much did soddin' Seagram win? Five thousand? Ten thousand?'

'Keep yer voice down, Stevie,' Charlie Sawyer frowned. 'I ain't saying Roper was paid anything; yer might 'ave beat him fair an' square. Anyway, what's the good o' shouting about it? Mister Seagram's entitled ter bet on his own boxer – like a racehorse owner. It's when an owner makes secret bets on the *other* bloke's horse that questions get arst.'

Whatever Steve Bundy's indignation, people were beginning to take serious notice. With the realisation that the war was going to last at least through 1915, newspapers were settling down to a less hysterical pattern, and sports journalists were creeping back to their columns. In the early days of patriotic euphoria many hundreds of professional and amateur sportsmen, anticipating only a few weeks of hostilities, had enlisted in 'Pals' battalions', intended to group together men of similar interests, and were probably now regretting it. Familiar personalities had disappeared from public knowledge, lost among the teeming flood of khaki, and new, emerging names had to be searched for and applauded.

Nobody knew much about the young boxer Steve Bundy, who seemed to be punching his way through the middleweight division with contemptuous ease; none of his fights had gone full distance. The Blackfriars promoter, Mo Lyons, confessed that he had taught Bundy all he knew before urging him in the direction of more golden horizons, and Private Johnnie Spong, Royal Fusiliers – who had done a bit himself – frequently reminded his platoon fellows of the advice and encouragement he had given the prospective champion. 'If it hadn't been fer me,' he assured everyone, 'Steve Bundy wouldn't 'ave got nowhere.' Johnnie Spong got as far as Neuve Chapelle, but no further.

Freddie Keegan of Bristol and a Canadian, Lou Delaney, were disposed of in quick succession – both honestly, Steve Bundy decided. The Canadian, indeed, in the space of three rounds, had reopened the old scar over his eye, and the attending doctor had advised that if the sutured wound was not given a full six months in which to knit firmly, any subsequent scar would be of low vitality and always vulnerable. Mr Seagram nodded. 'That can't be allowed to happen,' he agreed, and it was not. Hooker Laski, only four weeks later, strenuously avoided hitting Steve Bundy to the head before retiring reluctantly with an alleged broken hand.

Then, during the week of the first Gallipoli landings, two things happened. Steve Bundy received a perfumed note of invitation from Lady Llanstephan, inviting him to join her for a few days at her Newmarket house, and in Aldwych a young lady presented him with a white feather. The first he allowed Mr Seagram to decline politely on his behalf, pleading prior engagements. The second, of which he told nobody, stung him sharply.

'D' yer remember Sailor Hobbs?' asked Charlie Sawyer, as Steve Bundy sought to release his irritation by punishing a suspended punch-bag. 'He was called back to the Navy, and he went down on the *Good Hope*.'

Steve Bundy lashed out savagely. 'Hobbs was a bloody good bloke, an' he was straight. He told me, after our fight, that he 'ad a wife, four kids and a widdered mother in Southend, an' the loser's end o' the purse was eight quid – only I didn't care much then.'

'Well,' Charlie shrugged, 'tearing an 'ole in that bag ain't going ter change anything. Anyway, Mister Seagram wants ter see yer in his office, ter talk about yer next fight.' He waited until the other had peeled off his gloves and reached for his coat. 'It's the big one, Stevie,' he said, quietly, 'like I told yer about.'

Steve Bundy stood motionless for several moments with eyes narrowed. Then he drew a deep breath. 'Ah, yes,' he nodded. 'I remember.'

In the office above Albemarle Street Mr Seagram looked up from his desk and smiled. 'Come in, Steve, and sit down.' It was the first time he had addressed the younger man by his first name, the first time he had offered a seat.

'Now,' he beamed. 'You've been doing pretty well since you've been fighting for me, haven't you? And I'd not be surprised if you had a nice little nest-egg tucked away in the Post Office. Two hundred? – and that's not to mention tailored suits, a watch and chain, and an invitation from Lady Llanstephan.' He chuckled. 'A bit better than the Mile End Road, eh?'

Steve Bundy's silence presumably indicated agreement.

'Some of the papers are saying that you're only a couple of fights away from the British title,' Seagram went on, 'but we're not going to rush our fences, Steve. Frankly, I think you need a little more experience with top-line men, and that's why I've arranged a return match with Chris Craddock.'

'Craddock?' Steve Bundy frowned. 'But I put 'im down in five, Mister Seagram.'

Seagram's eyes were distant. He pinched the end from a cigar. 'We-ell, yes, you did – although it might be more accurate to say that Craddock went down in five. You'll recall, Steve, that you went in as a substitute; you should never been in the same ring as Craddock. That's why I made a little arrangement. You would win your first fight with Craddock and he would win the return—'

'Yer mean yer paid 'im ter throw the fight,' Steve Bundy said.

'If I hadn't, Steve, he would have hammered you to pulp.' Seagram placed the tips of his fingers together. 'Now, this time—'

'Then yer paid Matt Roper,' Bundy interrupted again, 'and Hooker Laski.'

Seagram was mildly impatient. 'Steve, these are matters that don't concern you. As I said, you've done well for yourself, and you can do better – just so long as you do as you're told. Now, listen. Craddock's not fought since he lost to you last August; you've won five fights inside the distance and the sports writers are all climbing on the Bundy wagon. A lot of money is going to be put on you, and the odds will shorten. You'll start firm favourite, understand?'

'But your money's going on Craddock, Mister Seagram.'

Seagram ignored the suggestion. 'I still think Craddock knows too much for you, Steve, but I'm not quite as confident as I was eight months ago. You've improved by a mile; you might just get home a right hand and put Craddock down. No' – he shook his head – 'I'm not telling you to throw the fight, Steve. I want you to put up a good show, but don't be *too determined*, understand? Before the night, we'll work out something. If your eye cuts again, all the better. We can throw in the towel.'

Steve Bundy sat in silence, frowning. Then, at last, he decided. 'No, Mister Seagram. I don't mind fightin' Craddock – or anyone else – but I'm only fightin' ter win.' He brightened. 'Why don't yer put yer money on me, instead? Jes' say, an' I'll *flatten* Craddock.'

'Even if I were certain of you winning,' Seagram snapped, 'the odds will be all wrong. Anyway, the thing's already settled with Craddock.'

'But it ain't settled with me,' Steve Bundy shrugged. 'I ain't going ter lose if I can 'elp it. Yer'll 'ave ter find someone else ter fight Craddock that yer *can* pay off.'

'Bundy, you don't understand.' Seagram paused to allow his anger to quieten. 'It has to be you. You don't suppose I promote fights just so that people can buy tickets to watch? Of course not. I've invested in you; your fight record has cost money. I arranged for you to beat Craddock once, which suggests to the public that you'll beat him again. Don't you see? Craddock has kept his part of the deal and he'll expect us to keep ours. Don't worry. Losing one fight isn't going to do you much harm.' He smiled. 'And wouldn't you like to double that two hundred you've got saved? Better still, I'll put two hundred on Craddock for you – very discreetly. Think of that. Next time you receive an invitation from Lady Llanstephan you'll be able to drive down to Newmarket in your own motorcar.'

Steve Bundy rose to his feet. 'No.'

'You'll fight Craddock, like I say,' Seagram insisted. 'You seem to forget you're under contract.'

Steve Bundy had never really understood what a contract was. He had signed a typewritten paper but, at the time, had been unwilling to imply doubt in Mr Seagram's integrity by reading it. 'Well,' he said, 'I ain't any more.'

Seagram flushed. 'If you revoke your contract, Bundy, you'll never fight for anyone else.'

They faced each other, unspeaking, for several moments. Then Bundy grinned. 'Oh yes, I will, Mister Seagram – yer needn't sweat. I know jes' where ter get a new contrack. The purse ain't much, nor's the grub, but nobody'll tell me ter throw a fight, neither. D'yer remember that German, Max Kunze, that I never got ter meet?' He sniffed. 'Well, I might, after all.'

At the nearest Post Office he presented a demand for two hundred pounds from his account, a sum that necessitated three days' notice of withdrawal, and instructed that the money be sent to a Southend address. 'Mrs Sailor Hobbs', he wrote laboriously, but with a feeling of intense satisfaction. He recalled the old woman with no feet who sat on the pavement outside Lockhart's in the Mile End Road. Sod it – there wasn't much difference between his last few pence then and two hundred quid now. It made a bloke feel good. Righteous.

He knew exactly what he wanted to do. It was bleedin' Fate. There was a naval recruiting office in the Strand; he had seen it briefly, a few days earlier, when that posh young tart had given him a white feather and a smirk, but he'd not known about Sailor Hobbs then.

He walked from Albemarle Street and his legs felt good for fifteen rounds. Twenty, if yer like. Right now, he'd knock seven kinds of shit out o' Jack Johnson.

Outside the recruiting office stood two elderly naval reservists in uniform. They were inviting every passing young man to confront a mirror, fixed to the wall between them. The mirror was flanked by the words, 'Photograph of the Man We Want. Roll Up. Join the Royal Navy.'

Ten months of war, however, had creamed off all the eager patriots; the young men that now walked the Strand were more wary. It was easy to cross the street.

'Heave ho, heave ho,' one of the grey-haired sailors greeted Steve Bundy, not too confidently. 'Yer can get yer life on the ocean wave 'ere. No waiting. The Navy afloat, the Royal Naval Division, or the Royal Marines. We pays yer money an' you takes yer pick. Yer've got jes' the right legs fer bell-bottom trousers, mate. Jes' think of it – rollin' down the Ol' Kent Road with yer benjie on the back of yer 'ead, and all the tarts chasin' yer ter touch yer dickie—'

'If I sign now, can I go terday?' Steve Bundy asked. He winked. 'I don't want ter miss any promotion.'

'Blimey,' the man marvelled. 'We'll send a signal ter Jellicoe, ter tell 'im yer coming.' He lowered his voice.

'Fer Chris' sake, mate, don't sign fer the RN Division. It's the trenches. Anything else, but not that.'

He signed inside – but not, he emphasised, for the RN Division, then sat in a bare waiting-room for two hours with a handful of others who talked with a nervous bravado that he found infectious. A petty officer marched them to Charing Cross Hospital where, in another bare room, he coughed with a doctor's hand in his groin, was thumbed and prodded, weighed and measured, hung by his hands and pedalled with his legs, touched his toes and read letters from a card. The doctor briefly fingered the pink scar over his eye, but made no comment.

'Now,' said a Royal Marine sergeant, when they had dressed. 'I'm going ter put yer on a train fer Deal. Yer'll be locked in, see, so's yer won't fall out. We 'ave yer welfare at 'eart. Yer'd better all do a piss before yer start – and *try* ter march in step.'

'What's Deal, Sergeant?' Steve Bundy enquired. 'Is that a Navy training place?'

'Navy?' the sergeant snorted. 'What's the Navy got ter do with it? Yer've jes' joined the Royal Marines. The *Royals*, mate. The *Corps*.'

Seven

From the bridge wing of the obsolete battleship *London*, Rear-Admiral St John Primrose levelled his binoculars at the near shore-line of low, mustard-coloured hills stippled with grey, untidy scrub and a few clumps of stunted pine above which the hot sky of startling blueness was marred by the drifting smoke of shell bursts. Contrasts shocked the eyes; white-hot sun and incandescent sky, turquoise Aegean, the flare of white surf, gullied hills of gold shadowing to sepia and bronze. Gulls floated overhead, wheeling.

Between the ship and the narrow ribbon of beach the shallows were dotted with small craft – steam launches towing strings of life-boats, drifters, cutters under oars, lighters, and even dinghies. Further to seaward were the equally old *Queen* and *Prince of Wales* with torpedo nets out, and several destroyers, *Chelmer*, *Ribble* and *Scourge*, blinking their signal lamps at each other. Two days earlier their decks had been crowded with troops, Australians and New Zealanders, who had scrambled ashore in pre-dawn darkness like eager, undisciplined schoolboys on holiday, but many had not seen the sun rise over the broken cliffs of the Gallipoli Peninsula. Their bodies lay in the loose sand and rubble of the beach or drifted in the tidal flow, scythed down by the fire of Turkish machine-guns or carried under and drowned by the weight of their equipment.

12,000 Australian infantry and two Indian Army mountain batteries had landed during that first day, another 8000 infantry on the second, but, in error, they had waded ashore further north than the intended mile-long beach of Gaba Tepe. The boats had grounded in a small bay overhung by cliffs that the Turks called Ari Burnu but which, forever after, would be known as Anzac Cove. Company after disorganised company had swarmed inland, scattering among the confusion of ravines and gullies that led only to more sand dunes and scrub-covered cliffs. By daylight many detachments were lost, out of touch with their flanking units and cut off from following supports, pinned down by machine-gun fire and a probing howitzer barrage. As the sun climbed higher and the Turks rallied, a battery of 105 mm guns began shelling from the far side of the peninsula.

'It won't do,' Primrose said, to nobody in particular. 'It's bloody, utter chaos. What the hell are we supposed to be firing at?' The Anzacs' uncoordinated advance had bogged down in terrain of which their ship-borne commanders knew nothing or, worse, had completely misleading information. Intelligence from the fighting areas was sketchy, ambiguous. Orders conflicted with orders and desperate appeals from the troops for fire support met with blank stares because the references meant nothing; there were no maps. Anzac Cove, now, was littered with stores hauled from the boats by beach-parties – rations, ammunition, medical supplies, water. There must soon follow horses, mules and fodder, but the cove was being drenched with fire from hidden enemy positions. The sea for fifty yards from shore, an aeroplane pilot reported, was dyed red with blood, but the ships' gun-crews waited for orders that never came, because nobody knew the dispositions of either friend or enemy. It could only be assumed, the staff officers shrugged, that everything was going according to plan, or somebody would say so, wouldn't they?

'If the mountain won't come to Mohamed,' Primrose gritted, 'we'll go to the bloody mountain.' He turned to his gunnery officer. 'You and I'll go ashore and see what the score is. The Turks must have observation posts for directing their artillery fire; we'll see if we can chart them for our guns. And we want locations for our own OPs to spot the enemy fire from across the peninsula. Those four-point-ones have got to be silenced or there's going to be even more chase-arse than there is now.' He paused. 'My compliments to the Captain. I'd like to take a pinnace away as soon as possible, please.'

Crawling among the forward positions of a battle zone was no task for a greying Rear-Admiral, but Lieutenant George Pope knew better than to argue, and so would *London*'s captain. When Sinjin Primrose sent his compliments to someone, that person instantly stopped whatever he was doing and complied. On this occasion the Captain was asleep in his sea cabin after fourteen hours on the bridge but, roused, he reached for his telephone to tell the Officer of the Watch to order away a pinnace. Then he gazed wearily at Pope. 'Good God,' he heaved. 'He's going ashore to look for enemy OPs? Haven't we got two damn divisions of infantry already doing that?'

Pope agreed. He was just as weary. Primrose was as durable and unfeeling as a leather seaboot, and vociferously critical of lesser mortals, in which category Pope conceded himself to be. Earlier, if the older man had never been easy to please, at least he had always been approachable, but since Mudros, from where the invasion fleet of transports and warships had sailed, he had not been even that. Despite Pope's long, and latterly more entrenched, relationship, he had never been addressed by his first name if there existed the remotest chance of such a laxity being overheard by a third person. Since Mudros he had hardly been addressed at all. The Rear-Admiral consulted his yeoman of signals more frequently than he did his gunnery officer, which raised a few eyebrows on *London*'s bridge.

Something, George Pope was aware, had changed Primrose's attitude towards him from merely discreet to coldly hostile. He wished he knew what he had done, or failed to do, to offend his exacting uncle by marriage.

He had always been uncertain about Imogen's regard for him. She usually addressed him as 'dear George', or 'George dear', but extended the familiarity to others, including a persistent young deck officer of the Mercantile Marine named Hedley Bellman, who visited Portsmouth on a number of occasions. George Pope knew exactly why, and also knew that Bellman recognised a rival in him. He had borne young Bellman no ill-will and went to some pains to be civil and even to allow him Imogen's undisturbed company, so far as possible, whenever he came. Bellman's visits, by necessity, were infrequent, and George Pope did not believe that he represented a serious threat to his own prospects.

He did not, that was, until Imogen began exchanging letters with Sub-Lieutenant Bellman of HMS *Aboukir*. Occasional visits to Portsmouth were one thing, he reasoned. Bellman was a shy young man and unlikely to throw himself on his knees with a proposal. Letters, however, were something different. George Pope knew how easy it was to say things in letters that could not dared be said in a drawing room. It was time, he decided, to make a firm move.

Yet he was uncertain about Imogen's regard for him. Being dear George proved nothing. By the same token, he confessed to himself, he could not in all honesty swear that he *loved* Imogen. She was of physically breath-catching appearance, a Dresden-china shepherdess with wide blue eyes, hair of a golden splendour that might be unbelievable if he did not know it to be true, and a figure that could not fail to generate erotic speculation in the most pious of men. Imogen also had a twinkling wit, and that, he realised, was the word that really described her. Imogen twinkled. She would be a polished hostess, pour tea with delicate skill, discuss opera and avant-garde authors. He recalled his father's brief references to women like that, and also to his own mother, who, despite cucumber sandwiches and custard, had ridden a hard-mouthed hunter better than most men, pedalled a bicycle in bloomers, and taken fencing lessons. She had shown the Australians a thing or two and, after the initial shock, the Australians had loved her. In due course, George Pope knew, he must return, but he feared that Imogen and a cultural wilderness like Australia would be incompatible. It was even more probable that George Pope and Imogen were incompatible.

With such poor prospects of marital happiness, why did he feel such anxiety to lay claim to her? George Pope could fabricate a number of reasons, and did, but truthfully there was only one.

He did not desire her carnally; he was not confident that he could play man to any woman, however attractive. There was something lacking in him.

No, that was not entirely true. For several years, plagued by embarrassing skin rashes, mercifully usually below the neck-line, he had carefully avoided exposing himself before even masculine eyes in gymnasium, shower bath or sports field. He had a poor appetite, and experienced bouts of nausea; his hair was thinning. More worrying, he was beginning to forget simple things, men's names, routine orders, not yet with any serious consequences, but there might be, one day.

It was all attributable, he knew, to the concussion he had suffered aboard *Albion*. Since then, he had never subdued the nervous twitch of a face muscle that the tinkle of a fire gong provoked, nor the apprehension he experienced as he lifted himself through the hatch of a turret into the hated smell of oiled steel and polished brasswork, but he disciplined himself. There must be others, he told himself, who felt the same. It was just a matter of emotional control. These gunnery ratings, poorly educated and crude-mannered, who probed with matchsticks at dulled ears as the shell hoists crashed within inches of them – were they better men than him?

He could, of course, have requested a transfer to a different speciality, perhaps torpedoes, or signals, or navigation, or ask to be drafted to minelaying or the surveying service, but it would mean explanations. Warships, he had always told his father, were platforms for guns and nothing else. All other activities – engine-room, wireless, code-books, cables, steering, boats – were all subsidiary, all merely servants to the one thing that made a ship of war different to any other; her guns. No, he determined, to abandon gunnery would be to abandon every ambition he had nursed. He might just as well have remained in Australia, aboard the old *Encounter*, and chugged around the Great Barrier Reef.

And there was only one reason for wanting Imogen Primrose. The thought of another's lusting hands plucking the petals from that exquisite flower was insufferable.

In the event, it had all happened more quickly than was comfortable. He had chosen a moment when St John Primrose was in a mellow mood. The RN Gunnery School XV had just beaten the Royal Engineers with bone-crushing zest, the field-gun's crew had taken four seconds from Devonport's best time, and a confident rumour had it that the new battleships being laid down were to be mounted with fifteen-inch guns. For the moment, all things were bright and beautiful for Rear-Admiral Primrose.

He stared at George Pope. 'May you do *what*?' he snorted.

'Pay your addresses to my niece? Dammit, man, do I understand that you want to propose to Imogen? If so, *say* so.'

'Yes, sir,' George Pope nodded, and felt his lip twitch. 'That is – if you have no objection—'

'Goddammit, your father didn't ask anyone if he might pay his addresses to my fiancée. He *fought* me for her.'

George Pope was taken aback. 'Yes, sir—'

'*Tell* her she's going to marry you, but don't make too much fuss over it. We shall want a new turret drill and ammunition handling procedure prepared before the fifteen-inch breeches arrive from Elswick – so there's going to be no time for billing and coo-ing. Then there's the whaler's crew to be worked up for the summer regatta, and then these confounded Turkish crews we're expected to teach thirteen-five drill. They don't eat pork or bacon, I'm told – so get the labels on the tins changed, and we'll say the bacon is salted goat. If they don't believe it, give 'em sardines—'

The pinnace grounded, panting, in two feet of water that floated with debris which was unwise to examine too closely. The stoker lifted his head above the after hatch but lowered it again as a shell from an unseen enemy gun smashed into the sea fifty yards away. 'Return to the ship,' Primrose ordered the midshipman, who had been hoping for an opportunity to search for souvenirs on the beach. 'We may be several hours. Tell my yeoman to watch for our return at this point.' With George Pope he waded ashore. He was wearing a pistol, Pope had already noted, and hoped it did not mean that the old boy intended to exchange shots with the Turks, although nothing would have surprised him.

The shingle was littered with the wood of broken boats, ammunition boxes, abandoned equipment, piles of stores of every description, punctured water-cans, spent cartridges. Other boats were beaching, with men hauling off crates and sacks and, burdened, hurrying across the open expanse of foreshore to the comparative security of the cliffs under which were tents, more piles of stores, a field hospital and lines of prostrate wounded waiting to be embarked after dark. Every few seconds a spatter of bullets tore up the sand, or a mushroom of dust and shale was lifted skyward by a falling shell. At a discreet distance from the field hospital was a growing pyramid of hastily-swathed corpses, attracting thousands of flies. It was hot, with a choking smell of dust, chloroform, cordite and rottenness. 'God, this is terrible,' George Pope said. Primrose only grunted.

'If you two Poms want ter live ter collect yer bloody pensions,' shouted an irreverent Australian voice, 'yer'd better watch yer arses. Them Johnnies is using real bullets.' Primrose only grunted again.

They crossed a shallow gully in which a long, twisting file of Australian infantrymen waited, smoking and talking, and pushed on, followed by the men's curious eyes. George Pope could not guess what his superior intended to do and did not wish to enquire. He was already beginning to feel jaded. Ahead, beyond the immediate sand hills, they could see the brown hump of Koja Chemen Tepe, the highest point of the Sari Bair range. Behind them the sea was no longer in sight. They passed more men, some crouched in rifle pits, a few sleeping with bush hats over faces. At least, George Pope presumed they were sleeping. A machine-gun was chuttering somewhere to their left. There were more dead, more flies humming.

Sinjin Primrose halted at last. They were alone, standing among rubble and scrub. The older man put his hands behind his back and thrust out his chin. 'Have you had a letter from Imogen?' he barked.

Surprised, George Pope frowned. 'No, sir – that is, not since Malta.'

'I have,' Primrose said. 'I had a letter in Mudros.'

George Pope gazed back, uncomprehending. Odd things

happened to mail all the time. Primrose had surely not brought him to this desolate place simply to announce that he had received a letter from his niece? Still, he nodded. 'I'm glad, sir. She's well, I hope?'

The Rear-Admiral rocked gently on his heels, his eyes on Pope. Then, to the other's astonishment, he began to unfasten the flap of his holster. George Pope glanced quickly around; he could see nobody.

Primrose levelled his pistol at Pope's chest. 'Imogen has contracted a disease,' he rasped. 'An obscene disease that only a man could have given her.'

Imogen? An obscene disease? Pope grappled for some sort of interpretation. Had he heard it correctly? He stared at the pistol, then at Primrose's grim face. 'She's contracted a disease from a *man*? Well, it wasn't—' He stopped.

'It wasn't you? You're suggesting that she got it from someone else? In a brothel, say – or in an alleyway behind the seamen's hostel?'

Pope shook his head desperately. 'Of course not. But are you sure? Sir, I mean—'

'I'm sure,' Primrose affirmed. 'And it took a lot of damn courage for Imogen to write about it.' He sucked in his breath. 'By the grace of God, and in ignorance, she went to the doctor who has known her since the day she was born, and she'll not be queueing with whores and vagrants to be leered at in some damn charity hospital. She's going to be cured, but it'll take a long time – and it'll be a humiliation that'll scar her for life.' He paused. 'That's what you've done to Imogen.'

It was still, even now, nightmarishly unbelievable. But perhaps he, Pope, had jumped to the wrong conclusion. He could feel the muscle in his jowl flickering madly.

'Sir' – he spoke very deliberately – 'are you saying that Imogen has' – he swallowed – '*syphilis*?'

Sinjin Primrose ignored the question. 'Only three people,

other than Imogen, know about it. There are going to be only two. I'm going to kill you.' The gun in his hand rose slightly. 'Yes, I'll report that you were struck down by an enemy bullet; nobody will question it, and there'll be no post-mortem. I'll write to your father – I have a considerable regard for him, and I'll tell him you were killed on active service. I owe him that. And if your mother is watching, she'll understand. As for you, Goddammit, you'll be buried alongside men whose boots you're not fit to lick. I apologise to them; they don't deserve you.' He drew in his breath again, but his eyes were hard. 'It's no different to shooting a rabid dog.'

This was not really happening, George Pope assured himself. It was like some ludicrous scene from a cheap-jack melodrama. 'Sir – really!' he protested, and tried to laugh.

On the lower, westward slope of Chunuk Bair the Turkish rifleman had waited, alone, for thirty hours because his officer had ordered him to, when his company retired, and it was impossible for him to reason that by now he had been abandoned and forgotten. There must be others, isolated like himself, in the surrounding labyrinth of sandhills; all day he had heard rifle fire and an occasional chatter of a machine-gun, and was comforted – although there was no doubt that the English had passed him on both sides and closed behind, cutting off his retreat but without being aware of his presence. *Maaleesh*. It was written.

There was only a mouthful of water remaining in his canteen, and he was very hungry, but he could see the Aegean, distant, flashing gold, and he could see the enemy ships – the big, clumsy transports, the sheepdog destroyers and the scores of smaller craft that crawled like water-beetles. He had not realised that there were so many ships in the whole world.

His dirty khaki blended excellently with the terrain. He had found a length of corrugated iron to roof his sniper's nest, and spread it with sandy earth that had dried in minutes under the hot sun and was indistinguishable from any other few yards of arid hillside. Stay here, his officer had ordered. He had stayed.

He had a fine Mauser rifle with a telescopic sight—only one had been issued to each battalion, but was he not the battalion's finest marksman who had taken the prize from the hands of Pasha Liman von Sanders?

The curving beach of Ari Burnu was hidden from him by the cliffs that overhung it. Incoming craft vanished from sight several hundred yards from shore, but he had momentary glimpses of bodies of troops advancing inland, khaki-clad like himself, at first ill-disciplined and ignoring caution until Turkish bullets had torn them down in swathes. Now most of them had gone to earth, clinging to dead ground; he could hear their shouts, and the boats were still coming. Soon, he suspected, the English would advance again and, sooner or later, by sheer weight of numbers, they would overrun the few remaining Turkish positions. For him, survival was unlikely; he had his rifle and sixty cartridges and would remain in this dark, oven-hot cavity until his company counter-attacked or until a grenade buried him. It was written.

He stirred occasionally to ease the growing cramp in his legs. Several times he had been tempted to fire, but each time the range had been more than a thousand yards, and even with a telescopic sight it had been risky; he had no wish to compromise himself, not yet. When the time came, he would want to shoot an English general, or at least a colonel, but at a thousand yards they all looked the same. Like his fellows, he had been surprised that the English all wore drab khaki; photographs and caricatures had always shown them in scarlet tunics and tall, bearskin hats – either monstrously fat with handlebar moustaches or beanpole thin and falling over over-size swords.

It was becoming insufferably hot under the canopy of corrugated iron and sand. He could smell his own fetid body, but he no longer sweated. He thought of the mouthful of warm water in his canteen, but not yet.

He wrenched his thoughts away from the mouthful of water. Barely fifty yards from him two men had appeared from nowhere, had halted, and seemed to be engaged in conversation, facing each other. Neither was in khaki, but in dark blue or black, with white caps. It was odd that they should be here; they were, he recognised, naval officers – but why here? And they were English. No Moslem wore head covering that denied his face to the sun. He pushed his rifle hard into his shoulder. This was very easy, but he waited.

Curiously, the two men did not seem to be components of the day's savage activity. They appeared unaware of their surroundings, or at least uncaring, and were simply talking as if in a different place, a different time. One of them had gold on his hat; perhaps he was the Bayuk Amiral who had brought the enemy ships to the Dardenelles. He was stocky, broad-shouldered, with a white spike of a beard and the arrogant posture of all cartoon English milords. The other was younger, slimmer. The crouched Turkish sniper made a whisper adjustment to his telescopic sight. Then, to his surprise, the white-bearded Amiral drew a pistol from a holster at his waist and levelled it at his companion.

It was wise to anticipate that only one shot would be effective, the sniper knew. When one man fell, the other would almost certainly throw himself behind cover. So it had to be the Amiral. He placed the cross-wires of his sight over the coloured splash of medal ribbons on the Amiral's chest, held his breath, then squeezed the trigger.

The bullet struck Sinjin Primrose high in the chest, spinning him. He gave a surprised, pained shout, fell to his knees, then sank forward to all fours. 'Goddamm,' he choked, his face twisting. He made an effort to lift himself back to his knees, but could not; his left shoulder was useless. In his right hand, however, he still clutched the pistol.

George Pope stared only momentarily, interpreting the situation even before his stricken companion, and threw himself also to the ground. A second bullet kicked up the sand only inches from his outflung foot. Frantically, he looked about him for sanctuary, but Primrose, on knees and elbows, was struggling to raise his pistol again. Helplessly, Pope watched the wavering muzzle turn towards him, behind it the angry eyes of his accuser. He tensed, but in that moment saw the other's face jolted backward by a third bullet that smashed through cheek, jaw and skull, spattering blood. Sinjin Primrose was dead instantly, with eyes glazed and stubby white beard red-drenched.

Shocked, George Pope clung to the earth, then realised that there was no sense in doing so; he must be as visible to the hidden marksman as Primrose had been. There was a rock-strewn depression several yards away from which, earlier, the two men had climbed. He scrambled for it, tearing the skin from his hands and expecting every second the hammer-blow of a bullet in his back, but now he was safe, plunging to the earth yet again and unashamedly crawling. Perhaps, he speculated feverishly, he should have tried to have brought back Primrose's body. Would someone ask why he had abandoned a Rear-Admiral's corpse? Had he really been dead? He'd *looked* dead. Jesus Christ, yes, he was dead—

Distant shouts and the distinctive tack-tack-tack of a Vickers machine-gun told him that he had regained the Australian line and, throwing all caution to the wind, he rose to his feet and ran blindly.

Eight

The war was seven weeks old when Donald Selley was released from detention, and he might do worse, the prison governor advised him, than enlist immediately in the service of his country; he was still only forty and able enough to make atonement for his obliquity. Donald Selley promised, penitently, that he would go to a recruiting office directly from the prison gate, but when that gate closed behind him his first objective was the nearest tavern. A haughty gentleman of the Prisoners' Aid Society had given him four-and-sixpence, and he had not tasted a drop for six months.

Four-and-sixpence was a niggardly sum with which to celebrate his freedom, and, when he had spent it, his reawakened craving was unsatisfied. He wanted whisky; a man was entitled to whisky after six months of abstinence. He had been deprived, victimised. Resentment smouldered within him, fanned by his frustration at having failed to save a copper for the tram to Leith. He walked, generating a vague conviction that somebody was responsible and somebody was going to be sorry.

He pulled his cap firmly to his ears to hide a head shorn only the previous day so that nobody would fail to recognise a discharged convict. Somebody was going to be sorry. Bluidy hell. Enlist in the army, did that bastard of a governor say? Donald Selley laughed bitterly. By the time he reached Inkerman Street he was ready to put a fist into the face of the first person that spoke to him.

The house was silent and the door locked, but he forced it open easily. The interior, he noted, was neater and cleaner than he had ever known it, which affronted him even more. There was a battered phonograph that he did not recognise, a glass chimney around the gas-light, a length of cheap matting in front of the stove and, luxuriously, a chequered cotton cloth on the table, albeit stained. Donald Selley walked from scullery to living room, then climbed the narrow stairs.

He was looking for provocation, and he found it. In the room he had shared with his wife the bed's blankets were turned down. Mary Selley would have risen at four in the morning, but there was no doubt that she had left someone else still occupying the bed who, subsequently, had abandoned it in disarray. Both pillows, plainly, had been used; both sides of the bed had been slept upon. Mary Selley, undeniably, had shared the night with another.

And only last night? How many other nights during the past six months had his wife whored with some man? – aye, and the pair of them laughing at the thought of Donald Selley on a pallet of planks in a cold prison cell and safely locked away. Bluidy hell, and he'd been a faithful husband, except for a few times, and this was what a man got for it when his back was turned. Donald Selley's righteous revulsion choked him. Bluidy hell, somebody was going to be sorry.

Even more than vengeance, however, he craved for alcohol, and he was penniless. He returned below, took the phonograph under his arm, then walked to a pawnbroker's establishment three streets away. The pawnbroker displayed little enthusiasm. People didn't want old phonographs these days, he sniffed. They wanted gramophones. If Donald

Selley had brought a gramophone, now, that would be different. He'd never sell a phonograph, not these days. What did Selley want for it? A *pound*? The man laughed. Five shillings – and that was more than it was worth.

Life was just one injustice after another, Donald Selley simmered, as he repaired to the Montrose Arms. Five shillings wouldn't buy enough whisky to sweeten his spit. There was more irritation to come. The potman grinned at him. 'So it's yesel', is it? Och, we thocht ye'd joined the Gordon Highlanders, mon – or wuz it the Gaol-hoose Grenadiers?' He guffawed, searching the bar-room for applause.

It required only a short time for Donald Selley to drink his way through five shillings. The duty on whisky had been raised, which was a diabolical penalty for a man who had been allowed no opportunity for drinking any for six months. Society was determined to exercise its spite on Donald Selley, one way or another.

Could he have credit? The man across the bar shook his head. Not for a man just out of prison, with no work and few prospects of any. How would Selley settle his tally? The opening months of the war, paradoxically, had seen a significant increase in unemployment. Hundreds of local men, with no prison records, were idle, while thousands of Belgian and French refugees were pouring into the country, willing to work for half the wages of an Englishman or Scot. Credit, did he say?

He leaned forward with a confiding wink. 'That laddie o' yours – Albert? – that's the under-manager o' Coleman's Bakery, ye ken? He's the money fer a pint or tae o' ordinary most nights. And ye lassie – Harriet? Och, man, the Leith Company's paying guid. Whit's a man like yesel' doing, asking fer credit, when ye family's bringing hame wages?' He winked again. 'Who's the man in ye hoose? Yesel'? Och, who did ye go ter bluidy prison for? Who's been earning money, an' living in ye hoose – while ye've been on skilly?'

Of course the man was right, Donald Selley realised. He should of thought of it before. Hadn't he gone to prison because he'd surrendered to temptation for his family's sake? And the police had been vindictive because one of them had not found the prosperous corpse first. In six months he'd had neither a visit nor a letter from his wife, while she had been whoring, his elder son swilling ale in the Montrose Arms and his daughter spending good money on phonographs and table-cloths. Bluidy hell.

Young Martin and Kate, outside the house, observed their father's approach and ran for the next street. Six months of enforced abstention had weakened his tolerance, and he was more befuddled than he might have conceded. They had seen that unsteady gait before, and knew what it threatened. In an hour or so they would return, tentatively, by which time he would have smashed everything within reach and then collapsed in a drunken stupor on an upstairs bed – and if he was sufficiently comatose they might investigate his pockets for coppers he had overlooked.

It was darkening, and Mary Selley, fortunately for her, was debating the potential of her firmly-clutched purse among market stalls lit by guttering acetylene flares – potatoes and bread, bacon scraps and salt belly, flour, oatmeal, barley and dried peas, a sheep's head, condensed milk, sugar, margarine, jam, suet, yellow soap – the list was monotonously the same every week, but the Selleys, with three earning, were living better, recently, than most of their neighbours in Inkerman Street. With stringent care she might even buy boots from Macintyre's oilshop. Hob-nailed boots from Macintyre's were the indisputable hallmark of Inkerman Street's elite.

Like his mother, Albert was ignorant of the date of Donald Selley's release from prison. He knew the time had been approaching but had tried not to think about it, and by tacit consent it had not been discussed. Albert entered the Montrose Arms a mere thirty seconds after Donald Selley had pugnaciously left it, a fact with which the potman acquainted him immediately and with relish.

'Ah, yes,' Albert nodded, as if the event was of no great concern, but he shuddered mentally. The day had come at last, then, and he had not prepared himself for it. Had those six months of calm passed so quickly? For certain, he was not going to hasten after his father. 'He was his usual sel' – boozed,' the potman enjoyed divulging. Albert took a pint of ordinary and drank it slowly as he brooded over the situation. His conclusions were not very different to those already reached by Martin and Kate. Given time and a wide berth, Donald Selley would surrender to drunken, snoring sleep; it was just a matter of time. Albert took another pint of ordinary.

It was harshly unfortunate that when Donald Selley regained the house in Inkerman Street, only Harriet, unwarned, awaited him.

For eight or nine weeks Harriet had been tormented by fears that had nothing to do with Donald Selley; his sudden appearance only made her knowledge more terrifying – the knowledge that she was pregnant.

In the beginning she had not recognised the signs. Her knowledge of such things was sketchy and she had shrunk from confiding in her mother, but the women at the fish dock left her in no doubt. They had shaken knowing heads, their sympathy tinged with amusement. She'd been careless, the poor wee lassie, and now she had a bellyful o' arms and legs, and no ring on her finger – and only fourteen, ye ken? They sniffed, with eyes distant. Aye, weel, if ye played wi' fire, ye could get yesel' burned.

What, she had pleaded, could she do? Well, they mused, there was something called 'Ippy-kack', brewed strong in hot water and taken in large doses, or there were Dover's Pills, or croton oil. Any of these screwed up the belly like wet string. Then there were strong mustard baths, or running up and down stairs, or large quantities of gin – or all of these simultaneously. If she and her condition survived these insults, then there only remained a visit to a certain old woman in Sevastopol Street, but – b'Christ, lassie – they'd not recommend that. It cost good money in advance and could lead only to a blood-drenched sheet in the infirmary and a medical student who had not the first notion of how to check a massive internal haemorrhage. No, lassie – only the most desperate went to the old woman in Sevastopol Street. It was better to let things run their course. Anyway, there were things that could be done wi' an unwanted bairn, when the time came. . . .

None of the off-hand suggestions seemed practicable to Harriet – at least, not with benefit of secrecy. No, she would wait just a little longer, just a while, to be really sure.

She could, of course, have achieved certainty one way or the other by consulting a doctor, but women seeking such advice were almost invariably escorted by another female, for decency's sake. Lassies of fourteen never went alone to a doctor for any reason.

But she was sure now. It was astonishing that nobody else in the little house seemed to observed any change in her. True, the thickening of her waistline was not yet very conspicuous, and fortunately her mother had always been absent during the morning bouts of retching in the outside water-closet. Was there nobody to whom she could turn for help? Fallen women who were pregnant, she seemed to recall, knocked on the doors of convents and begged for sanctuary and forgiveness, but she did not know of any convents, only of a few soot-grimed chapels to which the unforgiving righteous of Leith went in their Sunday blacks. Even the determined ladies of the Salvation Army who flourished tambourines outside the Montrose Arms and shouted for Jesus did not seem to offer quite what Harriet needed. Was there nobody in whom she could confide who would not insist on proclaiming to the world that a sinner had repented, and the Lord in His infinite mercy had stretched out His hand?

Aye, there's likely folk that'll take ye in, the women on the fish dock told her – the bluidy holy ones, ye ken, knowing ye canna go anywhere else wi'out a reference. And ye'll scrub an' scrape, an' carry coals from five in the morning until midnight, for pennies, wi' the auld man fingering ye arse when his wife's no looking or the boy frae schule loitering around ye bedroom every nicht. An' ye bedroom? It'll be under the tiles, an' so bluidy cauld ye'll sleep in ye clo'es. What was that? Ye bairn? Och, ye'll nae see ye bairn again, lassie. Aye, and in the end ye'll drop ye breeks for the auld man or the boy because, if ye dinna, they'll get rid of ye. When ye do – and ye will – the auld woman will know because it's happened before. She'll put ye on the street wi' ye bag, and the whole thing will start again wi' some other lassie. Yesel', weel, it's walkin' the streets for drunks an' sailors, most o' the time getting ye face smashed an' no money. . . .

Donald Selley gazed at her sullenly, swaying. 'Wha is she – ye bluidy mither?' He had goaded himself into a vicious confusion of emotions and was unsure of his priorities. He wanted money for whisky and he was going to thrash his wife for her whoring. Whichever he chose to do first, he would need his leather waist-belt. He unbuckled it.

'Feyther!' The colour in Harriet's face drained and nausea climbed into her throat. God, dear God, and I'm alone. 'We dinna know ye wuz coming—' She was unable to drag her eyes from the length of leather he wrapped around his knuckles. God, dear God, and there was nowhere to run.

'Are ye bluidy deaf ?' he snarled. 'Wha is she?'

Harriet did not know where her mother was. Mary Selley

might be seeking mutton pieces or cow cheek, or scrubbing a stairway, or pounding dirty sheets in some steaming wash-house. 'She's no here,' she said stupidly, and then gripped by terror, she urinated.

There was a moment of silence as Donald Selley eyed her contemptuously. 'Ye dirty little scab,' he slurred, and then his eyes narrowed. Despite his alcohol-dulled thinking he was aware of a change in his daughter that others, closer to her, had failed to observe because its progression had been so gradual. Harriet's breasts showed and her waist was gently swollen. Selley knew the early signs of pregnancy; he had cursed them savagely on other occasions, and Mary Selley had dreaded the moment.

Harriet shook her head, ashamed and desperate. 'I couldna help it,' she sobbed, 'I couldna—'

Donald Selley was no longer interested in Harriet's immediate predicament. Momentarily he was confused. Several things had been happening that he found difficult to keep in perspective simultaneously. How could Harriet be pregnant? She was only fourteen, wasn't she? – but he'd swear he wasn't mistaken. Aye, someone had taken the little bitch's breeks down, likely a trawlerman or a fish-dock porter, and she'd had her belly filled.

Where? In some trawler's fo'c'sle or the dock-gaffer's cuddy? – or upstairs here in Donald Selley's own house?

It was beyond belief, yet the evidence was here before his eyes. During his absence the house in Inkerman Street had become a whore-shop. His wife was taking men naked and laughing into her bed – *his* bed – and his daughter was pregnant from doing the same. What had that grinning mud-raker in the Montrose Arms said? 'Who's the man in ye hoose? Who's been earning money an' living in ye hoose while ye've been on skilly?'

Harriet saw his arm rise and she sobbed, flinging herself away, but there was no escape. The leather sang, tore savagely. She fell to her knees, her head in her arms, jerking and shrieking.

It was fully dark when Albert Selley emerged from the Montrose Arms, and there was the smell of fog in the air. Distant, a newsboy was shouting that the British were advancing across the Aisne with the enemy in full retreat, then adding the ominous words, 'heavy casualties', which would evoke a shiver in the hearts of all who had a man in France. Albert paused to light a cigarette in a cupped hand, delaying his return to Inkerman Street by a few more moments.

When, unwillingly, he reached the house it was silent and in total darkness. He was mildly surprised but relieved. A confrontation with his father, if inevitable, was at least postponed. Then he saw that Martin and Kate sat on the kerb, hunched and unmoving, with their eyes on the door, which was half open. Albert frowned at the door, then at the children. 'Wha's it, then?' he asked, between his teeth. Suddenly, something was wrong, and his belly twisted. Kate began to cry quietly.

Tentatively he pushed the door wider, then entered. From the dark living room beyond the little scullery came the sound of sobbing. It could only be Harriet; he had never heard his mother sob. He groped for the table, then the gas-cock above the mantel-piece, and struck a match. The gas lamp hissed into life, flooding the room with yellow light.

Harriet crouched low against the far wall, her hair disordered and eyes swollen with weeping. A sleeve of her dress was torn from a shoulder, and there were red wheals on her arms and throat that Albert recognised immediately. She raised her smeared face as the gaslight flared, then exploded into a new frenzy of lamentation.

There was nothing remarkable about a thrashing. 'Och,' he snorted, 'stop ye greetin'—' Then he halted, aghast.

Donald Selley lay sprawled and inert on the floor in front

of the brass fender with his knees doubled. His eyes were clenched, his mouth wide, showing his bad teeth, and his cap had fallen from his shaven head. One hand, still gripping his waist-belt, was flung wide. The other was clutched to his shirt-front. He was not in a drunken stupor. His jacket and the matting under him were soaked with fresh blood, and Harriet's gutting-knife was imbedded in his lower chest.

Albert stared, horrified, unable to move or speak. At last he did. 'Jesus Christ,' he choked, and retreated several paces so that the corpse was separated from him by the table. He drew a shuddering breath. 'Jesus Christ.'

'I didna mean ta, Albert,' Harriet jerked. 'I swear I didna mean ta – but he wud have killed me, Albert—' She began to sob again. 'He cud see I wuz pregnant—'

Albert had been about to bolt for the door and the darkness of the street – none of this was his concern – but his sister's last comment stayed him. 'Ye're *what*?' he asked. 'Did ye say ye're *pregnant*?' Nothing ever happened in halves.

It was an opportunity to transfer a measure of responsibility. 'Aye,' she accused, regaining belligerence, 'and ye know who's ta blame. It's all ye fault, Albert – all this. When I tell the polis—'

The police? Albert cringed mentally. 'Ye wouldna tell them about *that*, would ye?' He grappled for cohesive thought. 'Och, ye wuz willing – and how can ye prove it wuz me, anyway?' He had almost forgotten the corpse of Donald Selley. 'They'll no believe ye,' he gritted, shaking his head. 'It could ha' been anyone.'

'It wuz yesel' ' Harriet said. 'Martin knows.'

It wasn't really happening. It was a nightmare. In a few moments he would awaken sweating and trembling, then lay gratefully in the darkness. Albert shot a glance at his father's feet, at the clock that ticked over the stove, at the gaslight that hissed. He probed at his lips with the tip of his tongue. No, he wasn't going to awaken. It was real. Jesus Christ.

'Martin doesna see what ye do on the fish-dock,' he countered. The women who worked at the benches were notoriously promiscuous. 'Anyway, if it wuz me – and I'm no sayin' it wuz – ye dinna have ta say so. It'll be worse for ye, if ye do.' He lowered his voice. 'Ye can say it wuz a sailor fra a Swedish freighter, that ye've no seen since. Then, when ye told ye feyther, he tried ta kill ye, and ye only defended yesel', ye ken'. He forced a confiding grin. 'They'll no do much ta ye, Harriet, not wi' ye pregnant an a'—' He glanced at the clock again. Mary Selley would be returning from the Saturday market at any moment, and then the fat would be in the fire, no mistake.

Harriet lifted her head. She was dry-eyed. For several seconds she gazed at him, speculating, and then she nodded slowly. 'Aye, I'll say it wuz a sailor, Albert, if ye tell the polis it wuz yesel' that stabbed ye feyther.'

'Me?' Albert's jaw dropped. 'Och – ye're no serious—?'

She nodded again. 'Aye. I'll swear ye saved me fra being killed. Like ye said, they'll no do much. And it's fair.' It was bluidy men that took their pleasure, the women on the fish-dock had said, and the lasses that paid the price; it was always the bluidy same. But not this time, Harriet resolved. 'And I'll no say anythin' about the other – not about you, anyway. I'll say it wuz a sailor from a Swedish timber-ship that's no been back ta Leith since the war started.'

Albert was shocked. A few minutes earlier he had been standing with an elbow on the bar of the Montrose Arms, supping ale, and now, without warning, everything had exploded into disaster. He experienced not a shadow of remorse with regard to his father. A bluidy good riddance. But Harriet, now – there was a scheming little bitch for ye. He would never have thought her capable of such a cunning betrayal, and of her own brother, too. It undermined a man's faith in family loyalty.

'We-ell,' he said, and sucked his teeth.

'They canna blame ye for saving ye seester's life,' Harriet insisted, '*and* defending yesel'. There's plenty can say he wuz a mudderin' savage, wi' the whisky.' She paused thoughtfully. 'O' course, if I said I'm pregnant because ye forced me o' nights—'

The prospect was shuddering. Albert hesitated to trust Harriet's claim that he was responsible for her pregnancy; he could not even be sure that she was pregnant. If she were, the responsibility could be anyone's – seaman, tally-clerk, carter or any persuasive fish-dock lay-about. Why Albert Selley? Perhaps only because he was here, now. To be sure, he had fingered her a few times behind the hung blanket, and occasionally gone further – but *pregnancy*? She was a scheming little bitch, and no mistake. And what had she said? *Martin knows?*

For a brief moment he considered telling her to go to bluidy hell, but refrained. What he needed was time to think about it, but there was not much time remaining. Of course Harriet was right about Donald Selley. Given her supporting evidence, Albert would face only a manslaughter charge, and no court of session, surely, would condemn him for defending Harriet and himself, would it? Albert, fleetingly, visualised himself in the Edinburgh dock surrounded by policemen and bewigged lawyers. It was an awful picture which, however, had certain compensating colours. The judge might commend him for his gallantry, and he could have his picture in the *Evening News*, having his hand shaken by the Lord Provost. Reporters would flock to Coleman's to interview him, and he would be promoted to bakery manager.

The alternative was too awful to contemplate. Although sexual abnormalities were not uncommon in the congested circumstances of a slum environment, the subject was taboo. Newspapers publicised in careful detail all cases of murder, suicide, assault and rape but, by tacit agreement, never incest, and even in the most unscrupulous of communities a man guilty of such an offence became a pariah, an object of contempt. Harriet might be pregnant or she might not, Albert decided, but he had no choice. To be branded incestuous was infinitely worse than being charged with manslaughter.

There was a noise behind him and he turned. Mary Selley stood at the door of the living room, setting down her lumpy oil-cloth bag, then releasing the long pin that fastened her cloth cap to her grey, flattened hair. She looked at the corpse of Donald Selley, then at Albert, and finally Harriet.

'It's feyther,' Harriet confirmed. 'He wuz thrashing me because I'm pregnant, and Albert killed him.'

Mary Selley turned her tired eyes back to Albert. She nodded. 'Martin telled me. He's gone fer the polis. Ye'll tell them ye killed him?'

'Aye,' Albert said, relieved of any further uncertainty. 'I killed him. He'd have killed Harriet else.'

'He's nae loss.' Mary Selley nodded again, her face wooden. 'And Martin telled me aboot Harriet and yesel'. Ye've got her pregnant.'

'That wasna me!' Albert choked. 'Bluidy hell. It wuz a sailor from a Swedish ship. Harriet—?'

Briefly, Harriet met her mother's knowing gaze, then looked away. 'Och, we-ell,' she stammered, 'I'm no sure.' Her resolve of a few moments earlier was beginning to drain. There were so many factors to balance – the stabbing, the police, her pregnancy – and exactly what had young Martin confided to Mary Selley? What could she, Harriet, say about a Swedish sailor that was convincing? Would the police make enquiries at the fish-dock? 'I'm no sure,' she repeated, confused. What was the safest thing to say?

'Ye're bluidy sure!' Albert shouted, suddenly desperate. 'Ye said it yesel'. It wuz a sailor fra a Swedish ship that's no been back since the war—' There were ashes in his mouth; he was being betrayed.

Mary Selley remained astonishingly unmoved. 'I dinna want ta know anything,' she announced. 'Anything; ye ken?' She pushed an errant tendril of grey hair back into place. 'When the polis come, Albert will tell them he killed ye feyther, jus' like ye agreed, and nae doot they'll tak' him awa' ta Edinburgh. Whether they send him ta prison or no, he'll never come back ta this hoose.' She said it with finality. 'Harriet – ye'll have ye bairn, and ye'll work ta raise it decent. There'll be no creepin' round ta Sevastopol Street after dark, an' I'll no turn ye oot, but I never want ta know who the man wuz – ever. Aye, there'll be dirty talk fra the street, and likely never a husband for ye, but that's the price ye'll pay.' She gave the slightest of shrugs and glanced at the crumpled body of Donald Selley. 'But who wants a bluidy husband?'

From beyond the yard, outside, came the noise of cart-wheels on cobbles, men's voices, and Martin's falsetto. Albert stiffened. Mary Selley seated herself unhurriedly in the chair by the brass fender, her face expressionless.

Nine

'My son,' the Reverend Bellman told everyone proudly, 'is a survivor from the *Aboukir*,' and they looked at Hedley warily, as if he had just crawled out of the sea, and had seaweed on his boots. Elderly ladies were motherly, their elderly husbands very knowledgeable on the subject of submarine warfare, and small boys were rather distant; to have one's ship sunk was not very heroic. Hedley went down to Greenhithe to visit the old *Worcester* and lunch with her Commander – a privilege he had never enjoyed during his two years of training in her. He watched the cadets lowering and releasing boats, meticulously drilled, and refrained from commenting that the North Sea and the Atlantic were very different from the placid Thames, that when a stricken ship rolled over into an icy, heaving sea, when her decks were awash and there were no footholds, when the stokers were trapped below and half the hands dead, there was a fire amidships, choking smoke, the boats were smashed or jammed in their slings – well, it was all very different.

'I know what you're thinking, young Bellman,' said the Commander, who had served most of his sea years under sail. 'The first time I went around the Horn in a four-master it seemed that nothing I'd learned meant anything. But it did, of course. At least I had a blind faith in the judgement of my officers, and that's worth more than rubies when things get desperate.' He glanced at the cadets at the nearest davits, hauling enthusiastically. 'Still, God willing, the war will be finished before these youngsters go to sea.' Hedley Bellman was not sure; he recalled Sub-Lieutenant Bradley saying the same thing.

Temporarily he was without a ship. Unlike the Army, the Royal Navy suffered no shortage of men other than in a few specialised capacities, and had even landed a sizeable contingent of naval ratings, marines and armoured cars in Belgium to help halt the German advance. The Germans had been halted, but only just, and, after the first bruising flurry of blows, all armies were entrenching frantically to defend what they held, to draw breath and take stock. The war had not been finished by Christmas, which had come and gone, and if the Kaiser and failed in his promise to his soldiers that they would be home before the leaves fell, they had devoured almost all of Belgium and a vast area of France and showed no inclination to relinquish their spoils.

The letter, rubber-stamped by the naval censor, in company with a gas bill, several religious tracts and an appeal from the War Refugees Committee, arrived as he shared breakfast with his father.

'Sinjin Primrose – my word!' the Reverend Bellman exclaimed, and, engrossed, added marmalade to his egg. 'He's writing from HMS *London* – "where burning Sappho loved and sung"—' His brow furrowed. 'That's Byron, isn't it? He must be somewhere near Greece.'

'Mudros,' Hedley nodded. 'The Dardenelles landings.'

'My word,' the Reverend Bellman repeated, beaming. 'How splendid.' He returned to the letter. 'It's a month old, just think of it.'

Hedley pushed back his chair. 'You didn't know, then? I

saw it in *The Times*, and felt sure that you had – but I didn't want to be the first to mention it. Rear-Admiral Primrose was killed on active service. His name was on the Gallipoli list, and there was an obituary.'

The minister raised his eyes. 'You mean Sinjin Primrose is dead, Hedley? Then how—'

'I'm very sorry; I should have said something.' Hedley had his own reasons for not broaching the subject earlier. Any talk about Rear-Admiral Primrose would almost inevitably include references to Imogen Primrose – no, Imogen Pope – and she was someone he was anxious to forget. 'The letter must have been written just before he was killed. It's one of those distressing things that can happen – getting letters, I mean, from someone that's already dead.'

'Oh, dear,' the Reverend Bellman sighed. 'He was a fine man, a very fine man.' He returned his attention to the letter, and Hedley, watching, saw his frown deepen progressively. Then, quite suddenly, the minister stopped reading and stared blankly across the table at his son.

Hedley gazed back questioningly. 'Is there anything—?'

The older man seemed perplexed. He did not speak for several moments, but finally folded the letter and replaced it in its envelope. 'Sinjin Primrose's niece, Imogen,' he said slowly, 'will be coming to stay with us. I must write to her this morning. Did you know that her husband, Lieutenant Pope, was also aboard HMS *London*?'

Hedley did not, and would have claimed that he did not care if George Pope had been despatched to deepest Mongolia, but he was unable to control the flush that coloured his face. 'Pope?' he grunted. 'He's not dead, too, is he?'

'No.' The Reverend Bellman sighed again, almost regretfully. 'No – at least, I don't think so.'

'Then why is Imogen—?' The name clogged in his throat. Why was Imogen, who had married George Pope instead of Hedley Bellman, coming to stay at the needy Greenwich rectory? She had a husband, hadn't she? And her father-in-law was Sir Arthur Pope, wasn't he? – the millionaire of New South Wales who had equipped a hospital ship for the Suez theatre? Why should Imogen Pope come here?

Of course, he seethed, he had never been allowed an opportunity to propose to Imogen. Well, perhaps that wasn't quite true. He had written his proposal on paper often enough, and equally often tore it up. Then, while he was still balancing words and phrases, and tearing them up, Imogen had married George Pope.

The Reverend Bellman seemed to lack further interest in breakfast. 'The young lady has – er – been experiencing poor health.' He paused, uncertain. 'I don't think I can be more explicit, Hedley, if you'll forgive me. Sinjin Primrose asks that I take her under my wing until his return, and of course I must. She has no other relatives, you know.' He drew a slow breath. 'Now, unfortunately, he's not going to return.'

'But she has a husband,' Hedley suggested.

'Ye-es,' the other nodded.

'Then it can't be for long,' Hedley went on, mildly resentful. There must be thousands of women with husbands absent, and if Imogen chose to marry a naval officer like George Pope she must expect to be separated from him for periods of years. If she had only waited for Hedley Bellman to propose, her situation would have been different. Mercantile officers went overseas for weeks, sometimes months, but never for years. Hedley reached for the toast. 'The *London* will be returning for refitting as soon as the Gallipoli landings have been firmly established,' he decided. 'Say three months at most. Then Imogen will be off your hands.' He would rather not share the rectory with Imogen Pope, but, if he had to, he'd be damned if he would surrender his bedroom that overlooked the garden or his gas fire and his massive wardrobe, the huge, friendly bed that slumped in the middle. She could have the closet that faced the Woolwich road and the abattoir.

'My dear child,' the Reverend Bellman greeted her, and kissed her brow, while Hedley shook her hand self-consciously and then carried in her bags from the cab. Imogen was subdued, but she showed no signs of poor health. Indeed, she seemed more radiantly beautiful than ever, and black suited her. The minister did not enquire about her health, and Hedley, who was about to formally say, 'I trust you are well?' decided not to. Imogen offered him a scintillating smile. 'Hedley dear. You are well, I hope?' He stammered an affirmative.

The Reverend Bellman beamed paternally. 'Hedley will take your bags up to your room, my dear. It's a little small, I'm afraid, but—'

'Ah,' Hedley said. 'As a matter of fact, Father, I thought Imogen might prefer the room I'm in.' He reddened. 'I mean, as soon as I've moved my things out, of course. It's bigger, and there's quite a pleasant view, actually—' He could hardly believe what he was saying.

'Dear Hedley,' Imogen sighed, and he felt his knees weaken.

Of course, he told himself as he gazed from the closet window towards the Woolwich road and the abattoir, a chap had to be decent about things; there was no need to be churlish. The following day a large trunk was delivered by carrier, and he hauled it laboriously upstairs to the room he had yielded to Imogen. There was already ample evidence of feminine occupancy – a folded nightdress, flowers, a row of dainty shoes, oddly shaped bottles, and a smell of perfume which, under different circumstances, would have had him grimacing, but was today simply fragrant. It was strange, he noted, that a picture of Rear-Admiral Primrose stood on the bedside cabinet, but he could see none of George Pope.

'Hedley, dear, you're wonderful,' Imogen breathed, and gazed at him admiringly. 'I expect you're always having to do strong things on your ship.' Hedley shrugged modestly. 'And it was gallant of you, Hedley,' she went on, 'to give me your room. You must think I'm a horrible nuisance.'

'Not at all,' Hedley claimed, delighted. 'Actually, the bed's a bit odd. It's like a huge hammock. You'll find it difficult to keep out of the middle. That's fine for one person, but if there are two—' He stopped.

Her eyes were roguish. 'If I didn't know that you were a gentleman, Hedley, I *might* think you were taking a sounding, as Uncle Sinjin used to say. When I wanted him to take me to London I always pretended his uniform was getting shabby, and he needed to be measured for another – and, of course, I'd promise to go with him if we could just drop into Harrod's, then Burlingon Arcade, and then have lunch at the Royale and tea at Gunter's, then perhaps Drury Lane. Eventually he had four uniforms he had never worn, poor dear.' She smiled at him. 'I'm perfectly happy alone in a huge hammock.'

Neither his father nor Imogen had once referred to George Pope, her husband, Hedley puzzled, and he would have bitten off his own tongue before doing so.

On two occasions she had travelled into London alone for reasons not explained to him, although the Reverend Bellman seemed to know. Indeed, there seemed to be an understanding, almost a conspiracy, between Imogen and the minister to which Hedley was not a party. When Imogen had returned from her second absence, Hedley had inadvertently overheard her say to his father, 'I don't have to go again for three months, and that will probably be the last time.' The Reverend Bellman had patted her arm gently and replied, 'Wonderful, my dear. You've been very brave, and your uncle would be proud of you. Soon – perhaps when Hedley has gone – we must have a long talk about your future. You have to start again. If you choose to stay here, of course, I should be delighted.' Imogen had kissed his cheek.

Start again? It was all a little strange, Hedley considered. Mildly annoyed, he resolved to avoid displaying any interest in Imogen's affairs. If she and his father wished to exclude him from their confidence, then he would spare them the embarrassment of his curiousity. He wished he had a ship.

Imogen was beginning to regain some of her earlier vivacity. She abandoned mourning and teased Hedley into escorting her to the Haymarket Theatre and Madame Tussaud's, the Trocadero Restaurant and, of course, on shopping forays to Harrod's and Bond Street. Escorting Imogen was an experience to be savoured; she turned all heads. Men stared at her, then shot a speculative, envious glance at Hedley. Women fluttered fans anxiously and began talking loudly, and senior officers were unusually amicable towards a sub-lieutenant they would never normally have noticed. In response to other men's attention Imogen was graciously correct. Her lips smiled, he observed, but her eyes did not.

In France and Belgium the war of movement had halted and the armies snarled at each other from trenchlines that zig-zagged from the Channel coast to the Swiss frontier. Casualty lists were becoming progressively more horrifying and the gay optimism of 1914 had chilled. The Western Front was a horrendous maw that swallowed up tens of thousands of husbands, brothers and sons, and men were losing sight of the reason for which they had flocked to recruiting offices – the liberation of innocent Belgium. Posters on every wall still appealed to the noble concepts of honour, glory and tradition, but such idealism was wearing thin among the mud, misery and lice, the high explosives, the barbed wire and scything machine-gun fire of the trenches. 'Now, God be thanked Who has matched us with His hour,' brayed an obscure poet, and was immortalised.

Recruitment was not keeping pace with losses, and the posters were more insidiously accusing towards the reluctant male. 'The women of Britain say – GO! Enlist NOW!' From theatre stages high-stepping chorus-girls mocked, 'We don't want to lose you, but we think you ought to GO!'

The Gallipoli landings, undertaken with such confidence in April, had resulted in costly failure. Hedley wondered if George Pope was still aboard the old battleship *London*, which, he had heard, was about to be sent to reinforce the Italian blockade of the Adriatic. Hesitantly, he mentioned the fact to Imogen, who accepted the information with silent indifference; she declined to even shrug. It was all very strange.

Then, emerging from Simpson's Restaurant in the Strand, they saw a fashionably-dressed woman present a white feather to a young man who stared at it, then at its donor, uncomprehending. 'Serve your country,' she charged, 'or wear that.' The young man thrust the feather into a pocket and walked on. From outside the Royal Naval Recruiting Office, only yards away, an elderly leading seaman hawked and spat. 'What you soddin' need, matey,' he told the lady, 'is a bleedin' kick up yer crotch.' He saw Hedley Bellman, and apologised. 'Beggin' yer lady's pardon, sir, fer speakin' in French—' but Hedley grinned, winked.

The woman with the white feathers had turned her back on the seaman to look for new victims, only to find herself faced by an incensed Imogen. 'You despicable little harpy,' Imogen blazed. 'Safe, well-fed women don't have the right to goad men into going to war for them. There are women in France, nursing wounded, driving ambulances, serving in canteens and kitchens – and some of them have died. They have earned the right, we haven't. Instead of parading the pavement like a cheap whore, why aren't *you* serving your country? Because *you* can't face the mud and gas, the blood and death that our men have to?' She tore a feather from the several clutched in the other's hand. 'Why don't *you* wear one of these, you nasty little hypocrite?'

'Blimey,' the seaman marvelled. 'Put that in yer bleedin' pipe an' smoke it.'

Hedley steered Imogen away, discomfited as most men are by an angry dispute between women. Imogen spoke very little before they regained the rectory in Greenwich. The minister, a note told them, was visiting a local family that had lost a father in the fighting around Ypres. Imogen drew off her gloves. 'I embarrassed you, Hedley. I'm very sorry.'

He smiled. 'Of course not—'

'I behaved like a fishwife, but I meant what I said. Women like her make me ashamed of my sex.' She was still flushed and very beautiful. 'If we are to demand voting rights, and want to be treated as men's equals, then we must expect to lose some of the privileges and protection that women have always enjoyed. Do you know, Hedley, that the Russians are training women's infantry battalions?' She nodded. 'And that's where I'm going – to Russia.'

Hedley stared. 'Good God – to join an infantry battlion?'

'No,' she laughed. 'Doctor Elsie Inglis is taking a detachment of the Women's Reserve Ambulance Corps to the Russian front, and I've been accepted, providing I can equip myself. I can drive a Crossley tender.' She placed a finger on his cheek. 'That's why I want your leather seaboots, and some seaboot stockings, and that funny hat with the ear-flaps—'

'Imogen!'

'And I know you've got some long woollen unmentionables, Hedley. We have to wear trousers, you know.'

He continued to stare, aghast. It was totally incredible. The Russian front was a chaotic horror of corruption and inefficiency, primitive transport and poor communications, desperate shortages of food and munitions among frost-bite, typhus and shuddering battle losses. Hedley had seen some of those horsey English women in breeches and belted waterproofs who drove staff cars and ambulances, some of them even in France, and he grudgingly admired their pluck, but it was impossible to imagine the exquisite Imogen behind the wheel of a heavy Crossley or Dennis motor-truck in the sleet and freezing mud of Galicia.

Now, he realised, he knew the reason for her unexplained journeys into London. She was being very brave, the Reverend Bellman had said, and her uncle would be proud of her. But why the secrecy?

Hedley decided he needed a drink. There was only port and brandy in the sideboard, and he chose brandy. 'I know you've discussed it with my father,' he said, 'but are you quite sure you know what is involved?'

Imogen was surprised. 'I haven't discussed it with anyone, Hedley. You're the first to know.'

He was pouring himself a small brandy; he increased it to a large one. 'I thought—' he grappled.

'*What* did you think?' she enquired.

Hedley took a fortifying mouthful of Hennessey. He may as well say it and be damned. 'I thought, when you went into London alone, twice, that you might be petitioning for a divorce. I overheard my father saying something about your future, and starting again.' He drew a deep breath. 'I was still hoping, you see – because you've never mentioned your husband, and you came here – and everything was so cloak-and-dagger—' He paused again; it was all very difficult.

'Yes?' Imogen prompted quietly.

'Well,' he struggled on determinedly. 'Once, when you were writing to me in the old *Aboukir*, I'd made up my mind that I wanted to marry you. Then, before I could – or rather before I could propose – you married George Pope. I thought that was the end of it, until your uncle was killed and you came to the rectory. It soon became apparent – at least I *thought* it was apparent – that you had become estranged from your husband. Most women who have a man on war service talk about them, worry about them. They write and receive letters, and usually they treasure a picture. But you don't.' He shook his head. 'Of course I began to think what I *wanted* to think—'

'That I might soon be divorced, and then I'd be open to bids?'

'It wasn't as crude as that.' He frowned. 'Well – yes – I suppose it was. Look, Imogen—'

She had gone to the window, and stood with her back to him. 'You're right, Hedley,' she spoke carefully, 'about George and me. I never want to see him, or hear about him, ever again. As for divorce, I haven't really thought about it yet. I don't think so, because I would have to declare my reasons, and I couldn't. One of them would be as humiliating to me as it would to my husband, and the other simply wouldn't be believed. Afterwards, anyway, remarriage would be impossible. Nobody would wish to be even seen in my company.' She turned. 'No, Hedley – not even you, my dear.'

'That's nonsense,' Hedley retorted. 'Divorce is usually nasty. It's like going to the dentist, but the alternative's a lot worse. As for the reasons—' He shrugged. 'You've told my father, and he obviously doesn't think the blame's yours.'

'It's not a question of blame, and your father is a gentle, understanding man. I've told him only one of the reasons, which I'd be ashamed for you to know, Hedley, and I couldn't possibly tell a lawyer or a court judge. But I'll tell you the other reason.' Imogen faced him. 'I think George killed Uncle Sinjin.'

'You think—?' He gaped. 'You think *what*?'

'Uncle Sinjin wrote to me from Mudros – his last letter – which I didn't receive until after the notification of his death. He said that, soon, I'd be told that my husband had been killed in action, ashore in Gallipoli; he – Uncle Sinjin – swore that the shame of it would never be dragged through a divorce court. I knew what that meant. I knew Uncle Sinjin. But, then, *he* was dead and George wasn't. Later, I had another letter from *London*'s captain. He explained that Uncle Sinjin and George had gone ashore together, alone, and only George had returned.' Imogen lowered herself into a chair. 'I know what happened, Hedley.'

It was unfortunate that the Reverend Bellman's return had ended the conversation, which to Hedley was baffling, and there arose no opportunity for reopening it during the several days following. Then something happened that drove all thought of George Pope and Sinjin Primrose from Hedley's mind. He received his orders to join HMS *Invincible*, docked in Devonport.

'*Invincible!*' Hedley read the drafting order several times and, to make sure he was really the addressee, looked again at the buff envelope in which it had arrived. There was no accounting for it. *Invincible* was the flagship of Rear-Admiral the Honourable Horace Hood, CB, MVO, DSO, commanding the 3rd Battle-Cruiser Squadron, and, during this first year of the war, no other ship had hit the enemy harder, no other had raised glasses in celebration more often in every club lounge and beer-puddled tavern in the country. The name was one to be savoured, rolled around the tongue like good wine. *Invincible*, the scourge of the Kaiser's navy.

The war had been only four weeks old – four weeks of almost continuous retreat for the French and British armies – when *Invincible* and several sisters had destroyed the German cruisers *Mainz*, *Ariadne* and *Koln* off Heligoland with nonchalant ease. To a public bewildered by the depressing reports from the Continent the news of the success at sea had been intoxicating. And there were more stirring deeds to follow. Fourteen weeks later, off the Falkland

Islands, *Invincible* and *Inflexible* had annihilated the German East Asiatic Squadron commanded by Admiral Maximilian Graf von Spee. True, Hedley Bellman had heard doubts whispered about the British battle-cruisers' ability to absorb heavy punishment, but who could argue with success? What contribution could an Acting Sub-Lieutenant, Royal Naval Reserve, make to the legend of *Invincible*? Hedley thought of the old *Corinthian* with her clanking steam donkey-engine and rusting decks, of his useless days aboard the gouty *Aboukir*, and could recall no experience that qualified him for service in a crack battle-cruiser. The prospect was intimidating.

'My son,' the Reverend Bellman told everyone, 'has been ordered to join the battle-cruiser *Invincible* – under Rear-Admiral Hood, you know.' Hedley's stock among local small boys rose gratifyingly, and several church ladies began knitting industriously. 'I'm sorry I asked for your seaboots,' Imogen said, but he dismissed the apology gallantly; there would be a mountain of seaboots aboard *Invincible*. Guiltily, he realised that he had almost forgotten Imogen's commitment. Her circumstances at the Russian front, assuming she was in earnest, were likely to be far more harrowing than his own in a battle-cruiser.

He contrived to be alone with her. 'I've been thinking about everything, Imogen,' he began, but she shook her head. 'You mustn't, dear Hedley. You've lots of more important things to worry about than my silly affairs. If you're concerned about me going to Russia, please don't be. I'm sure we'll be miles behind the line with hundreds of Cossacks protecting us.'

'It's not just that,' Hedley insisted. 'It's the other business.' He shrugged. 'Hell, I don't want you to tell me anything that would be painful for you, and I suppose you must be pretty sick about men in general, but, you know, there's a lot of truth in the old platitude about time being a great healer.

What I mean is, well – you might be free to choose again, one day, and I just thought that, well—'

Imogen came to him and kissed him on the lips. It was the first time she had ever conceded such an intimacy. Then she regarded him gravely. 'My *dear* Hedley,' she whispered. 'First, I want you to come home safely. Will it help if I tell you that I wish – oh, I wish – that you had proposed to me when you wanted to?' She paused, her face thoughtful. 'There are so many uncertainties, my dear, and I need time, but I will give you a promise to take with you. When all the uncertainties have been resolved, and if – after everything has been explained – you still feel the same, and you still want to ask the same question, I promise I will listen very carefully.'

She brightened. 'Still, because you've been very sweet, I will tell you one little secret. Your father and I have planned to travel with you to Devonport, when you join the *Invincible*.' She squeezed his arm. 'I'll feel like Penelope, waving goodbye to Ulysses.'

They took a cab from the station to the dockyard's Albert Gate, then threaded a passage among railway lines, warehouses and rearing cranes, seeing the tall tripod foremast and massive funnels of *Invincible* long before they reached her berth.

Alongside the wall, she teemed with bluejackets and artisans. Bags and hammocks were piled on the upper deck, joining reservists soughts messdecks, dockyard workers shouted, and a collier waited to transfer 2000 tons of Welsh steam coal. On the jetty rail trucks and horse-drawn carts were off-spilling a confusion of stores – 60 tons of potatoes, 30 tons of fresh beef, 180 sides of bacon, 2400 pounds of margarine, a ton of salt cod and a half ton of kippers, 6 hundredweights of salt, macaroni, lard, tinned herrings, 720 dozen eggs, prunes, tapioca, slab cake, tinned apples. . . .

'My word,' the Reverend Bellman marvelled. 'Are those twelve-inch guns? They look more like twelve feet.' The minister had never been in close proximity to a battle-cruiser before. Neither, for that matter, had Hedley. He felt like a small boy on his first day at a new school. Imogen slid her hand into his.

Among the chaos Lieutenant-Commander Edward Bingham, the First Lieutenant, stood with his midshipman, attempting with only moderate success to establish the priorities of bunkering and ammunitioning, the sequence of hauling aboard the hundreds of tons of provisions in sacks, crates, boxes and barrels that never ceased to arrive. 'A more hopeless looking ship,' he snarled at his youthful subordinate, 'I never wish to see.' But he would have said that whatever the circumstances. Rear-Admiral Hood and his lady would be coming aboard this afternoon, an event which would coincide with coaling; the quarterdeck would be thick with grime and everyone choking in a pall of black dust. Bingham hoped that the Admiral's lady wasn't dressed à la Ascot, dammit. Perhaps the Royal Marine band and the call-boys had better be paraded at the dockyard gate—

Bingham was suddenly aware that he was being saluted hesitantly by a reservist junior officer. 'Begging your pardon, sir—'

The First Lieutenant glared ferociously. 'Who the bloody hell are you?' he spat, but then observed that, at the young officer's side, there stood the most exquisitely beautiful creature he had ever seen – golden, cool, blue-eyed, and shaped like a goddess. Bingham fumbled at the knot of his tie and prayed that his hat was on straight.

'Ah,' he said heartily, and returned the salute. 'Good morning.' There was also a clergyman, he noted, but *she* was absolutely superb. 'Are you joining?' He had never believed there were really women like this outside the pages of romantic books. Damn, he ought to have had his hair cut yesterday instead of responding to *Minotaur's* gin pennant.

'Sub-Lieutenant Bellman, sir,' Hedley explained, encouraged by the other's kindly countenance. 'Yessir, just joining. Should I report to anyone in particular?'

'It's not his first time, you know,' the Reverend Bellman beamed. 'Oh, no. He was Fourth Officer of the *Corinthian* – the Allan Steamship Company – and then served in *Aboukir*. Now he's been ordered to join the *Invincible*.'

'Good show.' The older officer nodded approvingly. 'I'm Bingham, the First Lieutenant.' Another bloody Saturday-night sailor, he simmered, full of knots, splices and nautical terminology but not much else. 'I really don't think the lady should go aboard.' He smiled at her in what he imagined to be a whimsical manner. In fact he would not have dared allow any lady to step over the gangway except the Rear-Admiral's. 'The decks are in a filthy mess, and the wardroom's a slum.' Wasn't the young muttonhead going to introduce him?

Apparently not. Infuriatingly, anyway, the fair enchantress had afforded him no more than an impersonal glance, as if he were no more than a barrel of pickled tongues. 'We'll say our goodbyes here, Hedley,' she decided, and took his arm. 'Don't forget Penelope. She unravelled her knitting every night.'

'Young Winstanley here will take you down to the Gunroom,' Bingham said, slightly less amiably. 'You'd normally report to the Gunnery Officer, Commander Dannreuther, but he'll not be back aboard until tomorrow. When you've stowed your gunny, I suggest you find the Officer of the Day, Lieutenant George Pope. He'll give you a course and speed.'

It was odd how all three stared at him, then silently at each other.

PART II

'Equal Speed Charlie London.'

Admiral Sir John Jellicoe's Flag Signal, Jutland, 1916.

Ten

She had been built in Vickers-Armstrong's Elswick yard on the Tyne, launched and named *Invincible* on 13 April 1907, and commissioned for sea on 20 March in the following year. *Invincible* was the first of the battle-cruisers, the name-ship of her class, which would always be referred to as the 'Invincibles', and the inspiration of Sir John Fisher, the embullient First Sea Lord, who had already given the Royal Navy the Dreadnought battleship, then the Super-Dreadnought, to render obsolete every other warship in the world – but, more deliberately, the warships of Imperial Germany.

To a British public intensely proud of its navy, *Invincible* seemed to fulfil all the desirable criteria of a powerful and formidable fighting ship; she looked every inch a thoroughbred. With her turbines generating 41,000 horse power, she achieved a mean 26.2 knots on her trials and later bettered 28 knots, a speed not matched by any large warship for the next decade. Her 12-inch main armament was supplemented by sixteen 4-inch guns, each of which could fire 12 shells per minute, and she carried a peacetime complement of 784 which would be increased to approximately a thousand for wartime service.

There were factors, however, of which an intensely proud public were blissfully ignorant. Experts had sucked their teeth when they saw the figures relating to the 'Invincibles' ' armour. Protection was only 6 inches amidships and 4 inches in the bows, with no armoured belt abaft the after turret. No deck was heavier than 2 inches, and areas of the main deck were only of ¾-inch steel.

The reason for such flimsy protection was that heavy armour and high speed could not live together in the same ship. The enhancement of either quality inevitably reduced the other, and if a speed of 28 knots was insisted upon then weight must be drastically reduced. Admiral Fisher had intended the 'Invincibles' to be employed in pursue-and-destroy operations against enemy heavy cruisers and commerce raiders, to perhaps overhaul and keep in touch with a fleeing enemy battle-fleet, engaging stragglers at long range. Speed, Fisher insisted, was the battle-cruisers' protection. With 28 knots and 12-inch guns they would be capable of annihilating anything that floated except battleships – and battleships would never be allowed to come within effective range.

Critics were less than reassured. The 'Invincibles' were not, as some enthusiasts seemed to think, fast battleships but merely heavily-armed fast cruisers which must never be taken within miles of an enemy battleship. Yet such ships, of 17,250 tons, devouring 500 tons of coal and 125 tons of oil per day when at speed, and requiring a thousand crew to man them, were surely too expensive for merely scouting, patrolling, or chasing an occasional marauder?

The trouble was that battle-cruisers *looked* like battleships. 'Vessels of this enormous size and cost,' observed Lord Thomas Brassey, one of the Civil Lords, 'are unsuitable for any of the duties of cruisers, but an even stronger objection to the repetition of the type is that an admiral having "Invincibles" in his fleet will be certain to put them in the line of battle, where their comparatively light protection will be a disadvantage and their high speed of no advantage.'

In short, he was saying, because it *looked* like a battleship, sooner or later a battle-cruiser would be asked to fight like a battleship.

But the crowds that cheered *Invincible* on that cold, sunny day as the whooping tugs eased her slowly down the Tyne had no such doubts. The finest ships in the world were built on Tyneside – and yez cud tell tha' ter Clydebank an' Birkenhead, an' a'. The race with Germany for naval supremacy was gathering momentum. Four more Dreadnoughts were building in British yards, to be followed by six in each of the next two years. The public bayed for eight. The British did not want to fight anyone but, by God, if they had to, then they had the money and they'd build the ships. *Invincible* turned her bows southward, towards Portsmouth and the Channel Fleet. Rosyth was being turned into a naval base, and the Germans were widening the Kiel Canal, which would allow their battle fleet to pass more easily between the Baltic and the North Sea.

Still, the war was not yet, although many knew that this was the Indian Summer of world peace, the last fleeting years of the old order. For more than a century the Royal Navy had been the policeman of the world's sea lanes, to the advantage albeit the jealousy of all other law-abiding nations, but had fought no major battles. Now, however, it was time to prepare for an enemy more sophisticated than the slave-runners, pirates, smugglers and minor revolutionaries of the Victorian era. To its credit, the Navy imposed upon itself a masochistic regime of reassessment, modernisation and retraining so that, when the war did come in 1914 – two years earlier than most experts had predicted – it was equipped, ready and more than willing.

In 1909 the name 'battle-cruiser' had not yet been coined. *Invincible* and her class sisters, *Indomitable* and *Inflexible*, were coyly referred to as 'fast armoured cruisers', and formed the 1st Cruiser Squadron of the Channel Fleet; but the Germans were not deceived. They laid down the 19,400 tons battle-cruiser *Von der Tann*, whereupon Britain countered with *Indefatigable*, *Australia* and *New Zealand*. Germany began building *Moltke* and *Goeben*. The Admiralty ordered *Lion* and *Princess Royal*, and Germany responded with *Seydlitz*, *Derfflinger* and *Lutzow*. Britain launched *Queen Mary* and *Tiger*. The war, now, was only a year away.

During March 1913, *Invincible* was involved in collision with the submarine C.34 in Stokes Bay, off Portsmouth, but no damage or casualties were suffered, which confirmed the opinion that she was a lucky ship. She was also comparatively roomy and comfortable, a good sea boat although not a particularly steady gun platform. All three ships experienced some inconvenience from smoke when they were at high speed, but this was a minor deficiency which could be corrected, it was speculated, by heightening the forward funnels. *Invincible*'s successive crews were proud of her reputation as the world's fastest capital ship; she was dubbed HMS Uncatchable.

In August 1914 there was no immediate collision of great battle fleets. German heavy units clung to Wilhelmshaven and the Jade, forbidden by the Kaiser to venture further to sea than the Horns Reef unless 'a favourable opportunity to strike offers itself'. Operations would be confined to submarine forays, minelaying, and the commerce-raiding of those few German ships still at sea when the war began, for as long as they could survive.

The British Grand Fleet, similarly cautious, withdrew on Scapa Flow, Cromarty and the Firth of Forth. Patrol and blockading duties were largely delegated to light forces and a mixed bag of obsolescent larger vessels based on East Coast harbours and the Channel.

Invincible's first orders had despatched her to Queenstown in southern Ireland, assigned to the monotonous task of halting and searching neutral ships and hopefully apprehending the progressively rarer German blockade-runners. Employing a battle-cruiser for such duties may have impressed the neutrals, but it was an expensive luxury and did little for the morale of *Invincible*'s crew. It seemed preposterous that this ocean tiger should be given such unflattering work when slow old ladies like *Aboukir*, *Cressy* and *Hogue* were flaunting themselves in enemy-dominated waters. It took a little longer for the Admiralty to reach the same conclusion. *Invincible* was transferred to the Humber.

The action off Heligoland Bight had followed almost immediately, the result of a swashbuckling British plan which did not quite achieve the success it deserved. Even so, three German cruisers and a destroyer had been sunk and a thousand men killed for the loss of thirty-five British. The battle-cruisers of Admiral Fisher, now retired, had been blooded.

On 1 November 1914 the old armoured cruiser *Good Hope*, the equally elderly light cruiser *Monmouth*, and an armed merchant ship, *Otranto*, had been destroyed with the total loss of their 1,600 crewmen off Coronel Bay, on the western coast of South America, by the German East Asiatic Squadron. The occasion would later be described as the Battle of Coronel, but it had been an annihilation.

The German squadron comprised the two heavy cruisers *Scharnhorst* and *Gneisenau* and three light cruisers, *Leipzig*, *Dresden* and *Nurnberg*, all under the able command of Admiral Graf von Spee.

Outpaced, outgunned and outranged, the British ships under Rear-Admiral Cradock had fought bravely but hopelessly. Cradock's last wireless message was, jauntily, 'I am about to attack the enemy now.' He did, flying the flag signal, 'Follow in the Admiral's wake', and perished with his ship.

In London, two days before, a vicious press campaign had achieved the resignation of the First Sea Lord, Prince Louis of Battenberg, German by birth but a naturalised Englishman and married to a granddaughter of Queen Victoria. To replace him, Lord Fisher of Kilverstone, now 74, was recalled from retirement.

Fisher, enthusiastically supported by the civil First Lord, Mr Winston Churchill, acted quickly to pinch out the dangerous threat posed by the German East Asiatic Squadron and, at the same time, avenge the disaster of Coronel. They ordered the two battle-cruisers *Invincible* and *Inflexible* to the South American station to hunt down von Spee, and a third, *Princess Royal*, to the West Indies to cover the Panama Canal.

Invincible was flying the flag of Rear-Admiral Sir Archibald Moore, but he was considered too junior for the task, and disembarked hurriedly to make room for Vice-Admiral Sir Frederick Doveton Sturdee, recently Chief of Staff at the Admiralty and nominally responsible for allowing Cradock's weak squadron to be matched against von Spee's. Fisher disliked Sturdee. 'You made these damn plans, Sturdee,' he snarled. 'Now go and carry them out!' The battle-cruisers, he added, would not return to the UK until von Spee had been wiped off the face of the earth.

The battle-cruisers would need coal and oil, ammunition and provisions for six months. *Invincible* and *Inflexible* flung off their moorings and steamed for Devonport, leaving dozens of libertymen ashore in Cromarty who would have to make the long journey southward, to rejoin their messes, by train.

The weather was raw, bitingly cold. Reaching Devonport before dawn on Sunday, 8 November, the twin battle-cruisers were thrust immediately into dry docks for their hulls to be scraped and repainted while, simultaneously, scores of dockyard technician swarmed aboard. Officers and men, reinforced by working parties from the nearby barracks, began working around the clock to fill bunkers and magazines to capacity. That afternoon Sturdee arrived and hoisted his flag in *Invincible*.

The Admiral Superintendent at Devonport had given as his opinion that the earliest possible date on which the ships could be made ready was Friday 13 November. Winston Churchill did not agree.

> 'To Commander-in-Chief Devonport from Admiralty. *Invincible* and *Inflexible* are to sail on Wednesday 11th. They are needed for war service and dockyard arrangements must be made to conform. If necessary dockyard men should be sent away in the ships to return as opportunity may offer. You are held responsible for the speedy despatch of these ships in a thoroughly efficient condition. Acknowledge. W.S.C.'

The two warships were ready a day earlier than even Churchill had demanded. During mid-forenoon on Tuesday 10th, with the crews coal-grimed and staggering with fatigue, Admiral Sturdee was informed that his command was ready for sea. He nodded. 'Very good. We sail at sixteen hundred.'

Plymouth Sound and the Channel, however, were choked with fog and, as a result of the hurried modifications, it was certain the ships' magnetic compasses were now unreliable. There had been no time for recalibration, and it would be madness to sail unless adjustments were made – which would take a whole day of swinging the ships around buoys – or at least until visibility had cleared. Then someone remembered a young American named Elmer Sperry who had been unsuccessfully trying to persuade the Admiralty to buy his newly-developed gyro compass. He was located at his

London hotel and bundled into a train with his odd device, and a few hours later a gyro compass was being installed in *Invincible* under the doubtful eyes of Captain Percy Beamish. Sperry would be still explaining his equipment as *Invincible* led *Inflexible* through the fog into the open sea, to be taken off by launch, cold, damp, but delightedly convinced that the world's biggest navy would now adopt his invention. It did.

Lady Sturdee and her daughter had come aboard *Invincible* for lunch while steam was being raised for twenty knots, decks were being hosed clean of coal dust and oil, and sea dutymen were being mustered. Only minutes before the last gangplank was removed, as a Royal Marine band brayed and harbour tugs made ready, eight teen-age midshipmen tumbled breathlessly onto the quarterdeck with their baggage. They had learned of the battle-cruisers' imminent departure in Exeter, forty miles away, and had raced that distance in taxi-cabs to report for duty.

Also, that forenoon, the Admiral Superintendent, stung by the implied rebuke in Churchill's order, and braver than he was wise, had taken a train to London to protest that it was impossible to brick up the battle-cruisers' fire-boxes in such a ridiculously short time. His insistence achieved him an interview with Lord Fisher, who listened briefly, drew out his watch, and then coldly informed his subordinate that *Invincible* and *Inflexible* were already steaming down-Channel. If the workmen had failed to complete their work they would remain on board until they had, to be dropped at the first convenient port of call to fend for themselves – and it was a matter of indifference to Fisher if they were dropped over the side.

The taverners and tradesmen of any seaport rarely extended credit to sailors; there was an old saying, 'First turn of the screws, all debts paid', which explained why. Sturdee's men, however, had been in Devonport too briefly to sample the shore-going distractions of Fore Street and Union Street. There had been no indiscreet gossip, but most of Devonport know that the crews had been issued with tropical whites and straw 'Benjies'. Many knew that Sturdee was to assume command of the newly-designated South Atlantic and South Pacific Fleet. The news of two weeks earlier, the unprecedented haste of the battle-cruisers' refit – all pointed to a two-and-two conclusion. Von Spee.

Von Spee might have been anywhere in the enormous expanse of the Pacific or South Atlantic, but incredibly both British and German squadrons – the uninformed hunters and the unsuspecting hunted – had closed on precisely the same pencilled mark on the chart, the harbour of Port Stanley in the Falkland Islands. The British intended to coal in anticipation of weeks of ocean searching. The Germans had planned to destroy the reportedly undefended Falklands radio station and coal stocks before conforming to Berlin's orders to attempt a return to Germany. It was a thousand-to-one coincidence. Sturdee's battle-cruisers, now joined by several cruisers, reached Port Stanley on 7 December. Von Spee's ships arrived on the following day. The British had 12-inch guns and a speed of 28½ knots. The Germans had 8.2-inch guns and 21 knots.

The issue was never in doubt from the moment of mutual recognition. Like Cradock before him, von Spee fought valiantly, cleverly but futilely, and died with some 2,200 of his officers and men. Coronel had been avenged and once again the battle-cruisers had decisively justified their building; the public were elated.

Few of the public, however, had seen the damage imposed on *Invincible* by only 8.2-inch projectiles. One had struck forward, on the water-line, and flooded both bow compartments. Another had penetrated the hull below water, under 'P' turret, flooding a bunker and giving the ship a list. A third destroyed a 4-inch gun and its mounting, then tore downwards through three decks. The wardroom, canteen and sick bay had been completely wrecked, and there were several fires. A number of shells had penetrated the upper deck at a steep angle of descent and then *gone out through the ship's side.* The German warships' gunnery, everyone agreed, had been remarkably accurate and consistent, and there was uneasy speculation on what might have been the battle-cruisers' fate if they had been matched against heavier calibre metal.

Eleven

Inside the steel cavern of 'X' turret's gun-house, Marine Corporal Steve Bundy, Gunlayer, polished the eye-lense of his range-finder, which, he had been confidently assured, would never be used in battle. He would merely read the enemy's range from a clock electrically repeated from the Gun Range Counter. He, Bundy, would never see the enemy; he would simply follow orders. Independent firing would only be necessary if the ship's gunnery control system had been destroyed, and then he would probably find his own, local sights fogged by spray, smoke and shell-splashes.

It was a good thing too, he decided. If he looked through the eye-lense of his range-finder he would see a tiny segment of the horizon, less than distinct, superimposed by vertical lines broken in the centre. If there was a ship in vision, that, too, would be broken in the centre unless his adjustment brought both halves to exactly coincide. Then he would be on target – except that there were complications like deflection, speed, course, and a dozen other changing factors beyond the calculation of a human brain, which were the business of the Fire Control Table, deep below the waterline, and something mysterious called trigonometry.

Steve Bundy was grateful for trigonometry. There was enough to think about in the deafening noise and stench of the turret when the fire-gongs tinkled. But there was something else. It was his eye, his right eye, which seemed to be increasingly obscured by a floating wisp of cotton wool, making visual concentration difficult. And the headaches, behind the scar. He had resolved repeatedly to see the Surgeon, but had never got to it. With luck, it might go away.

Mind, a gunlayer didn't need trigonometry, only imperturbability and an immediate and trained co-ordination of hand and eye, and Steve Bundy had all of that. Well, except for the eye. He felt mildly aggrieved. He hadn't asked to be a gun-crew number, had he? Christ, he hadn't asked to be a Royal Marine, but that was another bleedin' story. After the initial shock he had resigned himself to his predicament. Sod it. There was worse things than than being a Bootneck, although the sailors would have disputed it.

Mind, perhaps that bastard Hogg had done him, Bundy, a favour. The other seventy-nine of Benbow Company had been sent to Belgium. Thirty-one of them were now dead, two had no legs, four shared three arms between them, and ten would be coughing up fragments of gas-shredded lungs for years until they died blessing God for the mercy of it.

That bastard Hogg.

In the depot gymnasium the recruits of Benbow Company had been sitting cross-legged around the square of fibre matting on which two of their number sparred tentatively, when Warrant Officer Hogg entered and stood watching, tapping his swagger cane quietly against his thigh. 'Ogg by name and 'Ogg by bleedin' natcher, they had been warned by those of longer acquaintance, and that description, they now agreed, was exactly right. Hogg was big, ill-mannered, spiteful, and he had rank – the worst of all combinations. He stood all of six feet three inches in his woollen socks, ramrod taut and burly, with red hair, a thin moustache and pale blue, slightly protruberant eyes. He seldom conversed; he barked. Junior officers feared him, grateful that they were not required to dispute his methods once they had saluted and conceded, 'Thank you, Mister Hogg. Please carry on.'

The recruits had been paired off by height, not weight, and there was a marked lack of belligerence in their sparring which always infuriated Hogg. They were *idle*. Their marching and rifle drill were idle. Their boots and brasses were idle. Most of their gymnasium sparring was bloody idle because Hogg knew all about sparring. Warrant Officers were forbidden to ram a fist into a recruit's idle face, except in the gymnasium.

'Bloody *idle*,' he barked, and the unfortunate pair on the matting stopped their cautious circling, both inwardly cursing that they had to be the focus of attention when Hogg decided to demonstrate. Around them the other recruits sank lower into their buttocks, hoping to avoid notice.

Hogg unbuttoned his tunic. 'When I take this off,' he was fond of saying, 'you can forget I'm your senior officer.' It was a warning that he was about to bloody the face of some poor fool who would have no justification for complaint, and everyone knew it.

Of course, Steve Bundy rued, as he polished the brass rim of his range repeater, it had to happen, sooner or later. He remembered a Brazilian Wildcat, who had peeled off an exquisite, biscuit-coloured coat, but that was a long time ago. Well, it was last year, but it seemed like a long time ago.

'The ability to defend yourself without a weapon,' Hogg began, 'inspires alertness and confidence. Never be afraid of taking a hard knock.' He singled out one of the unfortunates on the matting. 'Alertness means watching your opponent, see, and confidence means hitting him hard as soon as he blinks.' He held up his left fist. 'Do you see this?' The recruit agreed that he did. 'It's my left hand,' Hogg nodded. 'And this – is my *right*.' The vicious blow caught the recruit full in the face, smashing lips against teeth and flinging him backward to sprawl among the nearest, seated spectators.

'He blinked,' Hogg explained. 'Never take your eyes off an opponent, see. I didn't, did I? Now, you—' He turned to the second man, who apprehensively retreated a pace. 'Don't run away, man—'

'Suppose the other bloke 'its yer first?' suggested a voice from the huddled onlookers. 'One day someone's going ter flatten yer.'

Warrant Officer Hogg turned slowly. 'Has that man got the guts to stand up?'

Steve Bundy stood up. 'I only arst a question,' he said.

'Quite right,' Hogg agreed. 'And you address me as "sir" – understand? However' – he smiled – 'for the purpose of this demonstration you can forget I'm your senior officer.' He beckoned. 'Come out here.'

Steve Bundy came.

'Now,' Hogg informed the recruits of Benbow Company, 'this Marine has asked what happens if your opponent *tries* to hit you first.' He was more than a head taller and three stones heavier than the stocky but very ordinary young man who stood before him gazing at the roof. 'I'm going to let him try, see, and he can forget that I'm—'

Steve Bundy's knotted fist slammed into the softness below Hogg's ribs with the velocity of a steam hammer. Hogg jack-knifed, his mouth gaped and his eyes rolled. He sobbed. 'Aaah!'

'Yer blinked,' Steve Bundy explained. 'And yer still ain't *alert*.' It was so easy; it was like taking cake from a bleedin' baby. He took his time, shifted weight, then rammed home an uppercut that snapped shut Hogg's open mouth like a steel trap, broke his jaw, imbedded his lower teeth firmly into his upper, and sprawled him, crumpled, drooling crimson and senseless against the wall bars, ten feet away.

Steve Bundy eyed his skinned knuckles. 'It's a soddin' good

job,' he speculated, 'that 'ee took 'ee's coat off, or I'd be on a fizzer.'

Warrant Officer Hogg, following a brief period in Sick Quarters, had gone on leave. The Adjutant had asked questions, but everyone, including the sergeant instructor, had affirmed that the whole affair had been one of those unfortunate accidents that could happen in any gymnasium – and apparently Hogg did not deny it. Subaltern officers grinned; Deal had become a pleasanter place, and Steve Bundy was embarrassed by the monstrous portions of stew and dumplings that overspilled his plate each day. Then someone recalled that there had been a Steve Bundy who had fought Sailor Hobbs and Battling Joe Marco. Was he really *the* Steve Bundy, the middleweight hope whose name had mysteriously disappeared from the sports pages of the *Star* and *Evening News*?

He denied it at first but, pressed, agreed that he had done a bit in the ring – and suddenly he was a celebrity, which was not unpleasant. Sergeants slapped his back and called him Steve. Corporals paid for his beer, and somehow the less desirable fatigues always seemed to pass him by. His brasses were polished and his webbing pipe-clayed. It was a soddin' pity, everyone lamented, that professional boxers were not permitted to fight competitively in service tournaments, because there was no doubt that Steve Bundy would knock the spit out of Stoker Murdoch, the Home Fleet champion, who ruled the roost from Portsmouth and had suggested that, to even the odds, he would fight bootnecks two at a time.

The Colonel Commandant sent for him.

'Stand easy, Bundy,' the Colonel said, and frowned thoughfully. 'I understand that, before enlistment, you were a contender for the British Middleweight Championship, and might even have fought for the world title in America.'

'Well, sir—'

'Splendid. I once did a little myself, y'know – at Wellington – so I know a bit about it.' The Colonel toyed with his steel-rimmed reading glasses reminiscently. It had been a long time ago. 'You're still a young man, Bundy. Presumably when the war's over you'll resume your boxing career?'

'Well, sir—'

The Colonel nodded. 'Good man.' He placed his hands behind his back. 'That's why I've sent for you, Bundy. I'd like to think that I helped someone along, you understand, particularly when there's an opportunity of putting the Americans' noses out of joint' – he chuckled – 'in more ways than one, eh?'

Steve Bundy chuckled politely.

'Now—' The Colonel frowned again. 'Benbow Company will be leaving Deal shortly, but not for service with the Fleet. They'll be going to France.' He paused. 'An increasing number of marines – and naval ratings – are being drafted to France to make good the casualties suffered by the RN Division. I don't have to tell you, Bundy, that a lot of men have been killed in the Ypres salient.'

Steve Bundy remembered. For Chris' sake, the sailor had urged him, don't sign for the RN Division. Anything else, but not that.

'Yessir,' he said.

'Yes. It's bloody foul that men who have volunteered to serve at sea should find themselves in the mud and gas of Flanders, and with no choice. Still, there's nothing we can do about it, Bundy.'

Steve Bundy offered no opinion.

'However, the Admiralty still likes to maintain a sea-going complement of Royal Marines – one turret manned in every ship, cruisers and above – and I'm permitted to draft selected men to Whale Island for heavy-calibre gunnery training. I'm sending you with the next detachment.'

Steve Bundy swallowed. 'Me, sir?' He was not sure whether to feel flattered or victimised. 'Sir, are you sure it's right? I mean—'

'No, I'm not sure it's right, Bundy, but the war could last another year, perhaps even two, and it's the élite of your generation that's volunteering to be killed and maimed – scholars, athletes, writers, teachers, the builders of this country's future – yes, and boxers too, Bundy. Too many of our finest young men have gone already. If I can save just a few from the worst of the holocaust, I will. And I have, just a few – two university dons, an Olympics medallist, a brilliant young lawyer, an author, a mathematician, and a man who went south with Scott. Now, they're in ships at sea, or in Hong Kong and Port Said – not willingly, you understand, but because I cooked the books, and I have no regrets. However, I mustn't discriminate only in favour of the highly educated; there are other qualities. Did you know that the wastage of the Napoleonic wars reduced the average height of French males by two inches?' The Colonel laughed, then shook his head. 'I fancy you don't understand, Bundy, but one day you might.'

Steve Bundy did understand, vaguely. Since he seldom penned anything more complicated than his own name and, arithmetically, had never progressed beyond his seven-times table, he would not have considered himself to be a member of his generation's élite. There were men in Benbow Division who had been clerks, travelling salesmen and even shop managers, whose post-war expectations might be thought to be eminently more promising than his own, but he would be a fool to spurn a reprieve from the carnage of Ypres. There were times when a bloke needed to keep his mouth shut.

'Gunlayers and trainers have to be non-comms,' the Colonel went on, 'and three-month recruits aren't usually rated corporals, so I'll have to give you a red-ink recommendation.' He sighed. 'That means you must refrain from sharing gymnasium accidents with warrant officers.' He raised his eyebrows over his spectacles questioningly.

'Yessir,' Steve Bundy agreed. 'Sir – about after the war—'

'After the war,' the Colonel nodded, 'assuming you achieve the end of the war, and resume your boxing, I'd be grateful if you'd do one thing for me, Bundy.' He paused. 'I've read about other boxers who call themselves *Gunboat* Smith, and *Sailor* Hobbs, or *Bombadier* Wells.' He paused again. 'If it's no trouble, could you call yourself *Marine* Bundy?'

Neither the events at Deal, however, nor the weeks that followed in HMS *Excellent*, Whale Island, had contributed anything to the cloudiness in his right eye that nobody else knew about. And the headaches. The training crew of which he had been a member was the gunnery school's best of 1915; he had a small medal on a ring to prove it, and only the best were drafted to Admiral Beatty's Invincibles and Splendid Cats. 'The Royal Marines man "X" turret,' Major Blackwood had told him. 'It's the smartest turret in the ship, and this ship's the finest in the Fleet. I don't expect to give orders twice and "X" turret doesn't accommodate passengers. Remember that, Bundy.'

Steve Bundy remembered. He just hoped, sod it, that he never had to use that range-finder.

Lieutenant George Pope had reached Malta before an opportunity arose to consult a civilian doctor; he had not dared to confide in a naval surgeon. In Valletta he walked a dozen streets, then saw the brass plate on the wall of a shabby house in Mattia Preti Square.

The surgery was very warm, airless and in shadow behind Venetian blinds lowered against the sun, and both men perspired. The Maltese doctor, a short, stout man with several gold teeth, hid his surprise at seeing a naval officer in his waiting room, but made no comment until he had completed his examination. He washed his hands with carbolic soap as George Pope buttoned his shirt.

'Yes, Lieutenant,' he spoke over his shoulder, 'I strongly suspect you have syphilis, probably in its latent stage, which means you contracted it some time ago. Why haven't you sought treatment before, and why have you come to me? The Navy's medical facilities are excellent.'

'I never realised it was – well – what it was.' George Pope frowned. 'Damn, it's not very obvious – just a general lassitude occasionally, thinning hair, sometimes a rash that seemed of no consequence. Why did it have to be syphilis?' He narrowed his eyes. 'Are you sure?'

'Sure?' The Maltese doctor shrugged. 'Medicine is a very inexact science, Lieutenant, but I have seen a great deal of syphilis, and I am not often wrong. Anyway, with your permission, I shall send a blood sample to Bighi for testing. We shall have confirmation in three or four days, but—'

'There's no time,' Pope said. 'My ship sails this evening.'

The doctor dropped his towel into an enamel bucket, then switched on an electric fan to agitate the warm air. 'Then I suggest you accept my diagnosis, Lieutenant. Your symptoms are not unusual. Syphilis is a great mimic, and often does not advertise itself. It is just possible that you will experience nothing worse than you have already, and will die in old age of something quite different – but let's not be stupidly optimistic. You will be merely living in a fool's paradise. Your condition seems to be quiescent, but at any moment it can explode – in your throat, your blood-vessels, heart, your daily behaviour – then *tabeo dorsalis*, which means incontinence, impotence, perhaps epilepsy, paralysis and insanity. It is not a pretty prognosis, Lieutenant.'

From beyond the window came the noise of iron-shod wheels grinding on cobbles and the slow clip-clop of hooves.

George Pope sucked breath through his teeth. 'It's impossible.'

'It really doesn't matter how you were infected, only that you are.' The doctor shrugged again. 'Only yesterday, in this surgery, I regretfully informed an unmarried young lady that she was pregnant, and she swore that it could only have happened when she was bathing in the sea, because she had *never* taken a lover. Well, it made no difference; she was still pregnant.' He was taking a small basin from a cabinet. 'However, pregnancy isn't contagious, Lieutenant. Syphilis is. I can give you an injection now, but it is very important that you obtain neoarsphenamine treatment as soon as possible, and you will have periodical blood tests for years.' He held up a hypodermic syringe to the light. 'You are a walking bacillus, Lieutenant – a threat to everyone with whom you associate. I wish I could put you behind locked doors.'

George Pope bridled. 'Now, look – I didn't come here—'

'To be insulted?' The little Maltese shook his head. 'Roll up your sleeve, please. No, you came to a back-street doctor because you were ashamed to face your surgeon-commander, probably weeks of confinement in an infectious diseases ward, and your service records notated accordingly. But even back-street doctors have ethics, Lieutenant. I might sympathise with some illiterate peasant labourer, but not with an English gentleman who has the world's finest medical facilities at his disposal.' He felt with his thumb for the basilic vein in the other's arm. 'I will also give you a letter for a practitioner in England, and it is imperative that you do go to a qualified doctor, not a quack, as soon as you arrive. If you wish, I can give you the addresses of three or four consultants.'

George Pope raised his head. 'I'm quite prepared to pay.'

'Oh, you will pay, Lieutenant,' the doctor smiled. 'For a

beginning, you may write me a cheque for five hundred pounds.'

'Five hundred—?' Pope stared.

Harsh sunlight flooded the room as the little doctor drew up the Venetian blind, and George Pope flinched. 'You can put on your coat,' the doctor said. 'Yes, five hundred, I think.' He stood, gazing from the window at the dun-coloured houses opposite and, beyond, the long bastion of Saint Salvatore that curtained Marsamxett Harbour. The sun glittered gold on the water's surface.

'I have several young patients – children,' he went on, 'with congenital syphilis. They are the offspring of diseased sailors who have since disappeared.' He turned. 'Ah, does the light hurt your eyes, Lieutenant? The children suffer from bone weaknesses, deformed teeth, deafness and semi-blindness – and none of it is their fault. They will never work or play normally, never marry, never have children of their own. They may never achieve adulthood and it might have been better had they never been born; they will always be treated as lepers – with pity, but at a distance.' He paused. 'Five hundred pounds will do a great deal for them.'

George Pope was silent for several moments, then groped for his cheque book. 'Five hundred pounds,' he nodded. 'And I'll make you a promise. If the treatment's successful, I'll send you another thousand.'

His letters to Imogen, sent to Portsmouth, had remained unanswered for eight months. He had wanted to explain a predicament that he did not understand himself, but it was plain that his pleas had been lost on her, and, he conceded, it was not surprising. Sinjin Primrose's body, recovered from Anzac Cove, had been buried on the Aegean island of Skyros and, thankfully, there had been no awkward questions about the Rear-Admiral's death. A few shook their heads; being shot on an enemy shore was just the end that the old boy would have wished for. George Pope left *London* at Otranto, no longer required and grateful to see her dirty smoke receding over the Adriatic horizon.

He needed the opinion of a doctor urgently, but not a naval doctor, and there had been no time to consult anyone in Otranto. In Malta he had a single day during which the ship coaled, and he had climbed the long steps from Lascaris Wharf, the sun hot on his shoulders, praying that everything was a mistake, that Imogen was wrong, and Sinjin Primrose had been wrong.

Well, at least he had money. Marriage, his father had written from Sydney, wasn't exactly a bloody disaster, but George could have the five thousand pounds for a wedding gift. In due course he must bring his bride to Australia. If she was Sinjin Primrose's niece, then she came from bloody good stock. He, Arthur Pope, would have to watch his bloody language and resign himself to cucumber sandwiches and bloody custard. . . .

To the intense relief of Albert Selley, who had not understood how any handful of town-bred youths, without the wit to recognise a starboard lamp from a steamed pudding, could be despatched directly from an Edinburgh recruiting office to a man-o'-war, HMS *Caledonia* was not a ship but a shabby collection of buildings in the shadow of the Forth Bridge, below Queensferry. Those of his companions who, on the twelve-mile journey, had begun to develop a nautical gait and talk about shore leave and tots of rum, were silenced – partly by the depressing situation but more by the spectacle of large and gaitered petty officers with savage voices and knotted ropes' ends swinging from their wrists.

That, however, had been only the beginning. Albert Selley and his fellows did not seriously resent a supper of hard biscuits and cocoa before being ordered to their beds in a corrugated iron barrack-hut so bitterly cold that their breath froze in the air as they cringed under their blankets. They were too exhausted after hours of double-marching from one obscure venue to another, to collect boots, vaccinations, oilskins, haircuts, next-of-kin cards, soap, prayer books and mattress covers. They were only mildly resentful, because they were so stupid with weariness, to be awakened by shouts and whistles at 5.30 in the morning, driven into icy communal showers, to breakfast on more hard biscuits and cocoa, and then be double-marched again between the same obscure locations as yesterday to have their genitals thumbed and their teeth probed, to accumulate caps and jerseys, tooth-powder and darning wool, mattresses to fill the mattress covers, ditty-bags and tin buckets, while their tormentors screamed thanks to Christ that there existed an Army. At the day's end nobody thought it diplomatic to enquire about shore leave or, indeed, had the energy for any such gratuitous physical activity.

The regimen did not become easier with the passage of time, although most of them hardened – or, more accurately, resigned themselves to it. One, latterly a postman from Forfar, did not. 'I'm nae gang ta be shunted aroon' like a bluidy black,' he declared after only a week. 'I'm gang ta desert.' He did, but was arrested within forty-eight hours, having spent the entire period in his own bed in Forfar. *Caledonia* saw him briefly when his warrant was read before the establishment, but never again.

At least, with uniforms, they looked something like sailors. They lowered boats, rowed them and raised them, blistered their hands on ropes and tore fingernails on wires. There was gun-drill with an old six-inch piece which bore the legend *Agamemnon 1876* engraved on its breech. They spliced, heaved leads, washed clothes, swabbed latrines and scoured decks with holystone, wolfed their food and were always hungry.

From Queensferry they could see the wide, sullen expanse

of the Forth, and in mid-river were anchored the grey monsters of Vice-Admiral Beatty's battle-cruiser squadrons which the petty officers, in rare moments of entente, pointed out as *Lion*, *Princess Royal*, *Queen Mary*, *Tiger*, *New Zealand* and *Indefatigable*. Only slightly less impressive were the light cruisers *Southampton*, *Birmingham*, *Nottingham* and *Dublin*. These, intimidatingly, were the ships of the real Navy, and their libertymen scorned the one, single-roomed tavern in Queensferry; they swarmed noisily to Edinburgh for headier recreations. The fledglings of HMS *Caledonia*, when released, practised their seafaring oaths in Queensferry. They were not yet ready for Edinburgh and the Fleet.

Then, finally, they had stood in the fine, drizzling rain outside the Regulating Office to receive their draft notes and hear the names of the ships to which they had assigned. They had speculated for weeks and most were disappointed or, at best, dubious. The ships' names that the Master-at-Arms read from the sheaf of orders in his hand were not those of Splendid Cats or the new and magnificent Queen Elizabeths, but uninspiring names like *Grasshopper*, *Redpole* and *Obedient*, which hardly generated visions of thunderous broadsides and shot-torn ensigns. They departed glumly to muster their hammocks and bags in the drill-shed, leaving Ordinary Seaman Selley, alone, with his oilskin collar upturned.

In the Master's-at-Arms hand there remained a single draft note, and to it was pinned a pink slip of paper that Albert Selley recognised.

'Ordinary Seaman Selley.' The Master-at-Arms looked up. 'Edinburgh Court o' Session. Probation for one year in cognizance of immediate enlistment in H.M.Forces.' He sniffed. 'I don't know what you done, Selley, and I don't know why the Navy has to take ticket-o'-leave men. It didn't happen in my day.' He folded the draft not carefully and pushed it into an envelope. 'It's not right. All them other sods have gone to destroyers and 'sweepers, but you're special. You've been drafted to the bleedin' *Invincible*. And that's not all. We've got to send a Regulating Petty Officer with you, all the way to soddin' Devonport, to make sure you get there.'

It had been two weeks or more before Sub-Lieutenant Hedley Bellman learned to find his way with confidence among the decks, flats and passageways of *Invincible*, to go from gun-room to cable-deck without finding himself in the paint store or the seamen's bathroom. The battle-cruiser was a labyrinth of steel caverns, ladders, water-tight doors and messdecks, artificially lit and ventilated, humidly warm, teeming with troglodytes who emerged, blinking in the sunlight, only when ordered to exercise, to raise boats or winch cables, and retiring rodent-like to their crowded warrens as soon as permitted. They ate, slept, kept watch, scarcely knowing the day or hour, or caring, conditioned to respond to bugles and whistles without questioning – and they had infinite faith in men like himself, Hedley Bellman, because he had a sliver of gold braid on his cuff and was thus a superior mortal.

He had experienced a shock when he met George Pope in *Invincible*'s wardroom-anteroom on that first day aboard, in Devonport. The last time he had seen Pope had been a few weeks before the start of the war, in Rear-Admiral Primrose's house, and in those intervening twenty months the man had aged beyond recognition. His hair had dulled and thinned, his face was lined, his hands nervous. He regarded Hedley Bellman blankly for several moments.

'Bellman? Hedley Bellman?'

'That's right. We have met – three or four times, briefly – in Portsmouth. It was the last summer before the war—'

'Ah! yes,' Pope nodded. 'I remember. You were the

merchant navy chap.' He forwned. 'Weren't you in *Aboukir*? You got off, then.' His voice was flat, distant. 'Anyway, the sun's over the yeardarm. Will you have a whisky?' He raised a hand. 'Steward – two whiskys, please – on my chit.'

'I read about Rear-Admiral Primrose,' Hedley said. Sooner or later the subject would have to be broached; it may as well be now. 'It was a rotten business. He was a solid old piece of teak. They don't make that kind any more.' He paused. 'Imogen—'

George Pope jerked a quick, startled glance at Hedley, then lifted his glass and emptied it with one gulp. 'I've just thought,' he muttered, and drew out his watch. 'Your bloke is Dannreuther, the Gunnery Officer. He'll be aboard tomorrow. Just shake down in the gunroom, will you, Bellman? Everything's a bit chaotic at the moment—' He turned, walked away, leaving Hedley staring after him.

Twelve

In the northerly Orkneys the dawn of Tuesday 30 May that rose over the vast and dreary anchorage of Scapa Flow promised nothing unusual. The misted hummocks of South Ronaldsay and Hoy were the same, scattered with wet sheep and mewling seabirds. In the sound, among the warships anchored like grey fortresses, bugles teetered reveille and whistles shrilled. The Fleet stirred. On a hundred quarterdecks the morning watchkeepers yawned, chilled, and sent away their messengers for coffee. The first drifter of the day, from Thurso on the mainland, nosed alongside Flotta's pontoon jetty, laden with sacks of mail and a handful of hunched, weary travellers whose stomachs after the journey across a heaving Pentland Firth would not be mollified by the sight of several ships' cutters being loaded with raw and bleeding beef – the morning 'blood boats', collecting three days' fresh meat.

The sun rose, probing weakly through overcast cloud but dispersing the dawn haze and giving hope that this would not be yet another day of drizzling rain; it always seemed to be raining in Scapa Flow. Yeomen of Signals turned their glasses towards *Iron Duke*, awaiting the preparative flag that gave five minutes warning of the eight o' clock colour-hoisting and the pealing bugle 'Still', when thousands froze and ensigns climbed simultaneously to every masthead. Seaman boys and midshipmen shivered in singlets, waited for the hated pipe, 'Hands to exercise', each asking what the hell this did for England.

Anchored in the Flow, sitting solidly at their moorings, were the sixteen super-dreadnoughts of the 1st and 4th Battle Squadrons, while another eight, the 2nd Battle Squadron, lay ninety miles to the southward, off Cromarty. Here they had waited since the first few weeks of the war for the Kaiser's High Seas Fleet to emerge from its harbours and offer battle. There had been several alarms, several brief forays, but the Germans had no desire to be caught at sea. Their chosen role was that of a fleet in being – always threatening to fight but never doing so. Fleet against fleet, they would be outnumbered and outgunned, and in attritional combat must be overwhelmed, while the British, however badly mauled, could still call on ample reserves and still hold the ring. So the Germans clung closely to their bases, venturing to sea only occasionally and quickly to taunt the enemy, then withdrawing again. The British glowered from Scapa Flow and Cromarty, frustrated. Their day would come, they vowed.

The day was Tuesday, 30 May.

There were three ships in Scapa Flow which were only temporary visitors and whose crews fervently wished to be elsewhere. They were *Invincible, Inflexible* and *Indomitable* – the 3rd Battle-Cruiser Squadron – brought north for full-calibre gunnery practice, which was not possible in the vicinity of their home anchorage, Rosyth. The battle-cruiser men were heartily sick of Scapa Flow, its drizzling rain, its monotonous, unchanging daily routine and total lack of shore-going recreations. They had no desire to kick footballs on wind-swept, waterlogged fields among screeching seagulls, or aimlessly walk damp decks because there was nowhere to walk ashore. They wanted Rosyth, so conveniently near to Edinburgh, Younger's beer and ready women. Scapa Flow might suit these buoy-swinging clods of battleships, but not Admiral Beatty's elite and swashbuckling Invincibles and Splendid Cats.

And Tuesday 30 May had dawned no differently to any other tedious Scapa Flow day.

The ships of both navies were equipped with spark transmitters and crystal detector receivers, but the Germans were careless with wireless communication, as they would be in a later war. More seriously, they were unaware that the Admiralty was in possession of the German Navy's ciphers – salvaged from a wrecked cruiser – and had erected a number of listening stations on the East coast which were not only intercepting enemy signal traffic but were able to roughly locate the source of wireless transmissions. The Admiralty was keenly interested in any sudden increase in German signals traffic, which might mean that the enemy was preparing to leave harbour. During the morning of Tuesday 30 May the Admiralty's coding experts reported that the German High Seas Fleet was indeed raising steam, had been ordered to assemble in the Outer Jade by 1900, and would probably put to sea during the early hours of the following morning.

The day for which the Royal Navy had waited for almost two years had arrived. This time, forewarned, the British would be steaming to a battle rendezvous before the unsuspecting enemy had even slipped his moorings.

A string of coloured bunting climbed to the yardarm of the flagship, *Iron Duke*. The battle-fleet, accompanied by the three visiting Invincibles, would slip and proceed at 2130. In Rosyth, also, Vice-Admiral Beatty hoisted the order to his remaining six battle-cruisers. 'Raise steam for 22 knots.'

In Scapa Flow the men of the Invincibles were incensed. Today, at last, the battle-cruisers were being unleashed, to roar ahead of the fleet and fasten their fangs on the enemy until the slower, heavier-armoured ships came up. That was the privileged task for which the battle-cruisers had been designed and their crews trained. Today, however, the 3rd Battle-Cruiser Squadron would not be accompanying its fellows, the 1st and 2nd, in spearheading the British sortie because it was two hundred miles away and, bitterly, the Invincibles must reduce themselves to the plodding gait of the battleships, the buoy-swinging clods of Scapa Flow.

The Marine postman had landed the last shore-going mail, returning with several incoming bags, but it would be an hour or more before mail call was sounded. There was smoke lifting from all funnels. Boats and side ladders had been hoisted inboard, booms secured, pennants hoisted, and shipwrights and artificers made last-minute adjustments to valves, hydrants, searchlights, pumps and breech-blocks. In the gathering gloom, signal lamps blinked from flag-decks, and on the forebridge of each towering superstructure the officers gathered – captains, navigators, officers of the watch, yeomen of signals and midshipmen, grouping in the tiny pools of light from the chart table and binnacle. The smell of warm oil came from open hatches, the hum of generators. Below, sixteen-year-old callboys moved through the messdecks and passageways, piping.

'Secure all scuttles and watertight doors. Special sea dutymen close up. Prepare for sea.'

The last shackles were knocked off and lines slipped. Slowly, in succession, the great ships moved towards the southerly gate of the Flow, first *Iron Duke*, followed by *Royal Oak*, *Superb*, *Canada*, *Benbow*, almost black now in the dusk but with a tumble of white at each bow as speed increased. Once clear of the Flow the battle squadrons would be joined by the destroyer flotillas steaming around from

Gutta Sound, jockeying for position among the giants, their funnels glowing and engine fans roaring in the night. All vessels darkened, with navigation lights lowered to mere glimmers hardly perceptible at two-cable stations.

Earlier, during the forenoon, Lieutenant George Pope had carefully written a cheque for one thousand pounds and sealed it into an envelope which he addressed to Dr Robert Spiro, Mattia Preti Square, Valletta. He had not expected to receive any letters by the last mail arrival, but when he came below after dismissing the fo'c'sle party there lay a letter on the pillow of his bunk. The manila envelope was bulky, and he broke it open with a thumb, mildly puzzled.

It contained several typewritten papers, the first headed 'Menley, Underhill & Ellis, Solicitors, Grays Inn.'

Corporal Steve Bundy's letter was post-marked Southend. 'It has taken me all this time to find where you was,' the cramped writing spelled, 'but Mr Sawyer said. It was kind to send the money when Sailor got sunk and it was a godsend make no mistake. Now I am getting married agen and he has a bit put aside and ses its only right you should have it back now theres no need. He works on the railway. When I saw Mr Sawyer he sed to tell you keep to the middle and dont stick your chin out. God bless you. Kitty Hobbs.'

Enclosed with the brief letter was a Post Office order for two hundred pounds.

Steve Bundy read the message twice, slowly, because his right eye was clouding badly. He had no illusions about his performance during the practice shoots of last week, and neither had Major Blackwood, 'X' turret's Officer of Quarters who sat in his bucket seat high behind the local range-finder with, above him, the turret hatch locked. It was always a matter of honour for Blackwood that the Royal Marines' guns should show ready to fire before the others, a requirement that depended on his gunlayers and trainers responding to the range clock quickly and precisely. At 20 knots and 8000 yards Corporal Bundy had been slow and unusually fumbling. The Marines' turret had achieved fewer hits than any of the other three, to the sailors' delight and Blackwood's anger. There had been jokes and winking commiseration in the wardroom, even a suggestion that perhaps gunnery was getting a little too technical for bootnecks. The Captain had said nothing, which was worse.

And it was too late to substitute Bundy now, Blackwood rued. In a few hours, God willing, the ship would be in action. It was too bloody late now.

In the seamen's messes on the main and lower decks all deadlights and hatches had been secured, lighting had been reduced and the atmosphere was already becoming stale. The Last Dog watchkeepers had finished their supper – soup, unidentifiable but hot and thick, corned beef hash and haricot beans – and cleared away messtraps. Some men sat, talking or laughing, while others, Middle watchmen, had slung their hammocks. A few had drifted away with buckets and towels to shower and change into clean underclothes; there was no knowing if there would be an opportunity later. The messdeck flats were too far forward to be much affected by the reciprocating throb of the engines, but ventilators whispered, breathing air already warm, and there was the gentlest of vibrations underfoot as the ship worked up to eighteen knots, then twenty.

Ordinary Seaman Albert Selley never received letters; none of his family had ever written one, so he did not feel deprived. Still, he sat under the mess-locker mentally reviewing all the things he didn't like. For a start he didn't like the Chief Bosun's Mate or the leading hand of the mess, both of whom seemed to think that Selley spend too much time devising ways of not doing anything, with the result that, in his jaundiced opinion, they ensured he did more than anyone.

Albert had never adapted to the brash camaraderie of a messdeck. *Caledonia* had been uncomfortable but *Invincible* was indescribably worse. He hadn't done anything to deserve this. He hadn't killed Donald Selley and should never have been arraigned before the Edinburgh Court of Session. Bluidy hell, he should never have been sent to the soddin' Navy; he ought to be at Coleman's Bakery. It was iniquitous. It was a bluidy cheat. If he ever deserted – it was the one possibility over which he enjoyed gloating – he'd not be caught in his bluidy bed. Just wait, he promised himself, until this soddin' ship returned to Rosyth, that's all. Just wait.

A pail of cocoa had come down from the galley and a tin of biscuits was being broken open. 'Kye up, fill yer boots,' the mess leading hand said, then laughed. 'It might be yer last bleedin' chance, Selley, ter wash up mess-traps before yer turn in—'

'Selley?' A Chief Petty Officer stood over him with a clip-board in hand. 'What's your action station?'

Albert switched off the snarl he had directed at the leading hand. 'Damage Control, Chief – in the Office Flat—' Christ.

'Not now, you ain't.' The Chief licked his pencil. 'You're 'Q' turret magazine, handling room – all right? It's the safest place in the bleedin' ship, unless it blows up – then yer won't know.' He looked up at Albert. 'Report ter Petty Officer Fawkes at first muster tomorrer—'

When the Chief Petty Officer had departed, the leading hand of the mess began to think. 'Fawkes? Mate, yer ain't going down the magazine wi' bleedin' Guy Fawkes, are yer?' He guffawed, then confided. 'Selley, me 'andsome, if yer can't find the cordite, don't strike a bleedin' match, fer Cris' sake—'

There had been no mail for Hedley Bellman. His father wrote weekly letters that resembled parish magazines, while those from Imogen, somewhere in the vicinity of Lemberg, reached him only after very long delays or, judging by their lack of continuity, did not reach him at all. She, at least, was well, and made light of conditions which he knew from accounts of the Carpathian battle theatre to be atrocious. Hedley, gloved and shrugged into his coat collar, watched the dawn rise from the Director Control Tower, high above the bridge. It was Wednesday, 31 May.

The sea was calm, and it would be warmer as the sun rose higher. A light mist reduced visibility to about ten miles, but perhaps that, too, would clear soon. *Invincible* led the line of three battle-cruisers, and Rear-Admiral the Hon Horace Hood had kept them at 20 knots all night, steering south-east, to draw ahead of the Grand Fleet by twenty miles. In company were the light cruisers *Chester* and *Canterbury*, and the destroyers *Shark*, *Acasta*, *Ophelia* and *Christopher* of the 4th Flotilla, the little ships plunging their bows gamely into the long swell as they kept station abeam, the hunched, oil-skinned men on their bridges protected from the wind and flung spray only by a flimsy canvas screen. From the steel box of the Tower, Hedley watched them, knowing that they would be tired and numbed, eye-smarting, as he had once on the bridge of the old *Corinthian* as she butted up-Channel into the teeth of a north-easterly. He pushed his chin deeper into his collar.

Hedley Bellman was the first of the Morning watchkeepers to reach the gunroom. It was empty except for the steward, clearing dirtied cups and plates from the table, and Lieutenant George Pope. Hedley had never before seen Pope in the gunroom; for months both, by unspoken agreement, had avoided each other, which was not difficult in a ship that accommodated a thousand men, and Hedley did not often enter the wardroom.

Pope glared at the steward, who vanished. 'This,' Pope said, brandishing a sheaf of papers, 'is a letter from solicitors. Imogen is petitioning for divorce. I don't even know where she is. Do you?'

Hedley hesitated, then, 'Six weeks ago she was with Brusilov's army. She wrote from somewhere called Rovno, wherever that might be, and was expecting to be sent to Tarnopol. I couldn't find that on the map, either. She seems to be in good health. You knew, of course, that she was with a field ambulance unit?'

The question was ignored. 'She's well, you say? You're sure of that?' Pope's eyes were narrowed.

Hedley shrugged. 'Well, she says so – and they wouldn't keep her at the front if she wasn't, would they? I think they're watched pretty closely.'

George Pope nodded slowly. 'And she must have been in good health before she went,' he calculated. Hedley did not see the relevance of the comment but, he agreed, she must have been. Pope's gaze still rested on him. 'Have you had anything to do with this divorce business?'

Hedley Bellman frowned. 'I haven't provoked it, if that's what you mean – I didn't even know for sure that it was happening – but if it does happen, and Imogen is free, I hope to marry her. I think I can make her happy.' He paused and then, without knowing why, added, 'I'm sorry.'

Hedley was expecting an angry exchange, but George Pope's face was expressionless. 'I see,' he said, and nodded again. The next moment any further discussion was impossible. Midshipmen Winstanley and Crowther had tumbled noisily through the door, dragging off their oilskins and shouting for the steward. 'If it's kedgeree again,' Winstanley threatened, 'it'll go straight through the scuttle. What's happened to all the eggs? We took on eight thousand last week. I know, because I personally counted 'em.' He shot a mischievous glance in the direction of George Pope. 'I suppose they all go to the wardroom. I hope they all get constipation.'

The three Invincibles ploughed on through the forenoon, their crews at first state of readiness. The long grey hulls were becoming streaked with salt and the funnels were blistering. Somewhere, far ahead, Admiral Beatty's six battle-cruisers were racing to intercept the German High Seas Fleet, and the Invincibles' rightful place was with them. It would be chastening to miss the first moment of contact with the enemy, an accident they would not be allowed to forget. Late in the forenoon Rear-Admiral the Hon. H.L.A. Hood, CB, MVO, DSO, came to *Invincible*'s bridge to join Captain Arthur Cay. He was a man of medium height, thick-set, with the kindly, ruddy face of an English farmer rather than that of one of the Navy's most capable younger admirals and scion of a distinguished family of fighting seamen. 'Nothing from the Flag yet, Arthur?' He glanced at the deck clock. 'He must be getting very warm.'

Cay, lean-framed and taller by half a head, recognised his superior's dilemma – the nagging desire to pile on speed, of which the Invincibles had an ample reserve, yet not place the squadron too far ahead of the following battleships for which it had been given screening responsibility. The battleships' maximum station-keeping speed was 20 knots.

At 1230 the hands were piped to dinner. Hood and Cay sent down for sandwiches.

Two hours passed with leaden slowness and the Fleet's wireless frequencies remained perversely silent. Annoyingly, the mist of morning had not dispersed and was even showing signs of thickening. Ahead, visibility was down to about eight miles, sometimes as little as two-and-a-half. On the flagdeck a signalman had bent flag Five to a halyard, the signal to open fire, ready for hoisting.

At 1425 a flush-faced Signals Lieutenant flung himself up

the bridge ladder. 'Signal from *Galatea* to *Lion*, sir—"*Two cruisers probably hostile in sight bearing ESE*." ' He swallowed. '*Galatea*'s leading the First Light Cruiser Squadron, sir – Admiral Beatty's screen.'

'Ah, yes, so she is,' Hood nodded, and with infuriating calmness turned to lift his glasses towards the destroyers, steaming ahead and in line abreast. 'Thank you, Lieutenant.' Everyone on the bridge stared at his back.

'These cordite charges, Selley,' said Petty Officer Fawkes, 'weighs three 'undred pounds each and cost a lot o' money. They're put in the hoppers, then turned through the turret trunk into the ammunition hoist cage, see. That lifts 'em up the trunk with the projectiles to the waiting trays in the working chamber, and then the hydraulic rams push 'em into the loading cages that goes up the rails to the gun. D'yer get that?' Albert Selley did not, but he nodded. 'If the hydraulic hoist fails,' Fawkes went on, 'there's a hand lifting winch to the working chamber and then a block an' tackle to the gun-house.' The petty officer grinned. 'Once yer down 'ere, Selley, there's no way yer can get out. Yer locked in. If the gun-house is hit, the Officer o' Quarters will order all doors closed and the magazine flooded.'

Albert Selley sniffed. 'Bluidy hell.'

Almost another hour passed before Rear-Admiral Hood lowered his glasses and turned from the forward screen. 'Increase to twenty-two knots, please.' Seconds later the speed signal was climbing to the yardarm and, astern and abeam, answering pennants fluttered.

'Execute,' Cay nodded. Everyone in the squadron, from the Rear-Admiral to the youngest seaman boy, now knew that their sister battle-cruisers, far ahead, were at grips with the enemy, and that the Invincibles, for certain, were going to be in battle today. Of course, battle-cruisers were not *expected* to fight battleships, but since the day the first had been launched, nine years before, nobody had ever seriously doubted that, when the gauntlet was down, they would.

Hood still stood at the screen, seldom moving – a lone figure that others did not approach unless for good reason. He was balancing probabilities, trying to interpret the situation ahead, of which he had only fragments of information intercepted by his wireless operators. The first major enemy formation, he knew, had been sighted – five battle-cruisers accompanied by torpedo craft – and at 1550 the British had opened fire at 12,000 yards. Hood was intensely anxious to further increase speed, but already he was widening the distance between his own squadron and the following Grand Fleet under Admiral Jellicoe, which meant he could find himself, unsupported, fighting battleships while leaving his own battle fleet without a screen.

He had not yet sent the squadron to action stations, an intense and fatiguing discipline that he would delay as long as possible, but the crews were anticipating it and men were drifting towards their battle quarters with their gas-masks, life-belts and goggles, rigging splinter mats and running out hoses, mustering damage control materials, stretchers, drugs and dressings, stand-by electrical and hydraulic gear.

Hood drew a deep breath at last, turned again, and the bridge personnel stiffened. 'Increase to twenty-four knots, please.'

He was going to gamble, and everyone knew it, everyone grinned. The signal to the squadron, however, had hardly been hoisted when the Signals Lieutenant, as if he had precisely chosen the moment, brought the order that had been hungrily awaited for hours.

'From CinC, *Iron Duke*, sir. We are to detach and proceed at utmost speed to support Admiral Beatty.'

'Thank you, Lieutenant.' Hood looked at Captain Cay. 'If you please, Arthur, we'll go to action stations at 1630.'

In 'Q' turret, amidships, Lieutenant George Pope, Officer of Quarters, gripped his bracing rail with white-knuckled hands and tried to divide his attention between the slit in his observation hood and the brass-rimmed repeaters that relayed gun-laying data from the Transmitting Station below the ship's waterline, the clatter of the cordite and shell hoists and the stinging hiss of hydraulic rams. He dreaded the order to engage. The steel cavern of the gun-house would be hot, reeking of cordite smoke, intolerable. Below him the two great gun breeches were closed, loaded, sunk into the wells that allowed their barrels to elevate twenty degrees above horizontal. To serve these two monsters, in magazine and shell-room, to hoist charges and projectiles, load and ram, train and lay, eighty men on several deck levels hauled, thrust, sweated and blasphemed, but beyond Pope's feet he could see the movements of only nine or ten – the seated breech-operators and loaders, sight-setters, trainers and layers. As the huge breeches closed and locked, red 'gun-ready' lamps would flicker in the Transmitting Station below and the Director Control Tower above the bridge. A bell tinkled with the innocence of a child's toy, and then there would be an awful concussion to stun his senses. The whole turret would lurch. Each gun, of sixty-five tons and heaving backward in recoil, would subdue, slide slowly forward again. Immediately the breeches would crash open, releasing a blast of hot cordite gas that flooded the chamber, stinging the eyes and throat. Fresh shells and cordite charges were already in the loading cages, and the range-pointers would jerk again.

He hated the turret. He hated its obscene noise, the pollution, the shuddering violence of the guns as they hurled their vicious missiles into a sky choked with leprous smoke, and hated himself for cringing each time the fire bell tinkled its warning. It was impossible that he was of flimsier fibre than the ratings below him who loaded, fired and reloaded to a pattern of time and motion from which every unnecessary movement had been eliminated, impassively unhurried and yet incredibly swift. He, George Pope, should not be here with a life-or-death authority over these better men, because when the battle began, he shivered, the nerves that he controlled with tensed muscles and gritted teeth could snap. He could reach upward for the clamped hatch-clips, then scramble desperately for that smoke-hazed circle of blue sky . . . .

Invincible, Indomitable and *Inflexible* had worked up to full speed, steering south-south-east now in order, hopefully, to turn between the enemy battle-fleet and its home base. *Canterbury* was five miles ahead – the squadron's eyes – *Chester* the same distance on the starboard bow, but out of sight, while the four destroyers were in line abreast, each of less than a thousand tons, armed with puny 4-inch guns and a pair of torpedo tubes but as eager as unleashed puppies. It was 1700, sunset was only two and a half hours away, and the perfidious, sea-clinging mist seemed to be growing even more dense than ever, but through it, from the south-west, they could hear the rumble of heavy gunfire. The Invincibles' turrets turned, their long barrels sniffing at the sky.

Then *Chester* reeled out of the haze, a floating shambles, ablaze with cordite fires and zig-zagging, but with her searchlight hammering a warning to the flagship. She was not alone.

'Four enemy three-funnelled cruisers, sir,' someone shouted. '*Wiesbaden* class.'

'Thank you,' acknowledged Rear-Admiral Hood, and smiled.

Chester turned across the path of her parent squadron. She had been badly mauled, but was drawing her four pursuers onto the guns of the battle-cruisers. Too late, the enemy light cruisers sighted through the swirling fog the ominous shapes of the three big ships, a mere 8000 yards away. They whirled frantically, seeking distance, but *Invincible* had already opened fire, followed in minutes by her sisters astern. *Wiesbaden*, torn to smoking wreckage, wallowed helplessly. *Pillau* had stopped, enveloped in a vast cloud of steam, and *Frankfurt* was reduced to a crawl. All four enemy vessels disappeared in the murk as they fell astern. Hood was after bigger fish, and he was about to find them.

Far below 'Q' turret, below barbette and upper deck, main deck and lower deck, below the waterline and the 7-inch armoured belt, Ordinary Seaman Albert Selley laboured, ill-tempered, in the cavern of the cordite handling room where bulkheads streamed with condensation and the atmosphere was dankly chill when a man paused for breath.

It was the safest place in the ship, the Chief had said, unless it blew up, and then nobody would survive to complain. Nonsense, ruled the experts. Cordite, unless confined within a gun-breech, never exploded; gelatinized smokeless powder only burned slowly however fierce the heat. Tests had proved it. Famous bluidy last words, Albert Selley snorted.

The cylindrical cordite charges for a 12-inch gun, each weighing 307 pounds, were encapsulated in pure silk, which left less glowing deposits in a gun-barrel, after firing, than any other known material, easily extinguished by the thrust of a wet mop – the woolly-headed bastard – that preceded the next loading. The charges were stowed in metal bins from which they were transferred to the hoist trays in the turret trunk, joining company with the 850-pound shells similarly taken from the magazine immediately below. Shells and charges were then hoisted by cage to the working chamber under the gun-house, where they were rolled off into waiting containers, hydraulically rammed into a second cage, and raised through the deck of the turret to the open gun breech.

Ignorant of the situation above decks, Albert Selley and his fellows worked fiercely, mechanically. *Invincible* carried a hundred rounds for each of her eight large guns, and the turret crews expected to receive those rounds at the rate of two per minute per gun. The rapid firing cycle was precisely timed to that rate of supply, and a delay for any reason meant the use of the emergency shells and cordite retained in the gun-house. It was a disrupting procedure that annoyed everyone from the Gunnery Officer in the Control Tower to the vociferous Gunner's Mate in the Magazine. Albert Selley, as he sweated, tried to calculate how long it would take to fire a hundred shells at two a minute, but his arithmetic was inadequate. He thought it might be two hundred minutes, no bluidy stand easy, and all for three pounds a bluidy month.

Above the shattering clatter of the hoist, the lifting winch, and the screech of cordite bins on the steel deck they could hear and feel the shudder of the guns, and the smell of burnt cordite seeped down the turret trunk through the flash doors that only partially screened the shaft. *Invincible* was firing to starboard, which meant, Ordinary Seaman Selley seethed, that the idle bastards in 'P' turret's magazine, on the port side amidships, were sitting on their arses doing nothing. And those sods who'd been drafted to *Grasshopper*, *Redpole* and *Obedient* didn't know their bluidy luck.

It was becoming clear to Rear-Admiral Hood that as a result of the fog and also the doubtful accuracy of the positional reports transmitted by Admiral Beatty's force, he had overshot the main battle area and was now probably to the south or south-east of the German fleet. This was not a bad situation, since it placed him directly across the enemy's line of retreat, but his first duty was to support the six ships led by Beatty's *Lion*, still unsighted. Hood, without hesitation, turned the Invincibles directly towards the sound of heaviest gunfire.

The squadron was now steaming at full speed into greying haze further thickened by intermittent, floating palls of gun-smoke through which the ships plunged and then emerged. There was a congestion of blurred shapes to port, but they were not battleships. Three flotillas of torpedo-boats, outriders of the German battle-fleet, launched themselves at the Invincibles, and the screen of British destroyers, *Shark*, *Acastra*, *Ophelia* and *Christopher*, wheeled immediately. With every gun firing that could bear, they hurled themselves at the enemy formation in counter-attack, regardless of the consequences because this was the role that justified their existence – the survival of the battle-cruisers. Met by such belligerence, the German flotillas, totalling thirty craft, fired off only twelve torpedoes before turning away, and only *Indomitable* observed that one missile had passed beneath her, a second passed ahead and a third astern. Then, within moments, the danger was astern and the Invincibles were through the torpedo-boat cordon, hidden by fog. In their rear *Shark* was a broken, water-logged hulk, sinking but with guns still firing, most of her crew dead. Captain Loftus Jones, dying, his left leg severed, saw that the ensign had become wrapped around the mast, and ordered that it should be disentangled to fly freely. Later, twice more torpedoed, *Shark* sank with her ensign still high, and there would be only six survivors.

The day was going well, so far. The Invincibles had annihilated a light cruiser squadron and shrugged off a torpedo attack. It was just after 1800, with two hours of daylight to come. Daylight, however, was not the same thing as visibility, and on *Invincible*'s bridge everyone, without debate, grappled with the same excrutiating question. Was there sufficient *time* remaining for Admiral Beatty's battle-cruisers, not yet joined by Hood's, to hold the German High Seas Fleet in play until Jellicoe's Dreadnoughts came up?

It was 1810.

'First and Second Battle-Cruiser Squadrons in sight to the south-westward, sir – about five miles and closing.'

All glasses rose immediately for the first glimpse of Beatty's Splendid Cats – and there they were, indistinct yet, but a brave sight, steaming in line ahead out of the curtain of funnel and cordite smoke, their guns pounding – first *Lion*, then *Princess Royal*, *Tiger*, *New Zealand*—

'There's only four,' someone jerked. 'Christ, only four—'

Awful seconds passed as mistrusting eyes counted again, calculated, but still refused to believe. '*Queen Mary* and *Indefatigable* are not in line, sir.'

Not in line? Then where—?

'They've taken punishment,' Captain Cay grunted. '*Lion*'s 'Q' turret's disabled, and the *P.R.*'s control top's holed. They'll be glad to see us, I shouldn't wonder.' Of the enemy with whom their scarred sisters were engaged they could only see the twinkling red flashes of gun salvoes through dark smoke cumulus, hiding all else, but the leaden sea was shredded by the white splashes of falling shells that reared upward, hung motionless, and then collapsed into vast lakes of white froth.

'From *Lion*, sir' – it was the Signals Lieutenant again. 'Take station ahead of me. Course 120, speed 25 knots. Enemy bearing SSE.'

It would have been a delicate manoeuvre to execute at modest speed and under the most favourable of circumstances, but to turn three battle cruisers into a U-turn inside Beatty's line, to forge ahead of the speeding flagship and then station those three big ships neatly in the van was an evolution to test the capabilities of any seaman, but Hood did it superbly. The Invincibles followed about as if they were exercising off Portland for the benefit of visiting royalty, gliding through the shell-pitted water and the leprous scud, navigating officers watching the next ahead and *Lion* on the quarter, an eye on the compass and the other on the revolutions repeater. Then they were on the station they had toiled to reach for the past twenty hours – at the head of Beatty's battle column.

On each bridge the midshipmen of the watch made the entry in the deck log. '1821. Course 120. Speed 25 knots. Enemy in sight bearing SSE, range 12,000 yards, closing.'

Lieutenant Sandford, *Invincible*'s Torpedo Officer, pointed beyond the starboard bow. 'That's *Lutzow*, sir, sure enough – and *Derfflinger*, the same class.' The Irishman was delighted. 'We're going to roast 'em, so we are!'

'Check, check, check.' Commander Hubert Dannreuther, the Gunnery Officer, spoke with lips close to his voicepipe. 'All guns broadside negative "P" turret. Target "A", battle-cruiser, bearing green oh-seven-two, range nine thousand, closing. We're ready to engage.'

'Enemy course one-oh-five,' the Rate Officer added. 'Speed twenty-four knots.'

'Stand by,' Dannreuther warned, watching the eight main battery gun-ready lamps. 'Confound this blasted smoke.' He turned his head. 'Sub, slope down to the pantry, will you? See if you can get a bucket of tea, there's a good lad. My mouth tastes like a stoker's sock.'

Sub-Lieutenant Hedley Bellman lowered himself through the lubber's hole of the control top, seventy feet above the upper deck, then swung to the ladder rungs that descended the port-side leg of the massive tripod. Almost immediately below him was the massive, volcanic maw of the forward funnel from which poured a tumbling, convoluting lava of brown smoke, solid enough, it seemed, to be walked on. He felt the searing heat of it; the sulphurous poison stung his throat. Only feet away the steam siren hissed and bubbled like a kettle almost aboil. It would have been wiser, he knew, to have used the ladder enclosed within the foremast, but he had a claustrophobic disinclination to commit himself to the long, dark shaft. He felt safer in the open.

Nobody would believe him, when he told them at home, that at this moment – when the two greatest battle-fleets the world had ever known were about to collide – he had been sent down to the wardroom pantry to fetch tea.

But he could see everything. At least, he could see, astern, the smoke-wreathed shapes of *Inflexible* and *Indomitable*. Beyond them, even more obscured, he recognised *Lion* and *Princess Royal*. There were other ships, splashed with red, in every direction, but impossible to identify. The hazed sea was ragged with water-spouts, and the level of noise, of rumbling gunfire and screaming shells, was so intense that his ears ached. A few minutes earlier, *Lion*'s lamp had blinked at them briefly, and Dannreuther had told him that *Queen Mary* and *Indefatigable* had been destroyed within thirty-five minutes of going into action. There were no details, and it was unbelievable.

He remembered those brave ships. He lowered himself, hand over hand, and then he remembered something else as his feet reached the upper deck. *Invincible* had been about to open fire. He distinctly heard the fire-gong's 'ting-ting'. A thunderous, intolerable roar had his senses cringing. His ears sang, his belly twisted like wet string. Shocked, he flung himself at the nearest door, grappled with its clips and raked a shin on the high coaming. It was the seamen's galley, but it did not matter; it was sanctuary.

A petty officer and several men of a damage control party were unrolling old, perforated hoses that would keep the decks drenched with water. They glanced up at him, only briefly interested. 'Are we winning, sir?' the petty officer enquired, and grinned at his subordinates. A sub-lieutenant was the lowest form of commissioned life, low enough for familiarity – especially a sub-lieutenant RNR with only a Temporary Certificate.

At a range of 12,000 yards, they'd told Corporal Steve Bundy on Whale Island, a 12-inch shell was in flight for a half minute, and in that time a target travelling at 25 knots had moved a quarter mile. Trigonometry was a bleedin' marvellous thing. He'd bet Johnnie Spong had never heard of trigonometry.

His right eye was blind, but it didn't matter. During the last few seconds of comparative quiet during which the guns had shortened range, Major Blackwood, informed by Director Control, had shouted that 'X' turret's very first salvo had achieved a direct hit on the German *Derfflinger*. The Marines had cheered. That'd show the bleedin' sailors which turret was top in *Invincible*.

It was a soddin' good thing, Steve Bundy decided, that he hadn't gone to the Ypres salient with Benbow Company. He might be bleedin' dead by now. When this lot was finished, and the ship was back in Rosyth, he'd get his eye looked at by the surgeon bloke. He was, after all, one of his generation's élite, one of the builders of the country's future. He'd been told that by a Colonel, who ought to know.

The fire-gong tinkled. 'Shoot!' Blackwood ordered, and the monsters below him roared, heaved, disgorging their vicious projectiles at the luckless enemy.

The Signals Lieutenant had climbed from the flagdeck yet again. '*Iron Duke* has wirelessed all ships, sir. "Equal Speed Charlie London".'

Rear-Admiral Hood lowered his glasses. 'Charlie London?'

'Course South East by East, sir.'

'Thank you.' Both Hood and Captain Cay went to the compass. Then Cay said, 'He's turning his divisions in succession to starboard, sir – into single line battle order. That must mean they're coming within range.'

'Then we've got 'em, Arthur,' the other grinned, 'if only

the light holds. Sir John's going to cross Scheer's T. We've got 'em.' It had all been worth while. He turned his glasses again towards the distant enemy line, nearer than his own flagship. 'And there *they* are, Arthur – *Lutzow*, *Derfflinger*, *Seydlitz*, *Molke*, *Von der Tann* – the Kaiser's beautiful ships. This is the moment we've waited for.'

The voice of Commander Dannreuther, the Gunnery Officer, barked from a near voicepipe. 'Director Control to Bridge. Enemy battleships in sight bearing green one two five, 8000 yards and opening fire. We've identified *König*, *Grosser Kurfürst* and *Kronprinz Wilhelm*, sir—'

Battleships should never be allowed to come within effective range of battle-cruisers....

Hood cupped his hands around the mouth of the voicepipe. 'Keep shooting, Dannreuther – keep at it. Every shot is telling.'

Thirteen

Following astern, men in *Inflexible* and *Indomitable* stared in horror. From the waist of their leading ship there blossomed a great crimson flower that swelled, climbed with awful slowness to 400 feet and lifted with it great baulks of armour, bulkheads and decking as easily as if they were swirling scraps of charred paper. Then the red flower died, leaving an immense brown pall of smoke that billowed grotesquely upward and outward, and as the following battle-cruisers came abeam and passed they were deluged with ashes falling as gently as snow. The smoke thinned, and through it could be glimpsed the blurred shape of *Invincible*. Her back had broken amidships, both bows and stern rearing above the filth-strewn surface of the sea. The two halves of her, in only 30 fathoms, stood almost vertically out of the water to a height of seventy feet for minutes until, surrendering, both plunged.

Dannreuther was hurtled from the Director Control position as if by catapult, arms and legs flailing helplessly, then crashed into the sea fifty yards from the ship and sank like a stone with senses numbed but knowing that this was the moment of death. At a depth of about thirty feet, however, he felt himself being drawn powerfully upward again, and broke surface among raining debris that he could do nothing to avoid but which, miraculously, left him untouched. All around and above was thick, choking smoke, and he was uncertain, yet, of the direction of the ship, but he struck out with a strength inspired by the sudden awareness that he might still live.

There was a shout. On a floating target of wood and canvas that he vaguely recalled being stowed in the tiller flat were three clinging men. He turned towards them, and they hauled him on to the precarious sanctuary. Despite the men's oil-blackened faces and wetly plastered hair, he recognised two of them. One was Rangefinder Dundridge, from his own action station and the other a Chief Petty Officer whose name he thought was Thompson. The third, in sodden blue overalls, he could not identify.

'It looks like we're the lot, sir,' Thompson panted, but Dannreuther was unable to speak. He lay on his back, heaving air into his lungs.

'Shure, and ye're not at all,' said another voice, and over the kerb of the raft rose the face of a nigger minstrel that carried a broad grin. Dannreuther sat upright. 'Sandford,' he croaked, 'only a damn Irishman could smile in a situation like this.'

'In Limerick,' Sandford declared, scrambling aboard the raft, 'the sun is shining, the birds are singing, and little children are playing. Begad, it's good to be alive.'

They gazed around them. They were on a tiny island that rose and fell in a sea floating with oil and burning cordite, splintered timber and unrecognisable refuse for hundreds of yards in every direction. Distantly, the darkening horizon flickered with gunfire still, and thunder rumbled, but the battle-cruisers had already swept past, and the last in line, *New Zealand*, was fading into the dusk to the south-east. It was cold, and they were alone.

Sandford struggled to all fours. 'Here come the battleships.' He pointed, then choked. 'Faith, it's a pity *they* couldn't have seen—'

Majestically the grey leviathans steamed out of the gold of the dying sun in a long, curving line that stretched beyond sight, flanked by light cruisers and flotillas of destroyers. They could see *Iron Duke* and *King George* V, *Royal Oak*, *Canada*, *Revenge*, *Agincourt*, ship after ship, and as the ebbing ribbons of successive bow waves lifted the flimsy hurdle, the five men rose to their knees and hoarsely cheered each passing squadron until they, too, vanished to the south-east, the haze closing behind them. They fell silent, once more alone and with darkness falling.

It was CPO Thompson who suddenly roused himself, his eyes narrowed. 'Isn't that a man there, sir?' He palmed the caked grease from his face. 'There – by that broken whaler—'

They all stared. 'Dammit, I think you're right, Thompson,' Dannreuther said. Minutes later they tugged the sixth survivor from the scummed sea. Outspread, he was as ludicrously oil-blackened as Sandford had been, his eyes clenched and vomit spilling from his lips as he sobbed for breath.

'Well, I'll eat my tall hat,' Sandford promised. 'It's young Bellman.'

'Bellman?' Dannreuther frowned, trying to remember. 'Ah, yes. Didn't I send you away for a bucket of tea?'

'Yes sir,' Hedley wheezed.

'So that's how it happened,' mused Sandford. 'Ye blew up the damn galley stove. Is that what ye did to *Aboukir* as well?'

Fourteen

'My son,' the Reverend Bellman told everyone proudly, 'is a survivor from the *Invincible,* you know. It's his second time.' It all showed that there were tangible advantages in having a line of communication with the Almighty; many men did not survive one sinking, not to speak of two. The Boy Scouts, the country's second line of defence, had turned the church hall into a first aid post and war messenger headquarters, resolutely equipped with bandages, iodine, semaphore flags and a bicycle, but there was a disheartening lack of casualties to be bandaged or messages to be pedalled. The Reverend Bellman raised morale by visiting the post every Friday evening. 'Twelve inch guns are not, as you may well think, only twelve inches long,' he assured them. 'Oh, no. It's the *bullets* that are twelve inches long. Just think of that.'

Hedley Bellman shrugged off an odd feeling of guilt with regard to his two escapes. That week in June had been one of the blackest of the war but, incredibly, within an hour of being hauled aboard the destroyer *Badger,* wrapped in blankets and sipping scalding cocoa generously laced with rum, he was belligerently advising an immediate torpedo attack on the German flagship, unaware that when the British fleet regained the Tyne and Forth three days later to land wounded, refuel and ammunition, they would be jeered and insulted by dockyard workers. The German Naval Press Bureau had already publicised claims of a great victory while the British Admiralty had mistakenly remained silent, and the silence was interpreted by many as a confession of defeat. Although, within twenty-four hours, Admiral Jellicoe was able to declare his ships ready in all respects for sea and a resumption of battle, and although the German High Seas Fleet never again ventured out of its harbours until it did so to finally surrender, the damage was done and would never be repaired.

Then, within days, had come the further, chilling news that Lord Kitchener had perished in the cruiser *Hampshire*, off the Orkneys, and it seemed that British fortunes could fall no lower. But they could, for the offensive on the Somme was about to begin, and by comparison the losses suffered at Jutland would fade into insignificance.

Hedley Bellman had walked ashore from *Badger* with Dannreuther, Sandford, Thompson and Dundridge. Only the Marine, whose name Hedley did not learn until he read an account of *Invincible*'s action several months later, needed to be disembarked by stretcher, and they never saw him again. The man had swallowed oil and had apparently been blinded in one eye – which was, however, no great price to pay for being blown out of the after 12-inch turret. It was a bloody shame, Dannreuther mused. He had recorded twenty hits on *Derfflinger*, and all *Von der Tann*'s guns had been disabled. If the German ships had reached harbour they'd not be out of dry dock for a year. They'd not forget *Invincible* in a hurry.

The five parted company, shaking hands and promising that they must meet again. Perhaps, after the war, they could enjoy a reunion every 31 May, in the evening. Hedley Bellman forgot the proposal within minutes.

He reached the quiet sanctuary of the Greenwich rectory after a depressing journey of delayed trains, few cabs and crowded omnibuses. The strains of war were beginning to show everywhere, in civilian shabbiness, shortages, khaki men with shoulders hunched under packs and rifles, women labourers, convoys of ambulances, military policemen and the same exhorting, accusing posters on every wall.

There was news, too, written, censored and rewritten until little more than gibberish, of a massive Franco-German confrontation in the Verdun area. 'The situation,' advised the newspapers, 'gives no cause for uneasiness.' It could be Germany's last, despairing effort, the death-throes of the Beast.

The great Russian offensive under Brusilov, which was to put Austria out of the war in six weeks, had foundered in the slime of the Pripet Marshes. Russia was bankrupt.

And the Somme was yet to come.

There had been no letters from Imogen for months – the muddied, crumpled letters that were rubber-stamped, opened, resealed, then opened and rubber-stamped again, marred by dirty fingers, mutilated by petty officials, and finally allowed the lowest of priorities in a transport system that was near to collapse. It was, as the Reverend Bellman told his son, a miracle that Imogen's letters arrived at all. Imogen, Hedley remembered, had his sea-boots, his ridiculous, padded hat with ear-flaps that he'd never worn, and two pairs of woollen long hose that he'd worn only once before deciding that chilled legs were to be preferred to four hours of itching during a middle watch.

The summer of 1916 passed into autumn, then into the third winter of the war, and Hedley had been assigned to minesweeping training in Devonport. The requisitioned trawlers with their worn decks and pipe-stem funnels had much in common with the old *Corinthian*; most of their crews had been fishermen and showed a marked reluctance to conform to naval standards of discipline and exactness. It was unlikely that *Girl Mary* or *Sally Foster* would ever exchange shots with an enemy, but the harvest for which they trawled in the western Channel was just as deadly, the task cold and wearying, unspectacular and seldom acknowledged.

Still, with luck, Hedley speculated, he might complete his war with the shabby little ships of the minesweeping service – a war of wasted years, wasted skills. Afterwards, it was being predicted, there were going to be a lot of new values, some good, others bad. For a start, there would be too few ships, and there would be many men with masters' tickets serving as mates and even second mates, queues of unemployed seamen, falling rates of pay and penny-pinching conditions afloat. Could the second mate of a rusting coaster or the Holyhead train-ferry offer marriage to Imogen Pope?

There was still no response to the letters that he wrote to Imogen through the British Red Cross, and the Society, in answer to his several enquiries, could offer little information. There were reports from the Eastern Front, but not the kind that should be publicised; they described dysentery, scurvy and lice, the amputation of frost-bitten feet in shallow trenches flooded with icy water, rations reduced to dried herrings and lentils. The British ambulance unit had been ordered to Bucharest, but there was no news of its arrival because Bucharest had been occupied by the enemy on 6 December.

Harriet had gone to Dr McGill because her mother insisted, and placed her shilling in the tray on the desk because the doctor avoided taking money in his hand. After examining her, McGill had asked questions, peering at her over his glasses, and then he had frowned and sucked his teeth, took down a book from a shelf, replaced it. He gazed at her for a long time, very thoughtfully, until she flushed. Finally he announced that he was not sure about pregnancy; she must come back in two weeks, in the meantime ensuring that she kept early hours, that she stopped thinking about it, and that her bowels were regular. She should take an infusion of senna pods.

Mary Selley was annoyed. It meant another shilling, and shillings didn't grow on trees, but there was no arguing with a doctor, and she, Mary Selley, was determined it would all be done right.

On Harriet's second visit the doctor followed exactly the same procedure as before. He asked the same questions and referred to the same book. Then he drew a deep breath and said, 'Pseudocyesis', which caused Harriet's mouth to drop open in horror. Was it serious? She whispered.

Dr McGill placed his hands behind his back. 'Pseudocyesis,' he repeated. 'It's a false pregnancy, lassie. Spurious, ye ken. I've not met it before in someone as young as yesel' – it's more usual in older women at the time o' menopause – but there's no doubt. Serious, did ye say?' He shook his head. 'Well, if ye were older it *could* mean a tumour, but I'd say it's constipation and flatulence caused by ye standing ten hours a day at ye bench, and with ye *obsessing* yesel' that ye're pregnant.' He waved dismissal. 'Do as I've told ye, lassie – senna pods, stop thinking about it, and leave ye shilling on the tray.'

By the time Harriet regained Inkerman Street she had given the situation considerable thought, but had reached only a confused conclusion. The doctor had said she suffered from pseudo-something, which was a force pregnancy. She had never heard of spurious, but she knew what constipation was; it was disappointingly undramatic. She decided to forget the part about constipation.

Albert ought to know. He was, after all, responsible. Neither she nor Mrs Selley had heard anything from him since he had been escorted from the Court of Session. He had not even turned to wave to them, and Harriet had no knowledge of his present whereabouts. Still, she reasoned, the Court of Session should know. They had sent him.

Harriet had always excelled in creative writing, the best in her school class in dictation and composition.

> Dear Albert: Nobody told where you went so I hope this letter reaches you safe. If it dont I will write another one. I am still working for Leith Fish but might go to the trams which are taking womin for conductors. The most important thing I have to tell you is I seen Dr McGill and he said a long word I did not know and then said it meant a force pregnancy. I thought after what happened you ought to know. Letters are now 1½d now. Donald Menzies was killit in France and Jamy Fraser has one arm. I hope you are keeping well: Harriet.

The letter took a long time in transit. The Clerk of the Edinburgh Court of Session passed it to the Probation Office, which redirected it to the naval recruiting authorities, who forwarded it to HMS *Caledonia*, where it was redirected to HMS *Invincible* c/o GPO London. The travel-stained missive had been lengthily pigeon-holed at each stage, but the GPO dutifully transmitted it to Rosyth whence, however, *Invincible* had departed for Scapa Flow. The cheap little envelope, its address almost obliterated by rubber stamps and scrawls, reached the Orkneys six hours after *Invincible* had led the Grand Fleet into the North Sea. Scapa Flow was empty of ships.

In 1916 the appearance of a telegraph boy in Inkerman Street had only one meaning. The poor of Leith wrote and received few letters, but the boy with the wallet at his belt from which he took the ominous red square of paper was a messenger of death. He had come four times before to

Inkerman Street. The children had paused in their noisy play and curtains had lifted. Eyes followed the boy's progress, watched him hesitate before one door, another, then closed in grateful relief as he passed beyond. There had been reports from elsewhere of people opening their doors and then, seeing who stood at the step, being felled by shock. The Post Office had already decided to change the colour of the accursed envelope from red to buff.

When the boy came to the Selley house he was received by young Martin, who knew exactly what the telegram meant – and the messenger's face confirmed it – but dared not tear it open. It meant that he, Martin, was now the man of the house; he could lay claim to his father's chair and put his feet on the brass fender. He was fourteen, big enough to exercise his authority, if he wanted, with his fist. There was nobody to deny him. He had plans, starting with the bath water. And Katie was thirteen, beginning to swell interestingly under her bodice. If he was right about the telegram, Martin calculated, there were going to be changes.

It was Harriet who read the telegram.

'The Admiralty regrets to inform you that Ordinary Seaman Albert Selley was killed in action on 31 May. . . .'

Martin's eyes rested gravely on Katie. Tomorrow.

The retreating Roumanians had left field guns, carts and scores of corpses on the frozen road between Lehliu and Budesti. The ground was too hard for burying, even if anyone cared, which was all to the advantage of the human flotsam that followed in the wake of the defeated troops – the irregulars, refugees, deserters, gipsies and dispossessed peasants of several nationalities who fought over abandoned baggage, looted the undefended and robbed the dead. The only law was the law of survival, and even the wounded were stripped and left nakedly dying so that another might live.

The corpse under the wrecked motor-truck had gone

unnoticed for days because successive scavengers had been distracted by the vehicle's scattered load, of meat extract, iodine, splints and dressings, Wincarnis wine, jars of unidentifiable tablets, and methylated spirit. The Cossacks agreed that the methylated spirit was far superior to Wincarnis. They spat out the tablets with oaths and made soup from the meat extract over a splendid fire fed by the splints and dressings.

The corpse, when it was uncovered, had stiffened to frozen rigidity and its clothing was difficult to remove, but a fine pair of leather knee-boots, a fleece-lined coat and a padded cap with ear-flaps justified effort and patience. It was only when the corpse was almost completely exposed that someone observed, disinterestedly, that it was female.

But *what* a female, another admired. No Slav or Serb or Magyar had hair of such fine-spun gold, a skin so white, so unblemished. See, such perfect teeth – and those delicate hands had never cut fodder, or hoed turnips, or watered cattle. Ah, Nikita, what a beauty she is, eh? Think, a man could grow old with a woman such as this, and always feel young. Ah, what a pity, Nikita. Is she Russian, you suppose, from St Petersburg? Or an Austrian from Vienna? But no matter. Now she is no more than any of these naked dead with their frozen eyes, and these are fine boots, fit for a general—

No longer did anyone gather under the gaslight in Stepney Green, to throw ha'pennies against the wall, argue the merits of Aston Villa and Preston North End, or merely stand with hands in pockets and collar upturned to leer at passing women. The younger male population of Stepney had been markedly reduced by events at Passchendaele, Arras, Cambrai and, most of all, on the Somme.

In time, of course, some of them might return. If they did, Steve Bundy would know. Every evening, before dusk, he pulled down the blind over the steamed window of the workmen's cookshop and, for a few moments, gazed up the darkening street. Not Johnnie Spong, but perhaps one or two of the others. In time.

He'd been bleedin' lucky. There was times, Steve Bundy told himself, when it was difficult for a bloke to believe his luck when it kept turning up trumps.

Like the turret, in which everything had ended for a lot of others. There were gaps in his recollection, but there were also moments he could recapture vividly – the guns firing like clockwork, the gun-house hazed with blue smoke, the fire-bells tinkling, and Major Blackwood shouting, above the clamour, that they were hitting.

Then there had been that other thing, the sudden grumbling noise from within the ship, forward, that they did not recognise. The deck-plates beneath them had shivered, the pointer of the range-dial he watched sank to zero and, instantly, all lights failed. 'Stand fast!' Blackwood had ordered, but there wasn't much soddin' choice, was there?

When they asked him, later, what had happened next, he could describe little that made sense except that he was being dragged from an oil-clogged sea, and he only vaguely remembered the hours of clinging to the wooden hurdle. After, there were more hours of retching exhaustedly in the humid below-decks of *Badger*, of drooling oil and brine—

He'd been bleedin' lucky, and no mistake. Like that official bloke, when he'd come out of hospital, who told him there was going to be a Government Pension Fund, and he, Steve Bundy, in compensation for being blinded in one eye, would probably receive three shillings a week for life.

For life! And they'd given him a nickel badge to pin to his lapel, so no more tarts would give him a white feather. It was a bleedin' joke; nobody *asked* him where he got his eye buggered so he wasn't going to say, was he?

Nor he wasn't going to say that, safely folded in his belt, he had a Post Office order for two hundred quid. That's what had set him up nice, with the cookshop.

Once, he'd had a night at Blackfriars, to smell liniment, sweat and tobacco smoke again, but it was all different. Mo Lyons had gone, and the old Major, and Palmer. He'd known none of the names on the bill, and there wasn't one of 'em that Charlie Sawyer would have given more than a derisive sniff. After that, he'd not gone to Albemarle Street; there was nothing more in the game for him, and he'd not want Charlie to tolerate him as a hanger-on. Anyway, he was a cookshop proprietor, one of the builders of the country's future.

He tied on his apron, glancing up the street as usual. There was nobody there yet, but there might be, one day, and there'd be pie, mash and gravy, and a few jugs. O'course, it'd never be quite the same.

Historical Postscript

HMS *Invincible* blew up at 1833 on the evening of 31 May 1916 with the loss of 1026 officers and men, including Rear-Admiral the Hon. H. Hood and Captain Arthur Cay. There were only six survivors, picked up that same evening by the destroyer *Badger*, which, believing they were Germans, took them aboard under armed guard.